PRIDE

WILLOW ASTER

Pride
Kingdoms of Sin, Book 4
Copyright © 2020 by Willow Aster
ISBN 13: 978-1-7335137-5-3

Cover by: Hang Le
Photography by: Wander Aguiar
Cover Model: Neil Ingham
Editing: Christine Estevez
Beta: Jennifer Mirabelli
Represented by: Brower Literary & Management

PREFACE

This book is a romance based entirely on fictional places. It is set in the present where there are monarchies in a world that doesn't operate quite like ours. There are no dragons or fairies, but there is lust, greed, pride, and wrath...something that exists in any world and has since the beginning of time.

Any mistakes I make in properly conveying royal practices and whatnot, I hope you will excuse and consider that in the kingdoms of Farrow, Niaps, Alidonia, and beyond, perhaps it's just the way it is.

List of Characters:

Safrin Family of Farrow:
    Neil* & Kathryn, father and mother
    Jadon, son of Neil and stepson of Kathryn
    Eden Safrin Catano, daughter, married to Luka Catano
    Ava, daughter

Catano Family of Niaps:
    Titus & Cecilia (Cece), father and mother

Basile, brother to Cecilia

Luka, son, married to Eden Safrin Catano

Mara, daughter, married to Elias Lancaster

Also in Niaps:

Brienne Jarvis, bodyguard to Eden

Elias Lancaster, advisor to Luka, married to Mara Catano Lancaster

Forbrush Family of Yuman:

Victros* & Anais, father and mother

Alex, son

Nadia, daughter

Gentry Barrington/Forbrush, son of Victros, boyfriend to Ava Safrin

Farthing Family of Alidonia:

Vance & Jonquil*, father and mother

Omar*, son

Delilah, daughter

Caulder, nephew, advisor to Vance

Otto Family of the Sea of Caninsula

Ralty & Sherai*

Shua, son

Solvang, daughter

*deceased

PROLOGUE

Jadon, age six

I bundle under the fur, as close as I can get to Mum while she sleeps. She's been sleeping a long time now and her body is cold. Usually we get warm when we cuddle, and sometimes we chat under the blanket, but she's quiet and I'm tired of lying here. I'm tired of being cold too.

Miss Lang raps on the door and I poke my head out of the blanket when she yells out, "Hurry, boy, it's cold out here."

I scramble to the door and fling it open, letting Lang come inside.

She comes to a quick stop when she sees Mum lying under the fur and puts her hand to her mouth as it opens in a silent scream. Her expression is confusing and I put my hand on her arm.

"What's the matter, Miss Lang?"

She clutches my shoulders and looks in my eyes. "You poor boy. When did she pass?"

"What...do you mean?" My face crumbles when tears start running down her face. I hate it when Mum or Miss Lang cries. "What's the matter?"

She wails louder and holds me to her chest, and I start sniffling too. I'm cold and tired and it's been quiet too long. The last thing I want is a wailing Miss Lang.

"You poor, poor boy," she repeats and I sigh, wiping my nose.

"You're going to wake Mother if you're not careful," I finally say.

"Your mother is dead, child. She's gone and I'm so, so sorry that she won't be coming back."

I take a deep breath and stare at my mother for a few moments, willing her to open her eyes.

"She's not gone! She's right there!" I run to my mother and hold her hand up. It feels strange and flops back down by her side. My eyes widen as I try to shake her awake. "Mum, wake up! Wake up!"

She lies there as still as can be and I lean into her neck and cry until I can't cry any more.

Miss Lang takes me to her house, dragging me out of mine, kicking and screaming.

"I can't leave Mum! She said we stick together, no matter what." I've said it in every way possible and still, Miss Lang insists that I cannot stay with Mum in our cottage any longer.

"It's time for Mum to go to heaven. We will have a funeral for her and say goodbye then," she says. "I need to get in touch with your family, you poor boy."

I want to tell her to stop calling me that, but it doesn't

matter, Mum will make her stop when I see her again. Mum *is* my family, the only family I've got.

"I want to see Mum," I repeat, as we walk into her dark place. I step over things on the floor and rub my arms as I try to get warm.

"You won't be seeing her again, child. I know you don't understand it now, but your mum is gone."

A few nights later, I meet a man whose hand trembles when he reaches out to shake mine.

"I'm Neil," he says.

His eyes are kind. When I shake his hand, I feel safer than I've felt since leaving Mum in our house.

"I'm so sorry I didn't know." His head bows and he presses his fingers to his eyes. When he lifts his head again, his eyes are wet and he looks sad. I frown at him and he pats my shoulder. "I didn't know about you until now or I would've been here sooner," he says. "Jadon, I'm your father, and I will take good care of you, I promise."

I swallow hard. I feel like crying. I miss Mum more than anything, but I've always wanted a dad. She told me it was just us though. I don't understand how I have a dad now, but I really want to go with him, so I don't say anything. He pats my shoulder again and takes a steadying breath.

"Are you ready to go to your new home? Your sisters will be excited to have a big brother."

"I've always asked Mum for a sister," I say excitedly. "How many are there?"

"There are two. One is a few years younger than you and the other is just a baby, but you'll like her too. Even though all she does is cry and smile." He laughs and I do too.

I can't believe I have a family. I run and get the bear I have and the little bag Miss Lang put my clothes in and rush to my father.

I still can't believe I have one.

———————

It takes a long time to get to my father's house. I fall asleep against his shoulder a few times on the way. And when we arrive, it's the biggest house I've ever seen. A *castle*.

My insides are shaky as I walk inside, holding Father's hand. A little girl runs up to me and holds out her doll. I smile and when I don't take the doll from her, she waves it in my face until I do. When it's in my hand, she snatches it back and runs circles around me.

"This is Eden. Someone is sure happy to meet you," Father says.

A woman walks in, holding a baby and I stare at her. She's beautiful and tall and the baby is so cute. I smile and the woman doesn't smile back, looking at my father. She stares at him for a few moments but doesn't say anything, instead turning around and walking out of the room with the baby.

"Kathryn and Ava," Father says. "She'll come around. It'll just...take time," he says under his breath.

Eden waves her doll in my face again and I start a game of peekaboo behind the doll, forgetting all about the woman and baby.

During the night, I hear the baby crying and leave my room to find her. I'm a little scared because Father tucked me in and I shouldn't be out of bed, but I find baby Ava's room not far from mine. I go inside and she's in her crib wailing. I look around, but no one else comes, so I reach over and hold onto her little hand. She stares up at me, eyes wide, and I sing a little song Mum always sang to me. She quietens and even smiles a little smile before eventually drifting off to sleep.

I fall asleep lying on the floor by her crib, just in case she cries again. I don't want her to feel like she's alone, the way I do without Mum.

CHAPTER ONE

Jadon

Present

I go visit Kathryn. She's being watched in the cottage to the east side of our property. She claims to be a bird in a cage, that I'm locking her up to torture her and to put her in her place. If I was that kind of person, I would've done it as soon as I became king.

Kathryn Safrin has hated me since the day I came to live in her house. I'm the illegitimate son of her husband, and as much as she loved him, she never forgave him for the affair he had while he was away at war for two years. Apparently, my mother never forgave him either, because he went back to his wife once the war was over. She never told him about me, and until the day he died, he did everything in his power to make sure I knew how much he loved me, to make up for those formative years in my life when I didn't have a father.

Kathryn isn't locked up because I hate her. I've never hated her—I've been *hurt* by her...there's a big difference—but I don't trust her right now. It's been a month since she tried to kill me and while I know it wasn't strictly her fault—she was kidnapped, given heavy hallucinogens, and hypnotized nightly with orders to kill me. My sister, Ava, also underwent the same brainwashing and she tried to *save* me when Kathryn shot me.

To me, the difference is clear and profound: Ava loves me and could never really hurt me, and my stepmother would love nothing more than to see me dead.

So yes, I do feel the need to supervise her recovery process a little longer, despite her manipulative attempts for freedom. The whole ordeal has been exhausting, not to mention an emotional lapse into the insecurity I felt growing up with Kathryn as my stepmother. It also feels like a distraction from what I should be focusing on: who was behind her kidnapping? And who is still out there waiting for the right moment to kill me?

There are probably too many enemies to count, but one was brave enough to kidnap my mother and my sister...neither in Farrow at the time, although that does little to ease my concerns over security since both Ava and our mother snuck back into the house without detection.

I'm walking along the path to the door, bracing myself for whatever mood Kathryn will be in, when my phone rings.

It's a number I don't recognize and I'm tempted to ignore it, but with my sister having been kidnapped before, I'm on the paranoid side and rarely avoid calls. Not many get past my team anyway, so if my phone rings, it's usually important.

There's always a small amount of fear that Ava will be taken again and that would put me in the ground. If anything happened to either of my sisters, I may as well take my sword to my gut and be done with it.

Enough morbidity, answer the damn phone.

"Jadon Safrin speaking."

"As in King Jadon?" An amused raspy feminine voice that sounds like feathers mixed with claws catches me by surprise.

"Who's asking?"

"This is Delilah Farthing."

"Delilah," my voice lilts at the end, "I was beginning to think you were merely a signature at the end of your family's endless emails getting *out* of meetings."

"Touché. I assure you, I'm more than a signature."

She sounds playful and I have to say, it surprises me. Her family has been an endless headache to my peace of mind.

"To what do I owe this surprise?"

"I think it's time we meet...somewhere neutral. Perhaps Ivalis or Grawlan?"

"What makes this time different? Forgive my bluntness, but I don't have time for another no-show." Every nerve in my body is on alert as I wait to hear her response. What are the Farthings up to now?

"My father is in remission, so I am freer than I've been in some time. However, I'd like to keep our meeting between us, if that's okay with you. Tensions are still...shall we say, to the ceiling? I don't know about you, but I love my kingdom and want to keep it in one piece. Something tells me you feel the same about yours."

"Is this a trick, Delilah? Because it seems to me, nothing would explode negotiations between our kingdoms more than your father finding out about us meeting behind his back."

"I'll put it this way: you don't *want* my father or my cousin, Caulder, knowing about our meeting. What I have to say is between you and me. Can you be discreet?"

I squeeze my forehead with my thumb and forefinger and look up at the blue sky. This could be a death trap I'm walking into, but it's a risk I'll have to take.

"Full of intrigue, Princess Delilah. Yes, I can be discreet. Question is, can you?"

"Ivalis, the day after tomorrow, noon, at the Cave of Stars. I'll be alone. Don't make me regret this...oh, and King?"

"Yes?"

"Watch your back."

Shit. What kind of game is this?

"Always do," I respond, my tone chilly. "I'll see you in Ivalis."

I walk into my stepmother's room already in a suspicious mood after that troubling conversation with Delilah. I'm distracted but on guard and when she glares at me as I enter, I try to tamp down the resentment that has steadily grown toward Kathryn. I've tried to be kind to her, tried to understand why she hated me when I became old enough to know how my father's infidelity must have hurt what seemed to be a flawless relationship...I've even tried to not care. But it all comes down to the simple fact that I have longed for a mother since the day my own died, and Kathryn will never want to fill that role.

Today when her upper lip sneers as I sit down across from her, starting our chess game where we last left off, I brace my heart for the rejection. You'd think I'd be a stone-cold wall of defense by now, but that doesn't seem to be my way.

"Hello, Kathryn. You're looking especially lovely today."

"I look dreadful and you know it. Now is not the time for false praise."

"I assure you, when it comes to your beauty, there is no such thing as false praise. Your attitude, however, is another thing altogether." I attempt a light tone, but when I make a move she doesn't like on the chessboard, she growls and I groan. It's hard work, being around her. Most days I wonder why I try.

"Let me out of here and I will be sweet as pie," she says, her lips curling into more of a grin than a sneer. It still rings fake.

"Still feel like killing me?" I cross my arms as I wait for her move. One of the guards in the room clears his throat and sounds like he's trying to cover a laugh. I shoot him a look. "Glad I can be your comic relief," I say dryly.

He bows his head, pinching his lips together. "The days are long, King Jadon." His voice is apologetic, but I hear his desperation.

Her doctors think the effects of the hallucinogens are clearing up, but the hypnosis she went through is another matter. Her hatred of me makes it harder to determine. My guards are ready for more exciting work spent somewhere other than these four walls watching the Queen Mother every day, but I don't know what to tell them.

I stand abruptly, shoving the chair back and then righting it when it almost falls backward. "I'll be seeing you, Kathryn."

"Jadon?" She stands too and one of the guards moves closer to her, so she can't make a move toward me without running into him.

"Yes?"

"Let me out of here and I will feel less like killing you."

I smile and her eyes flash. "As always, it's been an experience. Good day, everyone."

I step out of the cottage and it's like a thousand pounds immediately lift.

Duty #4,528 of a king's day completed.

I'm almost to the door of the castle, my guards a nice distance away. They knew by my mood when I left Kathryn to let me have extra space. A pitiful whine stops me in my tracks and I turn around, looking everywhere for the source. I don't see anything right away but move toward the sound. Under a tree sits a beautiful white dog, its large paw caught in a trap.

I get closer and she whimpers. "What have you gotten yourself into?" I ask, bending down. I carefully work on the trap, taking care to not hurt her in the process. When it finally releases, she licks my hand and face. "Oh my. Okay, that's enough. You're welcome." I laugh. Her paw is a bloody mess and I slowly pick her up. "You're quite heavy," I groan and it looks like she's smiling when she licks my face again.

I step out of the clearing and walk toward the house.

"See that she's taken to the vet right away, please," I tell

Quincie, one of the guards. "I'll take her to my office while you make arrangements."

"Sir, the dog is bleeding," Quincie says.

"Yes, I'm aware of that." I laugh. "My hands are covered in said blood."

"I just mean...do you really want to mess up your office?"

"Let me worry about that. Just please move quickly. I don't want this pup to suffer more than she already has."

I hurry to the office and pull a blanket off of the chair, setting it on the floor before carefully laying the dog on it. She looks up at me eagerly, her tail thumping loudly on the floor.

"I'm not getting attached until you get a clean bill of health," I tell her, rolling my eyes at how cute she is, even a complete mess.

When Quincie comes in a few minutes later and carries the dog out, I already miss her.

A sure sign that life as a king is not all it's cracked up to be. From death threats and meetings with future queens and murderous stepmothers...to a gaping hole in my chest where the loneliness constantly resides...this is my reality.

CHAPTER TWO

Delilah

I hang up with Jadon Safrin, thinking that went about as well as could be expected. I am already on the outskirts of Alidonia, having told my family I am going to pick out a new wardrobe in Valence. I'm traveling with a guard, but I plan to ditch him in Valence. I will still see a designer while I'm here, but I don't need several days to do it. I hope to be back before my guard even realizes I'm gone.

It's the riskiest thing I've ever done. Not following my father's plans and working on my own...it's definitely the stupidest idea I've had. But I want my father to see me as an equal in the family. I love him more than anything or anyone and would love nothing more than to help him accomplish his lifelong mission. His time is limited. He's been sick for a long time and when my mother passed away, my father became a shadow of his former self. I just *thought* that was a bad time. It was a thousand times worse when my brother died in a drowning accident two years later. The darkness consumed my father and nothing I did seemed to pull him out of it. When my cousin, Caulder, came to live with us, he was the only one who seemed to help. Now he and my father are as thick as thieves and it makes me happy that things have changed for the better with my dad's health, but I'd like to do my part to help. I'd like to see him stay this happy.

Caulder and my father want nothing more than for me to live a life of luxury and to give me every desire of my heart. I don't need all that, and I have a feeling meeting with my family's greatest enemy will either put my life in danger, or it will give me leverage.

I'm counting on leverage...

I will help bring my family to its fullest power by bringing King Jadon to his knees.

I want my father to see what an asset I am to this family. Not just a pretty face but someone to be reckoned with... someone who has just as much at stake and just as much to gain from ruling all of the kingdoms. I've been ready for this day since I first heard about the Safrins and Catanos. They're really the only two kingdoms standing in our way and with them now related to one another, if we bring down one, they both fall. Now that my father is healthy enough for me to travel, I can do my part.

I spend the better part of the morning doing what is expected of me: I pick out beautiful clothes. The attendant who brings each item I try on loves the outfit I arrived in and when I put it on before leaving, I see her looking at my jacket longingly.

"I'll trade outfits with you," I tell her.

"What?" Her forehead creases in the middle. "No, I couldn't possibly."

"Yes, you absolutely can. In fact, I insist!" I grin at her

shock and she laughs, eyes wide. I take off my jacket and start unbuttoning my blouse before shooing her out of the dressing room. "I'll leave my things outside the door. Put them on and then bring me your clothes."

She clasps her hands together in excitement and nods.

"I might need an extra jacket," I add before she leaves.

"Of course, I have one I think you'll like."

"Perfect."

When I'm leaving in my borrowed clothes minus the jacket, I call my father and he answers on the second ring.

"How's it going, little princess?" he asks.

"It's going well. I've picked out a few beautiful pieces."

"You'll need more than a few to get through the spring. No one wants to see you wear repeated outfits. You are our kingdom's icon. Make us proud."

I sigh, making sure the phone is far enough to not pick it up.

"Yes, Papa. I just think our money could be better served—"

"You let me worry about our money, precious. You are the vision of what every woman wants to be, not just in our kingdom, but in every kingdom. It sends a negative message to the people if you're seen in the same thing twice."

"Do you really think they care that much? I find that so hard to believe...especially for the people in our kingdom who struggle to afford food."

I normally don't press this with him—I don't like to upset him—but I know if we don't talk about it, he'll expect me to come home with no less than a dozen trunks. I try to pick accessories or accent pieces that will switch things up so he's none the wiser when I wear repeats, but something tells me he'll be watching to see how much I come home with.

For someone who has spent the past year in bed, nothing much gets past him right now.

"You give them hope. Yes, even more so to those who can't afford it."

He has that tone he gets when he's closed the subject and I know I've pushed back enough. I decide to call the designer later to add a few more outfits.

"You still think you'll be home tomorrow night or are you going to need more time to shop?" he asks, chuckling.

"I'll let you know if it looks like I'll be later, but I hope to stick with the schedule."

"Enjoy your trip, sweetheart. We miss you."

"I miss you too, Papa. Love you."

"I love you."

Ditching the guard goes like clockwork. I made sure Diego was the guard who accompanied me because he has a weakness for alcohol and women. I ensured he had both while I was shopping. When I'm ready to go to the hotel, he's already drunk and I make it a point of letting him know I'll be retiring early and enjoying a relaxing day in my room before we leave tomorrow night. He doesn't know I hired the beautiful girl he's been flirting with all day. She'll keep him drinking and happy until I return in time for our flight home. I watch him open his door and drunkenly tug her inside and then I get to work.

I throw on the jacket the attendant put in a bag for me and grin. The black nondescript jacket is perfect. Next, I put on the short black wig, careful to cover every strand of my white-blond hair. I put on more makeup than I normally wear and check my appearance one last time in the mirror by the door.

Pleased, I smile at myself in the mirror and turn at all angles to make sure my hair is completely covered.

The hardest part will be getting out of the hotel without anyone noticing me. I don't expect them to since I barely recognize myself. My guard and I have the whole floor to ourselves and when I go down the back staircase instead of the elevator, that solves the problem of seeing anyone. The stairway is empty and each step I take echoes. I look in every direction as I step into the parking garage, not sure where I am. We never enter through the main lobby, so it takes a minute to get my bearings.

Not a single person stops me or does a double take like they normally do. My hair has always given me away; I'll be using this wig a lot more often if it gives me this anonymity. Being seen as an equal by my father and my freedom are always just out of my grasp. I spend most of my time sheltered at home with guards twenty-four hours a day. I never do anything to cause my father worry, so doing this now gives me an incredible rush, but at the same time, I feel like I'm doing something horribly wrong.

You're twenty-two and have never done anything wrong in your life, live it up for once, I try to tell myself. And while it does feel exciting, I know the guilt of all of this will eventually catch up with me.

I take the train to Ivalis and it's around nine p.m. before I'm settled into my room for the night. The room itself would make Papa shudder, but it's not bad. It's not luxurious, but I'm sure there are far worse places out there. I think about the next day and how I'll get out of here undetected. I think I'll wear the wig and take it off right before I see

Jadon. I want him to know exactly who he's dealing with when we meet for the first time.

CHAPTER THREE

Jadon

I arrive in Ivalis early and check into a quaint hotel by the mountain. Quincie checks in for me, so I can stay as hidden as possible.

"Do you need me any longer, sir?" he asks once I'm in my room.

"No, I'm good for now, thank you. I'll be ready to leave tomorrow morning around this time."

He lowers his head and leaves the room, most likely wondering what I'm up to but too much of a gentleman to ask.

I've only been to the Cave of Stars once and it was when my father was king. I was fourteen and the cave felt otherworldly, the type of surroundings you'd find in a fairy tale or see on a fantasy show. Just as it sounds, it's a neutral location between royals in the caves of Ivalis with a ceiling of tarmagalcite that sparkles like a backdrop of endless stars. I arrive there an hour before I'm supposed to meet Princess Delilah, wanting to get a good look around.

I was surprised when she suggested this place. There are only a few territories such as this, where any of us could meet for as long as necessary without any threat to our kingdoms. Mostly used in a time of war, a noncombatant spot when it's a matter of life and death, it feels strange to come here when we're not in the middle of a crisis. But I suppose Farrow and Alidonia have been in a semi-crisis for years now. I'm still hoping it isn't pointing toward war, but with the recent threat on my life, I know better than to trust anyone.

When I step into the last opening before the Cave of Stars, I feel a wave of nostalgia for my father. I can still see him standing here, his excitement and dread about meeting with Titus Catano giving his eyes a crazed glaze.

"I brought you with me to have a witness, son," he said. "He cannot harm us here, but I'm sure the veiled threats will be flying. Just knowing you're with me will keep me levelheaded."

I remember my nerves rattling, the roar of my blood pumping in my head as we waited for his arrival. When Titus walked into the cave, he came alone but had enough swagger to fill a colosseum...sort of the way Luka was before he married my sister and she brought him down to earth a few hundred pegs or so.

Something Titus said stuck with me and I still think of it frequently. He told my father: "The problem with you, King Neil, is that you rule with your heart, not with your mind. You extend grace before justice and mercy before wisdom. If you keep it up, your kingdom will not stand."

And my father said something then that has also stayed with me. It's what I strive for as king. He said, "I'd rather die with my integrity intact and to love first, act later, than to inflict an iron fist on those who might have made a bad decision in haste. It might not always be the wisest decision, but it's the reason I can sleep at night with a clear conscience."

My father is dead now and I believe either Titus Catano or Vance Farthing was behind it—most likely the two of them were working together.

Do I still think my father was right? To rule with love first, thinking the best of people?

Yes and no.

I strive to love first, thinking the best of people, while also watching my back for them to do the worst.

So far, it is serving me well.

I hear her footsteps before I see her and I brace myself. Her tone on the phone was confusing, to say the least. Playful, but threatening? Almost like I'm a recreation she's decided to indulge in.

But when she steps through the entrance of the cave and is illuminated by the light of the stones, my breath catches in my throat despite all of my bravado.

The legend of Princess Delilah Farthing of Alidonia's beauty is no legend at all. It is unequivocally fact that she is the most beautiful woman I've ever seen. Pictures don't do her justice. In person, she is a force of nature with her shocking hair and violet eyes, and despite being petite, she looks like she could take on the whole world and still be the last one standing.

When she sees me waiting there, a small smile graces her lips and my fingertips dig into my palms to remind myself that I can't let her beauty get to me.

"You look like you were born to be showcased in the tarmagalcite, King Jadon," she says, her voice like music. "Perhaps I should've chosen another location where I would not be at such a disadvantage." She's teasing, but her appraising eye could almost make me think she likes what she sees as much as I do.

"Trust me, Lady Delilah, you are clearly in the advantage here. Your beauty quite precedes you. If we weren't sworn enemies, I would be forced to admit that you take my breath away."

Her chuckle is low and sets an explosion in my chest. "I wonder how candid you would be as a sworn friend."

"It's a shame we won't be allowed to know," I say softly. The words make me sad even as I say them in the same playful tone she's using. I shove those thoughts down deep where they can't surface again and clear my throat. "Why did you call this meeting, Lady—"

"Please, call me Delilah. That should be the one benefit of this divide between us...titles can surely be set aside here in the stars, no?"

"Very well. I've never been much for titles anyway."

She stares at me for a long time, long enough that I want to squirm but manage to fight it. I could force my agenda, but she called this meeting and I respect her for it...no matter what manipulation may lie behind it.

"It's no secret that my father hasn't been well and my cousin is becoming more of a leader in my kingdom every day. I have wanted to do my part for so long, but my father insists on protecting me." She shoots a rueful look at me and walks to the wall that has the most light bouncing off of the tarmagalcite. "I don't want him to have to work so hard. Keeping him healthy is very important to me and my cousin has taken on enough responsibility...that's why I'm here. I would like to extend a peace treaty among our kingdoms and have your assurance that you will forge the way with not only your people but the people of Niaps. The two of you are our biggest adversaries and if I had your word that we will not come to war, it would put my mind at ease."

She looks at me as if waiting for me to say something, but I'm too stunned by what she's saying to form a clear thought just yet. Either she is extremely naïve or she thinks I am; I have a feeling neither is true. I just don't know what game she's playing.

When she doesn't say anything else, the silence between us grows until it's an uncomfortable itch in the air.

Finally, she says, "Will you not respond to what I've said?"

I clasp my hands and press my lips together, willing myself to say this as clearly as possible.

"I have reason to believe your father was conspiring with Titus Catano in the murder of my father. I also believe your family is behind the recent kidnapping of my sister and stepmother, and the result was a murder attempt on my life. Now, if you want to discuss a peace treaty, you will have to convince me that your family really knows the meaning of peace and that the decree will be followed to the letter. Since it is you coming forward with this instead of someone who has the authority to do so, such as your father, I'm afraid I cannot agree to anything."

The softness leaves her features in an instant and I'm sure if we were in the light of day, I'd see her flushed cheeks. In this lighting, she looks pinched and pale, but the anger is still easy to see.

"And this conversation started out so well," she mutters.

"If you want to discuss your beauty, I can do that all day. However, I have a kingdom to run and my life to protect, so I'm afraid I'll have to say goodbye. I don't mean to offend when I say this, but beyond seeing you in person, I'm not sure what the purpose of this visit was. From the surface, it seems you are in way over your head. Please take this in the kindest way possible, because it has truly been an honor to meet you, but I ask that you never waste my time like this again."

I reach out and take her hand, kissing it and ignoring the rapid thumping of my heartbeat as I do so. I hear the quick intake of her breath and without waiting to see what other sorcery comes out of her mouth, I turn and walk out of the cave. When I reach the sunlight, I take a deep cleansing breath and shake my hands out in front of my body. Once I catch my bearings, I head back to the car and drive to the hotel, feeling a strange disappointment that I won't be seeing Delilah again.

CHAPTER FOUR

Jadon

The more I think about my conversation with Delilah, the more troubling I find it. Why did I rush out of there? I have so many questions. Why didn't I take advantage of us finally meeting to get some answers?

I step into the hall because I'm tired of pacing in my hotel room and run into a woman with short black hair.

"My apologies," I say, my hands on her arms.

She doesn't respond, and when I give her a closer look, she backs away, turning to walk in the other direction. I grab her arm and move until I can see her face again.

"Delilah? What are you doing here?"

She frowns and yanks her arm away. "No need to manhandle me. I'm staying here."

"Why the disguise and what were you doing outside my room?"

She levels me with a look that would put me in my place if I weren't so on guard.

"I'm staying in the room below this...I must have gotten off on the wrong floor."

"You expect me to believe that?" I put my hands on my hips and count to ten. Living with my stepmother has taught me this lesson well. Don't trust anyone until they earn it. "I regret leaving so hastily...without getting to the bottom of why you really called this meeting. I suggest you step into my room before I tell the authorities there was a woman lurking outside my room."

Her eyes flash like a little spitfire. She gets on her tiptoes and gets in my face. "You wouldn't dare."

"Oh, try me." I open my door and motion for her to step inside. "I'll give you five minutes to explain yourself and then we can say our goodbyes for good."

She huffs but walks into my room and sits on the loveseat by the window. She yanks her wig off and her hair spills down her back. The fact that she looks like a vision means nothing to me right now.

Yeah, you keep telling yourself that, buddy. I can hear my little sister in my head, calling me out for being so transparent.

"I have one question." I stay near the door so I'll have a quick escape should she try to—what could she really do? She's tiny and I'm sure she doesn't have a gun hidden in her dress anywhere.

She's the enemy, I remind myself.

"Well, are you going to stand there all day or are you going to ask your 'one question'?" she asks, her eyes nearly rolling back in her head.

I look at her for a few seconds longer and then go sit by her, pleased when she flushes as my shoulder brushes hers.

"Are you this cheeky with all the kings you meet?"

"No, something about you brings it out in me," she says, grinning. "Was that your question?"

This time I do groan. "No, it wasn't. Why did you tell me to watch my back?"

She shifts uncomfortably with that question, the lightness in her demeanor quickly shifting.

"It's been no secret that there was a threat on your life. I hoped I'd get to meet you before anything bad happened to you."

"And who do you suspect to be behind this? Can you admit there's a strong possibility that it's your father?"

"If it were my father, that would mean he has a good reason to protect himself. What have you threatened him with lately?"

It's as I suspected, she's here to fish, either of her own accord or to take information back to her father. I suspect he loves her too much to put her at this much risk, but he's a despicable man...maybe I'm giving him too much credit.

I need space and get up to stand in front of the window.

"I have never threatened your father. I've only ever come forward with talks of peace and to negotiate ways to move past the barriers between our kingdoms...there has been no threat from me. The last I knew, your father was very sick and wasn't in a position to be harmful, so I thought my life was in the clear for a while longer. This cousin of yours...he seems intent to carry things further than your father ever has. Do you find that to be true?"

Her expressions have shifted from hopeful to guarded to confused all in the course of seconds.

"How involved are you in the running of Alidonia, Delilah?"

Her shoulders falter for a second before she sits up straight, stoicism bouncing off of her. She's probably counting on me not noticing, but I try my best not to miss a thing when it comes to my adversaries. And the way I can't take my eyes off of her is only adding to my attention to detail. My eyes narrow on her hands fisting and unfisting and her face is flushed when I look at her again.

"I'm here, aren't I?"

I wait for her to say more and when she doesn't, I chuckle. "You say that as if it's an answer."

Her eyes flash with anger and she stands, stalking toward me until I wonder if she might mow me down. I hear her sharp intake of breath and force myself not to react to the nearness of her. She's extremely hard to ignore.

"What do you want?" I whisper. "Does your father even know you're here?"

Her chest rises and falls and I can't resist, I reach out and brush my fingers across her face. Her eyes close and her lips part and I have never been so fucking turned on in my life. When her eyes flutter open, my craving for her is so strong that I'm practically trembling inside. I school my features into indifference and wait for her next cue.

She leans in and I stop breathing for the seconds she stares up at me, our noses nearly touching.

"I don't want my father's last days to be spent stressing over what you're going to do next. Why is he so obsessed with you if not for your threatening him in some way? Back down and let us live in peace. Better yet, submit to my father and let's join kingdoms."

I frown at her, momentarily taken aback. When she continues to stare up at me with those eyes that remind me of the stones in the Cave of Stars, I clench my jaw shut and fold my arms across my chest, causing her to take a step back.

"Either you have been grossly misled or your naïveté is

appalling." The contempt drips from my voice and I don't bother anymore to contain it. "I'm not sure which is more detestable." The color rises in her cheeks and it gives me a small dose of satisfaction. "I suggest you go home, ask your daddy to fill you in on the way he conducts business, and let us take things from there."

If I thought her flushed skin was due to embarrassment, the way her eyes flash in the next instant proves me wrong.

"You're no better than any other man, thinking that I'm incapable of anything because I'm a woman. I assure you, I am fully capable."

"I have no doubt that if you were informed, you would be fully capable; however, all you have proven today is that you know nothing. You know nothing about me, and sadly, it seems you know nothing about your father...or in the case of the latter, I'd say that's probably a blessing since you can't choose who your father is." I soften my next words and attempt the mercy that usually comes easily to me...for some reason, she has me in a rage I don't typically feel toward anyone. "You're playing a dangerous game, Delilah. One you don't know the rules to, and one in which you don't have all of the information...please go home before someone is needlessly hurt."

I move past her and she reaches out and grabs my arm.

"Is that a threat?"

I sigh and feel the weight of what I have to do every day as king bearing down on my chest.

"For the last time, I am not a threat to you." I steady my eyes on her and pray that she's paying attention. "But I'd be worried about your family, once they find out you've been playing negotiator. Something tells me there's a reason you've been kept in the dark."

She pales and the way her skin can go from flushed to

white is fascinating. I swallow hard and attempt to think of something other than what her skin would do under my touch. What shade would her skin turn under the stubble of my chin or if I sucked her skin between my lips and gave it the hard bite that suddenly seems to be all I can think about...how many shades of pink?

"Please don't let anyone know about this meeting." Her voice shakes and the way she clenches my arm sends a bolt right through me. "What can I do to convince you that I have the right motives?"

"Go home and stay out of this."

I put my hand over hers and the way she looks up at me is almost beguiling enough for me to want to move mountains just to see her content. I drop my hand like it's on fire and her hand falls off of my arm as I walk toward the window.

"And if, God forbid, my father doesn't live and I become queen—will you be more forthright in your political aspirations toward my country?"

I rub my temples and focus on the colors of the sunset. We're going to just continue in these circles if we try to talk any longer.

"I've entertained this conversation long enough," I say with as much kindness as I can. "I'll ask you to close the door behind you on your way out."

A few seconds later, I hear the click of the door closing and take a deep breath, sagging into the window. *What was that?* I feel like I've run a marathon and am in last place, not sure where I went wrong. Watch my back indeed... somehow the attraction to Delilah Farthing feels far more dangerous than any recent attempts on my life.

CHAPTER FIVE

Delilah

I go home feeling defeated and like I have more questions than ever. My conversation with Jadon has plagued my thoughts all the way home. And what makes it worse is that I don't know how I'm going to find out the truth when I was supposed to have been on a shopping expedition...for a *wardrobe*, not gaining secrets from our greatest ally.

When I think of Jadon, my body turns to mush. I resort to a typical female, all giddy inside over a gorgeous man whose power seeps from his pores. I'm thoroughly ashamed of the way I fell captive to his charms; even when he wasn't being charming, the passion that exuded from him when he was abrasive was almost more powerful.

The only thing I really accomplished from this trip is knowing I could sneak out and none would be the wiser. Diego leaves as soon as my father greets us, his exhaustion from partying while we were away probably sending him straight to bed. And my father smiles warmly at me and hugs me as tight as his weak body can manage.

"Did you buy out all the shops?" he asks.

"Not quite. But I did get some nice things. Maybe I can take another trip later to fill in what I didn't find..."

He pats my cheek. "I'm glad you got away. You've spent too much of your time cooped up in this house, worried about me. It's time we have a little fun. I decided something while you were away."

"Oh?" I grin. I can tell by the mischief in his eyes that he's up to something and it makes me so happy to see the life back in his eyes.

"I've decided to throw a ball," he says, clasping his hands together. His smile is bigger than I've seen it in years and I hug him again.

"That's a great idea! Anything that makes you smile like this..." I lean back and beam at him.

"It'll be the biggest ball any of the kingdoms have ever seen...and all the key players will be here to witness it," he pauses to let his words sink in.

I put a hand to my throat when I realize what he's saying. "You're inviting all of the monarchies *here*? Is that wise?"

He throws back his head and laughs and I shiver, my nerves feeling whiplashed.

"Sweetheart, trust me, you won't have to worry about a thing. We will have more security than anyone knows what to do with, and you won't have to lift a finger for any of the arrangements unless you want to help with the planning. While you were gone, I handled most of that. You just need to show up and be your beautiful self."

I groan and scowl at him, which just makes him laugh harder.

"I'm capable of doing a lot more around here. I wish you'd let me," I shake my finger at him, "but I'm glad to see you excited about something. How about I take it from here and you just keep getting better. How much time do we have to plan this?"

"Invitations have already gone out and it will be in two weeks."

"What? No one will be able to arrange that with such short notice!"

"When the almighty King Farthing gets up from the dead, you don't think people want to see it for themselves? They will find a way to get here, mark my words."

He puts his arm around my shoulder and we walk into the living room.

"You probably didn't purchase something suitable for a ball of this magnitude on your trip," he teases. "We can have a selection of gowns brought in for you to consider...in the next few days, if you'd like."

"I can't believe you've done all of this in such a short amount of time." My eyes well with tears and as we sit on the couch, I take his hand. "Just a month ago, I thought I was losing you."

"I have at least six lives left," he says, laying his other hand on top of mine.

I look at my father, grateful that the color is in his cheeks, that he doesn't seem feverish, and that his body is beginning to fill out again after months of emaciation. His recovery is nothing short of remarkable.

"Thank you for fighting this sickness, Papa," I whisper, my words catching in my throat. "And for getting the best care. I-I don't know what I'd do without you."

"You'd be just fine without me. I've made sure Caulder knows the ins and outs of what will be required of both of you. You can lean on him for whatever support you need whenever the time comes."

"Hopefully that won't be for a long, long time. You're still young, after all." I smile when he makes a face. "I'm glad Caulder's here, but it's not the same as having you. He still thinks of me as his pesky younger cousin who is always trying to be in his business."

My father chuckles and looks so much like he used to in that moment. I study his features, trying to imagine the man Jadon thinks my father is...the monster he portrayed in his few words about him. The father I know is, at worst, over-protective and somewhat old-fashioned, but he could never be as evil as Jadon made him sound.

"Caulder will show you the proper respect when it's time," he laughs again, "but I think you're right, in his mind, you're still tattling on him for smoking behind the bushes."

"I haven't smoked behind the bushes in ages—are you still dredging up my past, Delilah?" Caulder walks in looking the part of a regal aristocrat, not a hair or thread out of place. He winks and pulls out a cigarette case from his pocket. "I don't have to go hide behind the bushes now, scared you'll rat me out again."

I get up, snatching the case out of his hands. I wave it in front of him. "These will kill you. I can't help it that I want the two men in my life to live forever."

He smirks and holds out his hand for the case. I roll my eyes but drop the case in his hand and he puts it back in his pocket.

"You're not queen yet...you're not the boss of me," he says it playfully, but something in his eyes makes me take a step back and I sit down by my father again, unsettled.

Caulder laughs then. "The two of you are a serious bunch today. We have a ball in two weeks. We should start drinking and being merry now...so it's not a shock to our system then." He goes to the bar and pulls out two glasses. He lifts an eye to my father and grins when he's rewarded with a brisk nod.

I frown and look at my dad. "The doctor said you shouldn't—"

"Oh, let the man breathe, Delilah. He's been laid up in that bed for months. Let him live a little." Caulder fills two glasses with brandy and when he brings my father his and doesn't hand me the other glass but clashes the glass with my father's and then finishes it in one gulp, I scowl at him.

"Thank you, that was so sweet of you to offer," I grumble. I stand up and walk to the bar. "Guess I'll get my own."

"There will come a day when I do all your bidding," Caulder says. "But as I said, that day is not here yet."

My face heats as I pour myself a drink and lift it to both of them. He's always saying things like that and it gets under my skin every time. I didn't ask to be the next in line. I wish it could be Caulder and he lets me know in these small ways all the time that he wishes the same thing. But in the next glance, he's grinning and sticking his tongue out at me and I relax; my cousin has always known how to push my buttons. Even more than my brother used to.

"To Papa's health." I lift my glass to them and let the liquid slide down my throat, enjoying the burn.

Again, Jadon's words about my father being behind the threat to his life and the murder of his father fights its way to the surface and I try to push it back down again. Jadon is my father's biggest enemy; of course, he'd try to plant doubt.

My cousin sits where I'd been sitting and he and my father resume a conversation they must've started the last time they were together. My mind wanders back to Jadon. I didn't like all the things that came out of his mouth, the seeds he tried to plant against my family, but the way he seemed to instinctively know I was in over my head and didn't throw me out...the forthcoming way he spoke to me... that's something that is sorely missing in my life. Having that for even the briefest amount of time was addicting.

And I'm craving more.

CHAPTER SIX

Jadon

When I return, the pup I left behind is waiting at the door, tail thumping like a drum stick against the floor.

"Well, look at you. You're looking much better." I bend down and pet her and her tail thumps faster. She stands up and circles around me, licking my face and when I stand up, she jumps up, her paws on my shoulders. "I'd never know you were hurt..." I lower her paws. "Sit, girl." She stares up at me and sits, tail resuming its steady beat. It's hard not to smile when she's so damn cute.

Jonz, who has recently done double duty as a guard and sometimes housekeeper, walks by and stops when he sees me with the dog. "As soon as I brought her back to the house from the vet, she ran to your office to look for you and then stationed herself in front of the door." Jonz shakes his head. "This is the most active she's been. I've actually been worried about her. She's hardly eaten."

As he says that, the dog goes to the nearby bowl that's

sitting by the door, and starts chowing down. I laugh and she turns to stare at me, tail wagging again.

"Aw, sweet girl, you are hard to resist." I reach out and pet her. "What should we call you?" Her snowy white fur is cleaner than when I left. The vet must have cleaned her up before sending her home. "You look like a snow queen, white as a ghost. I'd name you Ghost, but you deserve something more beautiful..." Delilah comes to mind and I'm tempted to name my dog Queenie after her, but it would make me think of the future queen even more than I already am.

I can't stop thinking about her. Night and day. She invades every brain cell. I'm supposed to be running the damn kingdom and I can't get her beautiful eyes and lips out of my head. The way her breasts curved with the light of the stones on the cave ceiling casting just the right brilliance across her...

"Okay, Star it is," I tell the dog. "From now on, you will be the only star I think about." She nudges me with her nose and I pet her. I start walking to my office and she follows.

Jonz laughs behind me. "Looks like she's just been waiting for you to get home."

A couple days later, I notice a stack of mail in the entryway. Usually it's brought to my office, but as I thumb through it, I realize it's been sitting here for a few days. An elaborate envelope is at the top and I open it first, taking the pile back to the office. Since Kathryn has been moved to a nearby facility, I've asked some of the staff to care for her so she doesn't feel so alone, but I probably should have someone here more often if I'm missing mail.

I slide a letter opener through the envelope and pull out a gem-studded invitation. When I read it all the way through, I blow out a long stream of air and sit down at my desk, reading it again to make sure I'm not imagining things.

A grand ball in less than two weeks at the Farthing castle in Alidonia.

It's a first in at least forty years that the Safrins have been invited to a Farthing event. I rub the gems absent-mindedly, imagining seeing Delilah again. Is this her doing? Did she plan our meeting so I'd be sure to come to Alidonia? Is this a setup?

I have to set it aside to get through a few meetings, but in the evening after supper, I call Luka and ask him if he received the invitation.

"I was just going to call you. I got the invitation a few days ago and haven't known what to think."

"We're going, right?" I ask, pulling up a picture of Delilah on my laptop. She looks younger in this picture...

"Do you think that's wise? What do you think this is about?"

"It's probably Farthing's way of saying *I'm healthy, I'm back, watch out.*" I grit my teeth and shake my head. "I think we should go and let him know we're not afraid of him. We're not backing down."

"Okay. If you say so. He *is* honor-bound to not harm any of us or our families while we're there. He won't break that vow. It's in the bloodstones," Luka says. "But I don't doubt that he's up to *something.*"

"I almost missed the invitation altogether...didn't even see it until today." My voice drifts off.

"You need to hire someone already. I feel like a broken record," he adds, laughing.

We end the call when Elias knocks on his door, ready for their meeting. Luka's become one of my closest confidantes since he married my sister. He has the same challenges I do, only he's ruling across the world in his kingdom of Niaps. Sometimes I wish we could scrap everything and have a good old-fashioned family vacation. My sister Ava and her boyfriend Gentry would be there too, and we could do normal things like—well, what do people even do on vacation? I've never been on one.

Luka is always telling me I need a right-hand man like Elias, his assistant, to help out with the day-to-day, but after my stepmother almost killed me on my own property, I haven't been as trusting of anyone. In fact, I've let most of my staff go.

I'd gotten used to the idea of thinking Farthing was no longer a threat with him being on his deathbed for such a long time, and now it's difficult to know otherwise. I've thought it should've been him dying instead of my father many times. I'm not sure there's one good bone in Vance Farthing's body.

Delilah sure seemed to think there is.

I pick up my phone and carry it to my bedroom. I want to talk to Delilah, ask her about this ridiculous ball, but I shouldn't call her. I take my second shower of the day just to distract myself from thinking about her. Doesn't work. What kind of crazy spell did she put on me?

I crawl into bed, my list for the next day already made. *Luka's right. I need a new assistant*, I remind myself. It's crazy not to do more delegating. Tomorrow.

I toss and turn and look at the clock a dozen times. What time is it in Alidonia? It's midnight here and I think it's eight there. I pick up my phone and do something really stupid.

What is this about a ball?

I immediately see the dots of her replying and my heart pounds. I wasn't sure if she'd bother responding.

Delilah: It's all my father's idea. I came home and he already had a party planned out. So far, there has been no RSVP from the Safrin family...does that mean you won't be in attendance?

I pause before answering, unsure of what to say. It feels almost like a conversation between friends and I have to remind myself to be cautious.

I'll be there. I hope it's truly as the invitation says and that this is simply a celebration of your father's life. Possibly a gesture of goodwill?

Delilah: I assure you that nothing bad will happen to you while you're here, King Jadon...I had no idea you were such a scaredy-cat.

I grin. I can just imagine her mouth quirking up as she makes a sassy comment, the way her eyes crinkle at the corners and her perfectly straight teeth shining. I run my hand through my hair and groan. I don't need to entertain thoughts of Delilah's smiling eyes or her mouth. But fuck me if I don't do it anyway.

I assure you I'm no pussy...although I have nothing against them personally.

There's nothing for several long seconds and I am about to punch my fist into the mattress when she starts typing.

Delilah: Do you turn every comment into a sexual innuendo or only late at night?

I curse out loud and toss the phone aside. I need to stop this now. I have better things to do, for jinga's sake. I haven't slept with Mavis in a month, but she's always willing and available. The problem with her is I think what started out as harmless fun seems to be her wanting more from me lately...which is why I've stayed away the past month.

Maybe I imagined that though—she swore she never expected a commitment from me. I could take her at her word and seek out her distraction—anything that will put a stop to this sudden obsession with Delilah.

My apologies. I shouldn't be texting this late at night.

Delilah: Don't apologize! It was just starting to get fun.

I draw in a deep breath and my eyes widen at the ceiling. I sit up in bed and stare at the phone again.

Well, do carry on then. I grin and wait to see what she has to say.

Delilah: Why are you never photographed with a lady besides your sisters, Lord Jadon?

My sisters make me look good. Why else?

Delilah: That doesn't work with me. Do you have commitment issues?

Damn. You don't mess around with small talk, do you?

Delilah: Once pussy is mentioned, no, I don't.

Fuck me. ***This IS Delilah Farthing, correct?***

Delilah: The one and only.

So you discuss pussy on a regular basis?

Delilah: I'm starting to think we're not just discussing scaredy-cats anymore.

I chuckle out loud and walk to the bar on the far side of my bedroom, pouring myself two fingers of whiskey. I tilt the glass back, savoring the last sips, and pour another finger. Another indulgence I don't usually allow myself. The burn down my throat feels like an adrenaline rush. I set the glass down and pick up the phone, ready for whatever is next.

Once you mentioned sexual innuendos, I'm pretty sure you were in on the joke. But we can pretend you're still sweet and innocent, if you'd prefer that.

Delilah: I'm plenty sweet and innocent, trust me. This is the best conversation I've had in my life. How sad is that?

I laugh and it sounds loud in my room this late at night, when the castle is sleeping. Not for the first time, I wish for a quaint cottage that would feel cozy and warm instead of this cavernous monstrosity. I imagine Delilah lying in her bed, smiling at her phone, while I'm over here hard as granite.

Something tells me you're not as innocent as you seem. This conversation being the main clue. Your secret meeting with me being the other. Don't get me wrong, I am here for it.

Delilah: Since I am but a lowly princess and not a KING, tell me how it works...you have someone at your disposal at all times and don't have to worry about hurting feelings or stringing anyone along? Everyone just knows you're allowed to do whatever you want?

Mavis comes to mind again and I cringe, feeling guilty that I even considered having sex with her again after realizing she might have feelings.

When you put it that way, I sound like a terrible person. Let me clear one thing up. You could never be considered lowly. Have you looked in a mirror lately? Lowly is the last thing you are. Goddess, more like. And on the topic of disposals...I don't regard any human as a waste. I have had mutually beneficial attachments that are maybe not the best option, but it's pretty impossible to find a wife while being king. I refuse to have an arranged marriage. It worked out for my sister, but she is one of the few. And how do I trust anyone?

Delilah: I can see I've hit a sore spot. But thank you for the compliment. I'm hardly a goddess, but I do appreciate your silky words. You're good, really good.

I assure you they're not just words.

It's quiet for a few moments and I wonder if I've said too much. Scratch that—I KNOW I've said too much. My skin is heated and I feel like I've just exposed my soul to the devil. A beautiful she-devil who seems to know how to get under my skin, but a devil nonetheless.

Enemy, enemy, enemy, I remind myself.

The phone dings again and I reluctantly pick it up.

Delilah: You are much nicer than I realized. What if you really are a good person?

Well, I should hope I am! It's really all I strive to be.

Delilah: Wouldn't it be crazy if all the things we've always heard about each other were never true at all, and we're actually both really good people deep down inside?

I think about that and about her father, who my father

always said was the worst human he'd ever met. What if that hasn't touched Delilah? How could it not? I shake my head and decide to put an end to this nonsense.

No one is ever all good or all bad. But our kingdoms are known enemies and I can't help but think your father is out to destroy me. So I guess it doesn't really matter if deep down you're good-hearted. We will always be on opposite sides of the fence. Goodnight, Delilah. I'll see you at the ball.

I turn the power off on my phone, but when I turn it on a few sleepless hours later, she hasn't responded anyway.

I can't help but regret what I said.

CHAPTER SEVEN

Jadon

Two weeks later

I haven't spoken to Delilah since that night. I've started working out at night until I can hardly move...anything to keep myself from texting her again. Her lure is more than it should be, that she can be speaking to me from across the world without saying anything at all.

I will be seeing her tonight and to say I'm apprehensive about it is an understatement. I will stay as far away from her as I can. Luka and Eden will be there, so I'm hoping I'll be distracted.

I tie an elaborate Farrow knot around my neck and smooth down my tux. I was tempted to cut my hair for the occasion, but I'm not willing to make any extra effort for the Farthings. My tux is black and my tie is gold, the colors keeping with our tradition for grand balls. It's been years since I've been to anything as elaborate as this and the fact that it's hosted at the Farthing castle has my nerves getting the better of me. I wish Father were by my side to face Farthing. He was the face of calm at all times. He knew what to say in every situation, and I'd give anything for his wisdom now. I force myself to sit and meditate in my hotel suite for a few moments before leaving.

Fifteen minutes before we're set to leave, I meet Luka and Eden in their penthouse suite. Luka has at least a dozen guards watching over us, which feels like overkill compared to my three, but I'm grateful he has extra protection for my sister.

Eden rushes forward when she sees me, her gown swishing as she sweeps across the marble floor. She wraps her arms around me and squeezes tight.

"You look beautiful."

"So do you. Who knew you could clean up so well?" she teases, straightening my jacket when she pulls away.

"Apparently, no one." I grin and look over her shoulder at Luka. He pulls me into a bear hug. "You're looking pretty decent yourself, Catano," I tell him.

"Ah, brother, it's good to see your face. We'll go in and make a formidable front—the Farthings won't know what hit them." He pounds me on the back and nods his approval as he checks out my suit. He's become quite the softie since marrying Eden, when he isn't talking politics.

"Let's not talk about hitting anyone," Eden says, giving both Luka and me a stern look.

"If they mess with you, all bets are off," he says, growling as he leans down and kisses her.

"Okay, that's enough. I can't even tell you to get a room since I'm in yours, but let's go before this gets more awkward than it already is." I open the door and Eden laughs, pulling away from Luka.

"I've always wanted to meet Princess Delilah," she says once we're seated in our limo.

"She's not what I expected," I say before I can stop myself.

"What do you mean?" she asks.

I look out the window and wish I'd kept my mouth shut. Eden is like a dog on a hunt when she tries to set me up with someone. If she catches a whiff of my interest in Delilah, she will be merciless about shutting that down. There's no reason for her to ever know a thing—I've shut it all completely down myself.

"I didn't know you'd met Delilah! When was this? What is she like?" The questions pour out of her and I level her with a look. "What?" She frowns.

"I'm sure she'll be just as enthralled with you and your gown and your—" I wave my hand toward her hair that is done up in her finest rose curls and twists, hoping flattery will distract her from the fact that I didn't answer any of her questions.

"Oh, you like my gown and hair?" she asks, grinning. "Why, thank you. It's like pulling teeth to get a compliment from you."

"I said you looked beautiful!" I laugh, rolling my eyes.

"You'd say that to anyone. You have to get specific with women, Jadon. This is why you're still single," she says, jabbing me in the stomach.

I jerk to the side and catch her finger before she can do it again. "Enough," I laugh, "you're as bad as Ava." I sigh. "I really wish she could be here tonight too. I'd feel better if we were all together."

"I know what you mean," Eden says. "I wish she was

too, but I'm also glad she's gotten as far from this life as possible. It's what she wanted more than anything."

I sigh again and sink deeper into my seat. My sister Ava never wanted the life of a royal, and I've tried my best to ensure she doesn't have to live that life. She endured too much in the past few months; now she deserves whatever her heart desires and she's getting that with her beloved Gentry. Still, I miss her. We used to talk just about every day and now we talk once a week.

Eden starts to say something and stops in mid-sentence with a loud gasp. The Farthing castle has just come into view, and it is unlike anything I've ever seen. The grandeur is out of this world, the turrets and columns sweeping up to the sky and standing proudly. The entirety of the Safrin castle could fit into the east wing.

"Holy shit," I mutter. "What have we gotten ourselves into?"

Luka sits up taller. "Only what we were born to do," he says. "Don't forget that, brother. Don't let this opulence intimidate you. They are mere flesh and blood, just like us. Only without the human decency," he adds under his breath.

The car pulls around the circular drive and Quincie steps out to open our door.

"Looking good, Quincie," I tell him and he nods.

"You too, King," he says. Man of few words.

I look up and up and up, taking in the architectural masterpiece. I may not like anything about the way this king has run his empire, but I can appreciate the beauty in his palace. And a palace it is. There is no detail left undone. We walk along the gold carpet and photographers snap pictures. I'm surprised by the photographers but relieved that no journalists line the carpet. It feels a bit more personal that way, but the journalists might also be waiting inside.

I see the king ahead and next to him stands a tall, good-looking younger man. He could be close to thirty, but it's hard to tell. When we get nearer, King Farthing steps forward and reaches out both hands.

"I'm honored to have your Lordships both grace my abode at once. Welcome, King Safrin." He bows deeply and I bow in return. "Welcome, King Catano." He bows toward Luka. And then his eyes widen when he sees Eden. "Queen Eden, songs are sung about your beauty. Now I know why." He kisses her hand and she lowers her head in respect.

We're introduced to Caulder, and his expression isn't as warm as the king's, but he smiles and has friendly pleasantries to offer, nothing of note. I get a slide of unease down my spine when he looks my way and I vow to get to the bottom of that...another time. While I'm a guest in their home I must behave as one.

We're ushered inside and I look around for Delilah but don't see her anywhere. The ballroom is as exquisite as the rest of the place and it's a lot to take in. We're led to a table that seats eight and Eden sits down while Luka and I stand behind her waiting for the king to enter. Most of the ballroom is full already.

Alex comes over a few minutes later, the newly-appointed king of Yuman since the death of his father. He whistles under his breath as he shakes my hand and then Luka's.

"What do you suppose this is all about?" he asks.

"No idea," Luka says. "Some sort of dick check most likely. I stand corrected, if we're going by castle size alone, he's the clear winner." Luka and Alex laugh and Eden rolls her eyes then glares at Luka. His laugh immediately dies down and he wipes a hand over his mouth. "My wife doesn't appreciate dick jokes."

"If you can at least hold the jokes until we're out of the Farthing ballroom, that would be greatly appreciated," she snaps, and he holds both hands up, pressing his lips together.

"Noted," he says. He looks at me and winks and I get a glare of my own from Eden when I start laughing.

"Don't you start too," she pleads. "Why can't you be more like King Alban over there?"

We all look over at King Alban, who is at least eighty years old and his chin is nearly touching his chest as he drifts to sleep.

"Dead, you mean?" Luka asks, his voice cracking with laughter. Eden shoots another look at him and I jab him in the side.

"If you don't want to be murdered in the enemy territory by your wife, I'd cut the jokes for now," I tell him through my teeth. My stomach is clenched as tight as a trap to avoid laughing, but I know my sister. She's nervous, and when she's nervous and angry, her temper comes out ahead.

"Finally, someone with sense," Eden says.

I grin at her and Luka groans.

But then I'm the one groaning next when the room titters with excitement. I feel the rush in my chest before I've even seen her and turn, knowing she's entered the room.

And oh my God, that woman. She is a work of art. Everything in me sparks to life when I see her.

Delilah.

CHAPTER EIGHT

Delilah

Last night, my dad switched things up on me. I'd spent a few days getting alterations done on the dress I chose, and right before bed, he knocked on my door and was carrying a long dress bag.

"You don't have to wear this. I know you've decided on something, but I was looking at this and it seemed like it would fit like it was made for you. Your mother's," he added.

When he unzipped the bag, my eyes widened. "It's her engagement gown."

He smiled at me fondly, proud that I remembered. I used to look at their old pictures all the time when she first died. It's been a while, but this dress isn't something I could ever forget.

"You really think it would fit me?"

He nodded and held it out for me to take. "Think about it. There is no pressure to wear it, but I know your mother would be honored if she were here."

I stared at it before bed, but I didn't feel comfortable trying it on. I wanted to wait until this morning when Papa said he'd have someone who could help me put it on, so I didn't rip any of the beading.

When someone knocks on my door and I open it to find a woman, I'm shocked.

"I'm Darcy." She lowers her head and curtsies.

"Nice to meet you. Please come in."

Even though I wouldn't expect a man to help me in my dress, it's still unusual to see a woman. Since my mother died, I've been the only woman in the house. I let her in, and she stops abruptly when she sees the gown hanging in the window.

"Your mother's gown," she whispers. Her eyes fill with tears. "She was a vision in that dress. You will wear it tonight?"

"Did you know my mother?" I hear the hope in my voice, the yearning that never goes away to know more about my mother.

"No, but I remember the pictures. You look so much like her."

"Thank you." I tuck away the disappointment and focus on the dress. "I need your help putting it on. Do you really think—" I put my fingers on the sheer fabric that would fall between my breasts, the beads the only thing covering up anything.

"Yes," she interrupts. "You must wear it. It is a great honor. This is the future queen's—"

She stops suddenly when there's another knock on the door.

"Come in," I say, straightening my robe.

My father walks in with a gorgeous floral beaded head-dress. I'd forgotten that in most of the pictures, my mom wore the beautiful heirloom. I gasp when he hands it to me.

"I don't want to do anything to mess it up."

"Anything can be fixed. If you want to wear it, it's yours." He beams at me and I swallow the lump in my throat.

"I'm so happy you're well, Papa. I think this is a wonderful idea, celebrating your life." I reach out and hug him and he pats me on the back while I sniffle.

When he steps back, he clears his throat and looks unsettled.

"Are you okay?" I ask. "You're not overdoing it, are you?"

He looks at the floor and shakes his head. "I'm fine, sweetheart. I'm happy to do something special for you tonight. This is a night you will long remember."

I crinkle my nose and grin at him, unused to his over-the-top sentimentality. He chuckles when he sees my face and points toward the door.

"I better leave you to get ready or you'll be late for your own party," he says.

"Your party," I correct.

He does an exaggerated nod. "Right. *My* party."

The dress is so revealing, it's hard to imagine my mother ever wearing this, but it fits perfectly. I feel like I'm slipping on a costume that is way more exquisite than anything I've worn, and once I slip the headdress over my waves, the floral beading catching the light just right, I feel like I've stepped back in the early days of Alidonian royalty.

"Wow," Darcy breathes. "I can't believe the resemblance to your mother. Dare I say even more beautiful," she whispers, her hand on her throat. "No one will be able to look away."

My father comes back a few minutes before I'm supposed to walk down to the ballroom. He stares at me, his mouth dropping when I open the door.

"Are you sure this is okay?" I ask.

"I'm so proud of you, baby girl," he says. He holds out his arm and I loop my hand through it. We walk toward the staircase and Caulder is standing at the bottom of the stairs, talking to a tall man with long blond hair. They both look up and watch as I slowly descend the stairs. The stranger looks me over so thoroughly, I feel way too exposed. I clasp my dad's arm tighter and focus on Caulder. He looks even cockier than usual.

"Delilah," he says, bowing low. He holds out his arm to his friend and nods toward Papa.

We reach the bottom and my dad puts his arm around the man. They all turn to face me and I feel my skin flush with all the attention.

"Allow me to introduce you to King Avaban of Blorl," my father says. "This is my beautiful daughter, Delilah."

King Avaban's eyes get stuck between my breasts, even as he's lowering his head in a bow. "She's a beauty all right," he says.

He takes my hand even though I haven't offered it and my skin gets clammy all over. I nearly pull it back before he can kiss it, but my father's expectant smile forces me to pause. I swallow hard, feeling a little sick and chalk it up to nerves and being severely grossed out by King Avaban. He looks about forty and the pervy vibes he's putting out are enough to make me want to run back to my bedroom.

Instead, I pull my hand away and give the slightest nod. He licks his lips and stares at my mouth, his eyes looking like ice.

"Well, we should get to the party, Papa," I say, smiling at my father. "We can't keep the guest of honor from all the guests."

He holds out his arm again and I take it, glad to be walking away from the Ice King even though I can still feel his eyes drilling holes through me.

King Avaban and Caulder go in ahead of us, saying something about a grand entrance, and then it is just Papa and me. It's quiet for a moment and I turn to my father one more time.

"You sure you're feeling up to this?"

"I've been waiting for this day for a long time," he says.

I laugh. "You must be feeling better...you've never wanted a party before."

"You'll see." He winks.

My head tilts as I'm about to ask what he's talking about when the double doors swing wide open and we are announced throughout the ballroom.

All is forgotten when I see him standing in the center of the room, his eyes sweeping over me like a caress. I shiver and this time, it's pure pleasure. King Jadon Safrin. I feel my heart begin to thud and the beginnings of a smile that I can't hide taking over my face.

Calm yourself. He's just a man. And the enemy at that.

There is a round of applause that draws me out of my stupor and I wave, trying to greet all the guests with a smile rather than just the one man who has captured my attention. A few of the guests line up to greet my father and me, and then we are ushered to our table, an elaborate feast already laid out on each table.

"You've outdone yourself, Papa," I tell him as I sit down, noticing Jadon is just one table away.

"I'm glad you're pleased," he says.

Our glasses are filled and our plates are piled high. I lift my hand to stop any more from being added to my plate; I already don't know how I'll get out of this dress if I eat anything. But Papa is so excited about all the delicacies offered, I try a little bit of everything.

"This is *shantas*...you've never had it because I couldn't find anyone who could make it as well as my grandmother... until this." He closes his eyes and savors the bite of meat-filled pastry with a creamy sauce.

I try a bite and groan. "Oh, that's the best thing I've ever tasted."

I feel eyes on me and look up to see Jadon staring at me. His blue eyes are brilliant even from a distance and his long black wavy hair shines like silk in the candlelight. He is the most perfect specimen of man I've ever seen and I wish I had the luxury of staring at him for as long as I want. There's a kindness about him that I wasn't expecting, that someone as built and brilliant as him could also be gentle is such a paradox. I must be fantasizing because all of my life I've been told the Safrins are fools of the winter, brutes who don't know the meaning of culture.

"I see you've caught the eye of King Safrin," Papa says, leaning into my ear. "I'm glad he's seeing your beauty first-hand, to know one more thing he's missing out on."

I rear back, looking at my father like I've been hit. "What are you saying?"

He shrugs. "Just that you are one more unattainable in this castle of all the things he must desire."

I set my glass down and stare at him. "I'd rather you not ever talk about me like I'm cattle, Father."

His eyes widen and he chuckles. He leans past me to look at Caulder and raises his glass. "Uh-oh, she's calling me Father now. Can't have our baby girl angry at the ball."

"Well then, don't say such ridiculous things," I snap.

Caulder laughs and my blood boils as I sit between the two of them, once again feeling like a child.

"Don't get your panties in a knot," Caulder says. "If you can even wear panties in that thing." He waves his fork up and down my dress and I want to stab him with the fork.

"Let's just enjoy the food and not talk for a while," I say. "The two of you are acting like barbarians."

They both laugh at that and I lean back in my chair, wishing I could be anywhere but here.

"It's almost time for my announcement," my father says when he takes one last swig of wine.

"Do you need help getting to the microphone or will someone bring one over?" I look toward the area that usually has the sound equipment.

He points to a mic stand next to our table and smiles. "It's moved closer and I'll be fine to walk that distance on my own. But stay close," he says.

He winks at Caulder and looks around the room to see if everyone is still eating or not. A few minutes later, he stands and walks to the mic. The room quickly silences.

"Welcome to Alidonia! I hope your evening in the Farthing castle will be a pleasing experience. On behalf of myself and my family, I would like to tell you how fortunate I am to have all of the kingdoms here to witness how healthy I am!" He raises his fist in the air and a polite applause goes around the room. "But that is not why I gathered you all here tonight." He looks at me and grins, the pride in his eyes making me smile back. "You all know how lovely my daughter Delilah is—and doesn't she look especially lovely tonight in her Alidonian headdress worn for generations before her—but I assure you, she will only get more beautiful as she blooms into womanhood."

I clasp my hands tightly together, uncertain of where he's going with this but not liking the direction. I feel conspicuous enough in this dress.

"She has always made me so proud. I've guarded her with my life, believing that no other could ever possibly take care of her as well as I can." He chuckles and shakes his head, looking at me fondly. "But there comes a day when every father must give up a small amount of control. At least enough for a husband to take charge, right?" He laughs again and I cringe inside, his ideas about a woman's place being the one snag we never seem to quite agree on. "So, with that thought in mind, I'd like to announce my daughter's engagement to none other than King Avaban of Blorl."

What? A cry escapes my mouth and I cover it, staring at my father in horror. He holds his arm out for me to come forward and on the other side of him, King Avaban is also stepping forward. Caulder nudges me from behind and when I turn and see the guests clapping, it all sounds very far away. Jadon is the only one I laser in on, his expression unreadable. My arm is suddenly gripped tightly and I turn in slow motion as Caulder forces me to walk to my father.

When I reach him, Papa holds out his hand and takes mine, firmly placing it over King Avaban's. With all three of our hands clasped together, he lifts them up in triumph.

"To this new union. Long may they reign!"

Cheers ring out throughout the room, while I stare on in confusion. I can't believe my father has done this to me. I try to rip my hand away, but he holds it tighter.

"Papa, I cannot do this," I hiss under my breath.

"Do not embarrass me, child. There are some things you have no control over, this is one of them," he says with gritted teeth.

King Avaban's eyes glitter as he stares at me, his expression a combination of contempt and arrogance. I don't even know this man's first name or anything about him other than the fact that he makes my skin crawl, and my father expects me to marry him.

I turn and my eyes meet Jadon's again, I need to see anyone other than the family who has betrayed me and the man they're auctioning me off to. I lift my head high and force myself to calm inside.

I will not succumb...I refuse to bow to this.

When the cheers die down, my father keeps talking. It's like a drone in the distance, his words meted out in my head.

My world has suddenly turned bleak.

I am terrified.

And my beloved father has broken my heart.

CHAPTER NINE

Jadon

I had no idea of what to expect at this ball, but hearing that Delilah is engaged to King Avaban of Blorl—I did not see that coming. When I first hear Farthing speak the words, an immediate rage comes over me that is completely unwarranted. For all I know, this could have long been in the works. But why then, have I felt any connection with Delilah at all, if that were the case?

Maybe she is used to toying with men's affections and I was merely something for her to bat around for fun.

It's not like anything beyond a mild flirtation happened anyway.

Even that was probably just her fishing for something to use against me.

But one look at the utter desolation on her face, her shock more apparent than anything, and I am filled with the urge to fight. Anyone will do, but at the moment, both King Farthing and King Avaban look like good options.

I try to focus on what Farthing is saying, but my eyes are glued on Delilah. A transformation takes place while we're standing there. She stands more noble than anyone I've ever seen, her neck like a swan and her head held high. She is a goddess and I believe that nothing could destroy her, except when her eyes reach mine...the truth is there for all to see. She would sooner die than marry this man.

I lock eyes with her and hope that I can convey to her even a small amount of peace. Not that anything I do could help her—who am I to her? But it's all I have. If I could hoist her over my shoulder and run out of here like a man on fire, I would do that in a heartbeat. I'm tempted to do just that. But I'd be dead in an instant and she'd be left to fend for herself anyway.

They go through a couple of customs I'm not familiar with, pouring sand on the ground for them to walk over and then lighting candles underneath Delilah and Avaban's joined hands. I don't like the smug look on Avaban's face; the contempt I've had for him is not quite up to Farthing's level, but it's right up there. He's an arrogant bastard with little to show for his attitude. He runs Blorl with an iron fist, with little regard for the less fortunate, which makes me see red. The thought of Delilah being forced to live in the dry, brown desert of Blorl after she's been used to the lush beauty of Alidonia is sad on its own merit. But imagining her living with Avaban makes it so much worse.

Everyone watches in rapt attention, and when Delilah pulls her hand away from Avaban's and causes the flame to flicker out, the gasp in the crowd circulates quickly around the room. She runs past me and her father follows but is still slow from his illness. Caulder holds his hand up to the crowd and the room hushes. My skin feels itchy from standing in this room and I rush toward the door, uncertain of what excuse I'll give if I'm stopped. The guard opens the door for me when I tell him I need to find the restroom and points down the long hallway. I see Delilah and her father talking and edge closer so I can hear them.

"How could you do this, Papa? I won't marry him!"

I can tell by the tone of her voice that she's about to cry, but she looks like fury in the thick of the storm. Her regal outfit only adds to the fire and I stop in mid-step, not caring if I'm caught staring.

"I've demanded very little of you in your life, sweetheart. This is not up for discussion. You will go back in there and put a smile on your face. You've embarrassed this family enough for one night; don't let the party end on this note."

"If I go back in there, it will be to say that you're forcing me against my will to marry that hideous man. Is that what you want?"

He grabs her arm and gets in her face and I rush forward, stopping myself when they both turn and see me standing there. In this lighting I can see that Farthing has aged considerably, but I'd guess it's the fault of the sickness more than time.

His features tighten when he sees me. "King Jadon, I'll kindly ask you to step away while my daughter and I finish this discussion."

Delilah pulls her arm away from him and then rubs it as she steps closer to me.

"Welcome to Alidonia, King Jadon." She bows her head. "I wonder if I could show you our museum of fine arts. You seem to have an eye for beauty." She smiles and God help me, it wreaks havoc on my mind and body when she does. She turns to her father and her smile drops. "Don't make a scene, Papa. We have a castle full of guests, it's time we think about them. I will show King Safrin the museum for a few moments in hopes of catching my breath."

She offers her hand to me and I tuck it in my arm, nodding at her father.

"If your father agrees, please, lead the way," I say, still looking at the king.

His face is red with anger, but he grits his teeth and nods. "Don't be long. Your future husband awaits."

Delilah squeezes my arm hard and I lead her away from her father before she can further anger him.

Once we're down the hall a few steps, she points toward the glass doors at the end of the hall. "It's just ahead," she says.

I feel her father's eyes on us while we walk away and breathe easier once we step through the glass doors. Floor-to-ceiling art covers the walls and the sight is something to behold. I'd be all about it if I didn't have Delilah standing in front of me. As soon as the doors close behind us, she walks to the right side until we're out of sight of her father. She pushes a button and music begins playing, along with a narrator describing the artwork in the room.

"We must walk, but I know where the cameras are. Follow my lead," she whispers frantically. "Help me. Please. I will not marry that man."

"Your father will have me and my family killed if we get you out of here," I tell her.

"I will die if I marry Avaban. There's something off about him. But even if he was wonderful, I don't want to marry someone I don't know! It's not kidnapping if I willingly go with you."

I reach out and straighten her headdress that is tilting slightly forward with her hurried movements. She comes to a standstill when my hands brush across her face and she reaches out and takes my hand in hers.

"Please," she whispers.

Her eyes fill with tears and there's no hesitation—I'll do whatever it takes to help her. She straightens the headdress again and we resume walking.

"Is there an attendant you trust?"

"I trust no one at this point. I don't know why I'm trusting *you*. My own father has betrayed me."

"As soon as you can, get out of this outfit. You look exquisite, but it draws too much attention." I try to ease the air with a teasing tone, but her expression remains rigid. "Cover your hair. All black would be best. Can you make it outside without being spotted—do you know a way out?"

She nods, waving her hand for me to keep going. I look at the artwork, but I'm not really seeing it. I feel the waves of tension coming off of her as if it's my own.

"Have your phone on hand, but leave everything else," I continue. "Make your way out of the east gate. If you can reach the ancestral stones, I'll have our driver stop there. Eden and Luka will keep him occupied while I get you in the trunk. We'll figure out the rest from there. If you aren't able to get that far, let me know and we'll stop sooner. Unless I hear differently, I'll wait as long as I can at the stones, but I think it's best that I leave here in an hour and a half...at the least. I'll make my rounds and try to leave as soon as I can after that."

She glances around, listening, then nods. "This recording will be done in a few minutes. If all of this fails for any reason, know that I appreciate your attempt to calm me. Even if it's for the wrong reasons—I'm not naïve, I know there could be a great gain for you to work against my father —but this has returned my heart rate to close to normal."

She attempts a smile and it doesn't quite reach her eyes, making me want to move heaven and earth to see a genuine smile from her again. She casts such a tragic figure, here among the masterpieces.

However, I check myself. *Never forget she is Vance Farthing's daughter.*

"This could all be a strange setup for you to drag *my* family down. For all I know, it could be another attempt on my life." I stop and turn toward her then, staring deep into her eyes. "We'll have to wait and see how this night ends to know the truth, I guess."

CHAPTER TEN

Jadon

When I enter the ballroom again, the string quartet is playing and conversation is still scattered with talk of the princess's engagement. Eden isn't at our table and I search the couples dancing, easily spotting her red hair in the crowd. I look around the room, checking the grand clock that hangs over the main wall like it's keeping watch over all. I need to pace myself, make sure I cover all the bases and still get us out of here on time.

I strategically speak to every dignitary, finding my allies first. It makes the first hour pass quickly. When I tackle the leaders who would love nothing more than to see me fail, I start with King Avaban. He's never done anything directly to me to display his stance against Farrow, but the fact that he's aligning with Farthing is a pretty clear indicator. I get in place to greet him, a small gathering surrounding him as the leaders who snivel after Farthing for his approval congratulate him. I see right through them, knowing they want an in with Farthing and think Avaban is the next best bet. I wait my turn, patiently smiling at those who walk away nervously. Cowards, the whole lot.

Luka moves into place next to me and we exchange a look. We talk every day even though our kingdoms are across the world from one another, and by now, I know he sees through this situation as much as I do...without knowing a thing about Delilah. Farthing must have something on Avaban and Avaban, as small as his kingdom is, must have something valuable to offer Farthing. The question is *what?* What is worth Farthing giving his beloved daughter away like a prized goat?

When it's our turn to greet Avaban, I let Luka step forward first and watch their interaction. Avaban is a cocky son of a bitch and holds Luka's stare without wavering.

Luka holds his hand out for me. "And my brother-in-law, King Jadon Safrin of Farrow. Brother, have you met Xang Avaban before?"

"We've met. It's now King Xang," he says with a tight clench to his jaw. "Jadon, thank you for your congratulations."

"It's King Jadon to you," I say with an easy shrug. "But who's keeping track? Congratulations on working your way to...would you consider this the top?" I frown and look around the grandeur of the room, the disgust dripping off of my face. What can I say? I don't like to pretend.

"I love my home, but I'm sure you'd agree Alidonia is one of the finest kingdoms in the world. I can understand why it'd be a little too fine for someone from Farrow." He laughs and his eyes take on a steely glint. "Even so, you can see why I'd want to cast my chances with this family, especially with Princess Delilah as the cherry on top."

He holds his hand out and I take it, squeezing it so firmly that Xang's eyes widen and his face turns red.

"She's a human being, not a dessert topping. I suggest you learn to treat her as such or your soon-to-be wife will want nothing to do with you." I let his hand go abruptly and step back, giving him a short bow. "I haven't had any quarrel with Blorl, I hope this alliance won't cause that to change." I don't wait for him to respond, stepping back and walking away before I cause an unnecessary fight.

I feel Luka's eyes on me as we walk away and I look everywhere but him.

"I'd like to leave soon if you and Eden are ready. I have something I need to tell you." We stop at our table and Eden walks up at the same time, her face flushed.

"They had tiny chettlecakes by the chocolate fountain. Did you try one?" she asks.

Luka and I both shake our heads.

"Jadon was too busy threatening Xang to think about that kind of dessert...dessert *toppings*, on the other hand." Luka snorts and I glare at him before turning to my sister. She looks at us confused, and like she's uncertain if this is a real argument or not.

"We need to leave." I look at the clock and we've gone past the hour and a half. Ten minutes over. "Now."

"Bossy much?" Eden says, laughing.

When I don't laugh with her, she puts her hand on my arm. "What's happened? You're so tense."

"I'll explain later. You guys go first. I'll follow quickly, but let's try not to make it obvious that we're leaving for the night." Someone passes, and I say loudly, "I'll grab one of those desserts on my way back from the washroom." Under my breath, I whisper, "Meet me at the car."

"I'll take one with chocolate on top," Eden says when a lady passes. She winks at me and I grin.

"I've missed you," I tell her.

She rubs my arm. "I've missed you too. Okay, Luka, I heard there's a fabulous museum. Should we go visit that?" She widens her eyes to see if we approve of her cover.

"Just look at the little liar you've created," Luka mutters, putting his arm around Eden's waist and pulling her close.

I chuckle under my breath. "Just go already, no need for more improvising."

They make their way out of the crowded room, Eden turning one more time to see if I'm following and when the color leaves her face, I look around knowing Farthing is most likely close.

"Your father would be proud of you for your bravery in coming here today." His voice sends a chill down my spine; he's far colder than he was when Delilah was around.

"I trusted you'd respect the code of honor," I tell him, taking his offered hand and shaking it. "Or know that the whole world would see you for who you really are should you choose *not* to respect it," I add.

The lines between his eyebrows deepen with his frown. "Your father always placed too high of a regard on honor..."

"We can leave my father out of this since he's too dead at someone else's hand to speak for himself...rumor has it you played a part in that, so I'd choose my words carefully if I were you."

"Haven't you heard the saying, 'Threaten not a man in his own castle?' Perhaps you're not as brave as I thought. Stupidity isn't a virtue."

"I'm not threatening anyone, merely suggesting you not start a war of words by discussing my father. Besides, this is a celebration of your daughter's engagement. If I had a glass,

I'd offer a toast on your behalf." I take a deep breath and glance at the clock again over the king's head. We're twenty minutes late for Delilah. I look past him and see Caulder walking toward us. "Looks like your nephew wants your time. Thank you for a lovely party, King Farthing. Enjoy the rest of your night. I heard there are chettlecakes for me to sample." I bow deeply and walk away. It wasn't my best performance, but he doesn't know me very well. Not enough to think my behavior was any odder than usual.

Several people stop me on my way out, but I make one polite excuse after the other.

Have you seen my sister?

I'm looking for my brother-in-law?

Beg pardon, my family is waiting in the museum.

I'm so sorry, I have chettlecake to gather.

Lies, all lies. And hopefully convincing enough to hide my departure.

Luka and Eden are already in the car when I get there.

"Took you forever," Eden starts.

I tap on the divider between us and the driver slides it open. I sent Quincie ahead of us to get the plane ready, so I don't recognize this guy, a local. "Can you please stop by the ancestral stones?"

"Sure. It would be much better to see it during the day though," he says.

"Thank you. I'd like to stop tonight, if you don't mind." I shut the divider and look at Luka and Eden, who are waiting for an explanation in the seat across from me. "Please follow my lead. What we're about to do will change the course of our future for a while. I'll give you a choice to help me or to go back to the hotel and know nothing."

"What's at the stones?" Eden asks.

"Princess Delilah," I whisper.

She gasps and they both lean forward in their seat and stare at me like I've lost my mind.

"What are you doing, Jadon?" Luka asks.

"She asked for my help."

"And you're sure this isn't a setup?" he asks.

"I guess we'll see when we get to the stones." I run my hands through my hair and tug the collar of my suit. "She didn't have a clue about this wedding until tonight and she says she can't marry him."

"And why did she ask *you* to help her?" Eden demands. "Don't you think that's a little suspicious?"

"I believe it's because she trusts me, but I could be way off," my voice dies down at the end. It all sounds a bit outlandish to me too, but the look on her face...her eyes when they pierced into me during the announcement. "If you could distract the driver, Luka. I'll take care of the rest."

In the next moment, the car stops and the driver opens the door. He peers down at me and waits for me to get out.

"Thank you," I say as I get out. "I'll just be a few moments. Eden, Luka, would you like to come with me?"

They both get out and then we all stand there in a circle, everyone looking at me for direction. I turn and can barely see the shadow of the stones, it's so dark.

"Eden, why don't you walk over with me? Our father always talked about this, remember?" I spew out the nonsense and hold out my hand for her to take.

"I'll wait here. Sounds like a family thing," Luka says. He starts chatting to the driver as Eden and I walk toward the stones.

"I feel like I did when we'd play games outside in the dark," she says, laughing nervously. "I never had to go to the bathroom before we started, but when I got nervous and excited, all of a sudden, the situation was desperate."

"Are you saying you need to squat behind the stones?" I ask dryly.

She hits my arm. "Gross. No, I was *not* saying that."

"Good, because it would be a huge fine if you were caught doing that," a voice whispers near us.

Eden screams and then clamps her hand over her mouth. "Sorry, you scared me. I promise I wasn't going to do any such thing. My brother here—"

Delilah giggles and my chest tightens. I smile despite the crazy situation we're in, wishing again that Ava were here with us. She'd love this little adventure.

"You made it," I say.

"At least a half hour before you did." She's so close her breath hits my neck and I feel the hair on the back of my neck stand up. "Was beginning to think you'd chickened out again."

"Now is not the time for sass," I say under my breath. "But well done. Good job, you. Now, let's get to the car. This poor driver is about to be knocked out and it'd be good if he was completely unaware. I'll make it quick and then you guys get in the car."

"What are you going to do with him?"

"Just watch."

She starts protesting and I turn to her, holding onto her arm. "Do you trust me? Slight change of plans, but it just hit me that this would be a safer option."

She pauses for only a second before saying softly, "I trust you."

I can practically hear the questions Eden is begging to ask, but she does me proud and plays her part. We get to the clearing and they hide behind the stones while I walk to the car.

"Where's my wife?" Luka asks.

"She wasn't quite done looking." I step up behind the driver and am grateful for the dark because he doesn't know what hits him.

As carefully as possible, I lower him to the ground and motion for Luka, Eden, and Delilah to come out of the shadows.

"Take them to the plane. We'll fly out tonight." I toss the keys to Luka and he catches them.

"I can't just leave you. What's your plan?" he asks.

"Hide her on the plane then you and Eden hurry back. Bring a first aid kit back...when this guy wakes up, we'll have him take us to the hotel and find another ride to the plane." I turn to Delilah. "Make sure you stay hidden or this could all end in a bigger mess." I squeeze Luka's arm. "Hurry. You're less than five minutes from the plane. Be back in twelve, max."

He groans and they get in the car, speeding off as soon as Delilah's door is closed.

Our driver groans and when he comes to, I kneel down.

"Are you okay?" I ask.

He sits up and holds his head. "What happened?"

"Are you sure you're ready to sit up? Someone came up behind you and knocked you out. I hit him and he took off running. Luka and Eden went to get help for you."

"You stayed for me?" the driver rubs his head and holds onto me for support. "You should've left me here and taken care of yourself. I'm so sorry. I shouldn't have stopped here."

"No apologies. You were only doing what I asked. I'm only sorry for the headache you might suffer."

Luka and Eden pull up a few minutes later and I breathe a little easier. We get in the car and Luka drives us to the hotel, the driver still holding his head. Luka points to the first aid kit he brought from the plane.

"I decided to just rush back myself. Are you okay, sir?" he asks. "Should we take you to the hospital?"

"I'm fine. I'm well enough to drive even. I don't need a doctor. I beg your forgiveness for not getting you safely to your hotel."

I lean up and put my hand on his shoulders and squeeze. "No apologies, remember?"

I feel like a bastard, but the guy doesn't seem to be suffering from much pain...only guilt. I wish we could've come up with a way that didn't involve someone else, but an alibi and rumor of a suspicious person who hit the driver by the stones was a necessary cover.

Luka pulls into the hotel parking lot and stops.

Now if we can just get out of here.

CHAPTER ELEVEN

Delilah

When an hour passes in a tiny closet in the bedroom of the Catano family jet, I start to worry that I'm stuck here for good. What if they were detained? Maybe someone saw me in the car with Luka. Maybe they're already searching the surrounding areas for me.

I turned off my phone tracker when I left the house and it's a good thing. My father started blowing up my phone about ten minutes ago. I would've turned it off by now, but I keep thinking Jadon might call. He's taking longer than I expected.

I pulled my hat off long ago and wish I'd taken off my sweatshirt before getting into the cramped space. I'd gladly strip everything off if I wasn't scared they'd choose that moment to get on board. I crack open the door to the closet and take in a deep breath, listening for any signs that someone else is on the plane with me. It's silent.

What if they're setting me up? It's not the first time I've

wondered if I should be trusting the Safrin family OR the Catano family in this getaway. Why couldn't I have chosen someone neutral?

The heat gets unbearable and I rush out of the closet, unable to take it in there for another second. I pace around the bedroom and get distracted by all the gold. My father would love this. I've always preferred silver, but the Farthing castle is outfitted in the finest gold, and I've heard the Catanos' is also. It isn't the first time the Farthings' and Catanos' love for opulence has been compared.

I crack open the bedroom door and peek out just as I hear something. I run back to the closet and step inside, taking another deep breath of air before shutting myself back inside. My heart is pumping fast and I regret not trying harder to talk sense into my father before leaving.

I know him though. He had his mind made up. It was scary how adamant he was about me marrying—

The door flings open and I sink back into the corner. Jadon holds his hand out and I take it, clutching my chest with my other hand.

"Heart a-attack," I stutter.

He pulls me out and somehow, I end up against his chest, staring up at him. His hand feels right at my waist as he looks me over, his other hand slightly brushing my hair away from my face.

"You appear to be in one piece," he says, smiling slightly.

I get lost in his pale blue eyes, finding myself sinking deeper into them. I sigh and he smiles bigger, but backs away slightly and everywhere I've been sweating is suddenly covered in goose bumps.

"This is the quietest you've been since we met,

Delilah." He frowns and tilts his head, studying me closer. "Say something. I'm beginning to worry."

I wave a hand and attempt to laugh, but it sounds like I'm choking. I cover my mouth and cough, knowing I'm acting so strangely but unable to stop myself.

"Fine. I'm fine," I repeat. "Hot."

He bites the inside of his cheek and smiles. I wonder if he's always this playful with everyone. He seems nothing like the serious king I've heard about or seen pictures of—in every picture of him on the Internet, his eyes look haunted and his full lips are pulled into a flat line. The lighthearted banter is the last thing I expected from him. Then again, I never imagined there'd be questionable texting between the two of us either. I still flush when I think about that conversation, and I've thought about it a *lot*.

All of it makes my heart trip over itself and I try to get a grip. I pick up the hat that fell in the closet and put it back on.

"We left our guards to cover for us—I'll message them shortly. It's just us on the plane. I mean the two of us and Luka and Eden. One of us will fly the plane. I voted for Luka so we could talk on the way, maybe come up with a plan for what comes next. Or do you have that worked out already?"

I step back and my legs hit the bed. I go with it and sit down. It feels good after standing for so long. He stands for a moment but then sits next to me, waiting for my answer.

"I wish I had a plan. As you can probably tell, I'm winging it. All of this has taken me by complete surprise."

He nods. "Any ideas why your dad would want to align himself with Avaban?"

"None at all. The only thing I've come up with that makes any sense to me at all is that he simply needed to get me out of the way. Marry me off and get me out of the house."

"Oh, I'd hoped Avaban would be moving right in here... that you wouldn't have to go to Blorl at all," he adds.

"I guess I left before finding out the details." My voice sounds angrier than I intended, but I'm too exhausted to take it back. There's something about Jadon talking about me being Avaban's wife like it's just a given that really sets me off. "And I am *not* going anywhere near Blorl."

"You didn't have the slightest hint this was coming? No mention of Xang leading up to the party or anything?" He studies my face intently, as if searching for the lies I must be telling.

I feel my skin heating with anger. "Xang?"

Jadon jaw ticks. "Xang *Avaban*?"

I hold up my hands, unable to hide my annoyance with him any longer. "I'd never met him until tonight!" My voice shakes and I lift my eyes to the ceiling, trying to keep my emotions at bay. "I apologize for taking it out on you. I'm in shock. My father isn't perfect, no one is, but I've never doubted his love for me. I've never doubted that he doesn't want the best for me. Now *everything* feels like a lie."

"I want to believe you. I think that's evident." Jadon walks to the door and looks back. "I can give you space. We'll be taking off in a few minutes. I'm not sure of the best way to handle all of this, but we'll have to discuss the options soon. I want to make sure you're safe, but I also have to take care of the needs of my people."

"I think I'd like to do a news conference soon...maybe somewhere neutral? And say publicly that I was not part of the discussion to marry Avaban...and that I refuse to do so."

He nods. "That sounds wise. Perhaps in the Sea of Caninsula? Or maybe Gynos would be even better. It

would be easy to get in and out of there. I can connect you
with their leader, unless you already have a way in."

"That would be wonderful, thank you."

He turns and I stand up.

"Jadon—"

I move closer to him and look down at his hands,
admiring his long fingers. They look strong and capable, like
they could span my waist on either side and touch.

He reaches out and touches my arm, dropping it quickly
when I look up.

"Thank you," I whisper. "I know what a risk this is for
you and I want you to know I'm grateful. I couldn't have—"

"You're welcome," he says, his eyes smiling. "Hey,
would you like to officially meet my sister?"

I let out a long breath, glad of the distraction. "Yes. I'd
love that."

We walk out of the room and sit across from Eden and
Luka. They are such a beautiful couple, it's hard not to
stare.

"Didn't know we'd be coming home with a princess,"
Eden says with a smile. "Delilah Farthing at that." She
shakes her head. "Mother will have a lot to say about this."

"We won't be telling Mother," Jadon says. "Best avoid
the topic of any Farthings altogether."

"What does she have against us?" I ask, looking at each
of them. Luka is studying me with a calculated stare, like
he's trying to figure out how I'm manipulating them even in
this moment.

"Everything," Jadon says.

"So why don't you hold that same thought?" I turn to
look at him and he looks at me for a moment before turning
toward Eden and Luka again.

"Who says I don't?" He laughs and when he stops, he

turns to me again and his eyes are still light. "For some reason, I believe you really need our help..."

It seems like he's going to say something else, but he just leaves it hanging.

"And?" I urge him to continue.

"And you're really hard to refuse."

I stare at him, my heart pounding harder as his eyes hold mine captive. When Eden clears her throat, we both turn to her and her eyes are wide.

"Well, well," she says.

"What is your plan?" Luka cuts to the chase.

They all look at me and I feel the heat go straight up my chest and face. "For tonight, is it okay if I just hide out a little longer until I come up with something?"

Luka leans forward and shakes his head. "Considering we might have your army on our tail by the time we reach Farrow, I'd say coming up with some sort of plan would be best," he says. "There have been threats on Jadon's life recently. Forgive me if I'm not as trusting as he is."

Eden pulls him back and takes his hand. He visibly calms when she does.

"If we're good to go, I'm going to get us in the air," Luka says. "Jadon, you're sure about this?"

Jadon nods. "I'm sure. Farrow, please. We'll take things from there."

Luka walks to the cockpit and we start rolling just a few minutes later.

The way Eden is assessing me makes me shift in my seat. I'm about to tell her to just say whatever it is she wants to say already when she speaks again.

"So, the two of you have met before?" It's hard to tell if she's asking a question or saying the obvious. She looks between Jadon and me and bites her bottom lip.

"Not too long ago," Jadon says.

"I see. And you've kept in touch?" She looks at me when she says this and it's like she can read all the naughty thoughts I've had about her brother. My face flushes and I nod.

"A little," I reply.

"And you're telling me all of this came about unexpectedly tonight...there was no premeditated getaway plan before we came?" She folds her arms across her chest and I'm suddenly seeing how the Queen of Niaps could be a very intimidating person.

I sit up taller and steady her with a glare of my own. She doesn't back down...not enough for my comfort.

"There was no plan for me to be a stowaway, no. You think I want this?"

"For all I know, this is exactly what you want...you get close to my brother and bring him down without your father having to lift a single finger."

"Eden," Jadon snaps, leaning forward. "Stop. There will be time for grilling Delilah later. Can't you see she's shaken?"

Eden rolls her eyes. "You've always had a soft spot for the downtrodden...I only hope this time doesn't destroy you. Don't forget who she is, brother."

"As if I ever could," he says, turning to face me.

CHAPTER TWELVE

Jadon

Hindsight is twenty-twenty is what they say, right? Who are *they* anyway? I've never lived my life wishing I'd done something differently. Call it a flaw or call it my greatest strength, but I try to think things through the first time and then rely heavily on my gut feelings. I am typically slow to act as a result because thinking things through so thoroughly often takes a testing of time and the wisdom to see through the bullshit.

The problem with everything regarding Delilah is simply this: I am not sure I'm capable of seeing her objectively.

I've never been drawn to a woman so intensely, this soon upon meeting. I've never felt the pull to protect as fiercely for anyone except my sisters, and I am in no way feeling familial toward Delilah. I've never thrown caution to the wind when my kingdom and family are all at stake, and I've never felt so in over my head as I do right now.

But I look at her and I know I'd do all of it again in a heartbeat. If it's a mistake, it's one I may pay for with my life, but if she's telling the truth and I'm saving her, giving my life would be worth it.

We land in Farrow in the early hours of the morning, and as we get in the car and I drive us all to the Safrin home, I can't help but wonder what she'll think of Farrow. The landscape is so different than Alidonia with the snow-capped mountains and the green fields surrounding the water. The curves up the mountain to home feel especially winding and I grin when Delilah gasps as she looks over the edge of a drastic drop.

No one speaks, the exhaustion from the night settling in. But when we pull into the driveway, Delilah sits up taller. She stares out the window, taking it all in. I'd give anything to know what she's thinking, the need to impress her colliding with my usual take-it-or-leave-it mentality.

"What will we tell the guards?" Eden asks.

"That we have a guest and they are to take the utmost care of her." I shoot Eden a look in the rearview mirror and she doesn't say anything else. "I kept the guards I trust completely. Everyone else that was questionable around the time of the shooting has been let go and I feel confident that those here now are capable of keeping their mouths shut."

"Because you hardly have anyone working for you now," Luka says.

"And it's a good thing, right? Less people to worry about spreading the news that Delilah is here."

Luka's jaw clenches as we step outside, quietly shutting our car doors behind us. It *is* strange not to have a guard coming out to greet us.

"At least let me send Uncle Basile and a few guards to help out," Luka says as we walk toward the house.

"Once Quincie and the others come in from Alidonia tomorrow, it'll be better." The house is quiet when we step inside. "The staff didn't expect us back until tomorrow night, so this is not all that unusual," I remind them. "But I think that's a good idea, Luka...I'll take you up on that if Basile is agreeable."

I don't say it out loud, but I am too isolated here.

"There was a shooting here recently?" Delilah asks, looking up at the tall ceilings in the foyer. "Who was shot?"

Luka and Eden both look at me and Delilah slowly realizes they're waiting for me to speak.

"Me." My voice is louder than I intended and I hold my hand out. "Why don't I show you to your room?"

"Oh, I didn't realize the attempt on your life was in your home. That's terrible. Were you hurt?" she asks as we walk up the stairs.

"Only my pride...and my heart," I say quietly.

She turns to face me then, even though I've opened the door to her room. She doesn't even look inside.

"It would've been easier if you'd been physically hurt then, wouldn't it?" She reaches out and touches my arm and I feel the warmth sink through my shirt.

"Much easier." I close my hand over hers and we stand there for a moment, our pain finding company. "After this with your father, you can understand how the hurt from our family can far surpass any physical threat."

"Who shot you?"

"My stepmother." I don't try to explain right away. Because even though I know my stepmother was drugged and hypnotized with orders to kill me, I've always known she didn't want me.

Part of me has always wondered if she wished I was dead, and now I know the truth.

"I'm so sorry. I-I didn't know. I can't imagine knowing someone in my family wants me dead. As angry as I am with my father right now, I believe he thinks he's doing what's best for me...even though he's wrong."

I nod and look down at our hands then reluctantly pull mine away. "My very existence proves my father's betrayal in his marriage. He loved my stepmother very much, but the fact that I was born proves that he wasn't faithful to her early in their marriage. I am a constant reminder of his affair. He tried to make it up to her until the day he died, but I am like salt in the wound."

"Where is your real mother?"

"I try really hard to remember my mother. I loved her very much. She died when I was six and she's never been spoken about in this house." I walk into the room and look back at her. "Do you think this will be okay? I'm right next door. This wing is separate from everything else and more private, but I didn't want you to be too far away from me. At least until I can get more security and we know what's happening with your father."

She steps in the room and still doesn't seem to see anything but me. She looks tiny and forlorn, exhaustion bending her shoulders—that or grief, I don't know her well enough to know for sure.

"I thought I knew my father so well," she whispers. "I have to find out why he's doing this."

"You let me know what you want your next step to be. I am offering you a refuge here for as long as you need it."

Her shoulders dip and she puts her hand to her mouth, her chest rising deeply with a breath. "Thank you. I think I'll sleep a while, and then hopefully I'll have more answers later."

I nod and start to back out of the door. "The bathroom is

through that door. You should find everything you need in there. I'll have Eden set a few changes of clothes outside your door. Find me when you wake up and we'll figure out the next step."

I close the door and put my hand on it, hesitant to leave her when she seems so sad.

I get to my room and even though I'm exhausted, I know I'm too wired to sleep. I text Ava, all of this concern over getting Delilah to safety making me worry about my little sister too.

You still loving traveling the world?

Ava: It's the best thing ever. It's the middle of the night there—why aren't you asleep?

Just thinking about you. No sign of anyone following you still?

Ava: Not even a slightly questionable sign. What about there? Anything unusual?

Only the enemy's daughter in my house. I start typing but delete the words. Finally, I just say, *So far nothing new. I wish I knew who was behind your abduction. I'd feel more at peace about everything right now.*

Ava: You okay? Is something going on that you're not telling me?

My little sister, always the most perceptive of all of us. She resists the monarchy more than us, but she'd probably be the one best suited to rule all the kingdoms combined.

Not sleeping. It's just got me extra melancholy. I love you, little one.

Ava: Love you too. You're worrying me. Should Gentry and I come home?

No. I'd feel terrible if you missed out on your trip of a lifetime because I'm having a weird night. Enjoy your trip! Just send more pictures. You've been slacking.

   Ava: Okay. Will do. :)

I lie down and when sleep finally comes, I dream that I'm being chased by King Farthing and Delilah.

CHAPTER THIRTEEN

Jadon

Despite my crazy dreams, I feel better when I wake up. I get a shower and when I walk past Delilah's room, I slow down, listening for any signs that she's awake. All is quiet. I walk downstairs and hear something being discussed in the dining room. When I walk inside, Luka, Eden, and Delilah stop talking and turn to look at me.

"What's going on?" I look at each of them and notice that most of the tension is gone between Eden and Delilah. *Interesting.*

"I'd like to do a news conference immediately. Word is already out that I'm missing," Delilah says.

"Did you decide where you'd like to do it?" I sit down across from her and she taps on the table with her fingertips.

"The Sea of Caninsula seems the easiest."

Luka nods and I look at the lunch I've missed. My stomach growls and I grab a piece of bread.

"The sooner, the better," Delilah adds.

I take a few bites and stand up. "I can have the plane ready immediately."

"I think we should take my plane," Luka says. "I don't want to cast any doubt on you—if they know it's your plane, they might come looking for her here."

I nod. "Okay. Do you have security in place in Niaps should her father come after *you*?"

"Yes," Luka says with a grin. "And Basile is on his way here, along with five of our guards. I'll sleep better knowing they're here."

"Thank you. It'll be good to see him," I add. I wave my hand. "Should we get going?"

"I think you should stay here," Delilah says. "Now that I know a little more about what you've been through recently, I don't want to put you in any more danger than I already have."

"I can't just sit here and wonder what's going on. I'll go crazy. And you're coming back here afterward...right?" The thought of her leaving so soon makes my head hurt.

She stands up and walks toward me. She smiles sheepishly when I look up. I forget about everyone else and stare at her.

"Jadon, you saved me last night and I'll always be grateful. It'd be best if I stayed somewhere neutral, so all of this doesn't come back on you. I'd feel terrible if I caused more of a divide between you and my father. Luka and Eden filled me in a little more on the history between our kingdoms than you have. I know my father has always talked about the Safrin family as the enemy, but now that I've met you for myself...I have found the most caring and selfless people. I just want to let him know that, somehow...once he gets this idea of me marrying Avaban out of his head, maybe I can reason with him about your family."

I stand up and grip her shoulders, staring at her in horror. "Let me make that choice for myself. I'd feel better with you here. Please just let me protect you until we know how your father is going to react to you leaving."

She swallows hard and eventually nods. "Okay. Let's see what happens after the news conference."

My hands drop and I take her hands in mine. She bites her bottom lip and looks so nervous, I can't take it. I lean down and hug her, wrapping my arms around her and feeling her sag into me. Over her shoulder, Luka and Eden are both staring at us in shock and I can't even pretend to care. I glare at Luka when he starts to smirk and he lifts a shoulder at me like, "What are you gonna do about it?"

When I pull back and look at Delilah, she smiles up at me and my heart thunders in response. This girl. Why does she affect me so much?

"I'll be on the plane and Eden is coming too. I don't want to leave her here without us," Luka says. "We can come back tonight and then we need to get back to Niaps tomorrow, if everything goes okay today."

"Let's do this." I grab an apple and bite into it as we walk down the hall and outside where the plane is waiting.

"Have you guys always been this close?" Delilah asks, pointing between Luka and me.

"It took a while for me to grow on Jadon," Luka says, grinning.

Eden snorts and pokes Luka in the side.

"Because you lead with asshole," she says. "It took a while for you to show your kindness."

He shrugs and I laugh because she's right and we all know it.

"Were you close to your brother?" Eden asks and Delilah's smile drops. "Sorry, is that too personal?"

"No, not at all. I wasn't very close to him. He was very close to my father and Caulder. I was closer to my father than to either of them, but being the only girl in the house after my mom passed away...they like to remind me that I don't need to bother myself with all of the stressful aspects of the kingdom. It gets exhausting, feeling like I'm in the dark all the time." She bites her lip and buckles her seat belt once we're all in place. "I'm thinking I must have been in the dark even more than I knew." Her voice fades and she looks out the window, deep in thought.

"Maybe forcing your dad's hand about this will be the best thing you've ever done," Eden says. She reaches out and squeezes Delilah's hand. "He needs to know you have a say in this. My marriage to Luka was an arranged one, but we both knew it was happening from a young age. Luka didn't want it, but I did." She laughs. "Until I married him, that is. Obviously, things worked out for us, but...you not having a clue until the party—I can't imagine that. I'm glad you got out of there."

Luka starts the plane and we're quiet until we're in the air. I work on my laptop while Eden and Delilah talk and when I set it aside, I lift my hands over my head and stretch.

"You look tired. Did you not sleep well last night?" she asks.

When I shake my head, she sighs.

"None of us did. I feel bad that I turned your trip to my country upside down. I would've enjoyed showing Alidonia to you," Delilah says and then clutches her chest, her face paling.

"What's wrong?" When she doesn't answer right away, I touch her arm and she looks at me, eyes wide.

"I just realized after this news conference, I may never be allowed in Alidonia again."

I take her hand in mine and ignore Eden's watchful eyes. "Let's not worry about that yet, okay? One roadblock at a time. I've been talking with the ambassador in Caninsula. They're prepared for you and willing to stand with us, should the need arise." I squeeze her hand and let it go.

"Thank you. That was fast. Why would they agree to this?" She pulls her sleeves over her hands.

"Are you cold? Here, I'll get a blanket." I stand and grab one off of the nearby couch, handing it to her.

"Thank you." She stares at me like I'm a mystery she hasn't figured out yet, and I know exactly how she feels. She's hard to read.

"You should both get some rest. It'll be a while yet before we land, and you'll need your wits about you, Delilah. The bed is ready for you if you need to take a nap."

"I'll be good here," Eden says, lowering her seat back. "You take the room, Delilah."

"I won't be able to sleep. You take it, Eden."

Eden laughs and looks at Delilah. "Why don't you at least try? Lie down and rest, if nothing else."

"I'd prefer to be in here with Jadon, if that's okay. I have questions about who I'll be meeting."

Eden lifts her seat up. "If you're sure." She smirks at me and I warn her with my expression to not say anything to embarrass me. "Later, brother." She leans down and kisses my cheek, whispering in my ear. "I dare you to think of another ten reasons to touch her." She laughs again and stands up, walking to the bedroom.

"Siblings." I laugh awkwardly, hoping to God Delilah didn't hear Eden. "They're impossible."

"Seems like you've got a pretty good deal going with yours. Are you close to your younger sister too?"

"Very." I nod and turn to face her. She's staring out the window, her gaze sorrowful. "You said you weren't very close to your brother?"

"I wanted to be. Does that count?"

I think of Kathryn and how I spent a lifetime striving to win her love. The thought of anyone causing Delilah to feel that way sends a spike through my heart.

"But you seem so easy to get along with." I came so close to saying *easy to love* but stopped myself in the nick of time. Where did that come from?

"I'm realizing how easy I've made it for my father and cousin to leave me out of the equation. They don't treat me the way you do Eden—the fact that you included her in getting me out of Alidonia...that would've never happened."

"So, your trip to see me really was a first step for you trying to take control somewhere? By what? Getting me into submission?" I grin when I see her flinch and know I've hit the nail on the head.

"Alidonia *is* the largest kingdom and the most powerful," she says quietly. Even though she seems embarrassed, I can tell she believes what she's saying. "My father obsesses over Farrow and you, so I wanted to make my own headway with you...prove to him that I'm capable of more."

"Delilah, you know I will never give up my kingdom to Alidonia, right?"

"Even if my father isn't king?"

A chill runs through me and I sit back in my seat, staring straight ahead. "Just when I start thinking I can trust you, I'm reminded that you're a Farthing through and through."

She shifts in her seat but doesn't say anything. I lean my

head back and think about what the implications of all I've done for Delilah could mean for my kingdom. When I risk another glance at her some time later, she's sound asleep, her face turned to mine.

She looks like an angel. I'd do well to remember that she's far from it.

CHAPTER FOURTEEN

Delilah

Ambassador Danes greets us at the airport and talks ninety miles an hour as we drive to a remote building nearby.

"King Otto is meeting us there and will have a few words to say at the end of your speech," Danes says. He looks at Jadon and Luka. "I'm assuming you have something prepared as well."

Luka and Jadon look at one another and nod. They seem to have a way of communicating without words and I'm envious of that. It's similar to my father and Caulder and I wonder for the hundredth time—how long have they been plotting my marriage to Avaban?

We're stopping before I'm ready, my mouth suddenly going dry at what I'm about to say. But I'm whisked to a back room apart from Jadon, which makes me nervous. He's treated me differently since I woke up and I miss the warmth that had started to form between us. I remember his hug in Farrow and I hope he's not changed his mind about helping me, because I feel like a fish out of water. It seems like every time we talk about our kingdoms, tensions rise. Something I said set him off and I wish I could take it back.

I put on a pantsuit Eden loaned me and feel like it makes me look at least ten years older. It's tighter and smarter than the whimsical pieces I usually wear, and I frown as I look in the mirror. Eden knocks and steps in, stopping in front of me.

"You don't like it?" she asks.

"It's just not me."

"I think that's good for today, don't you? Maybe your father will see this no-nonsense version of you and take notice."

"If only it were that simple. I hope you're right."

I reluctantly walk out of the cocoon of the dressing room into the room teeming with young journalists and camera crews from the various news stations from all over the world. I'm floored by what Jadon was able to set up in such a short amount of time. I told him what I wanted and he was making it happen while I slept. If I hope to be taken seriously at all, I'll have to learn to pull my own weight...

The room grows still as they notice me walking toward the microphone. I notice Jadon and Luka standing to the left side of the podium and a few other dignitaries that I vaguely recognize, along with King Otto, whom I've never met before. King Otto steps out to greet me and then turns to face the cameras.

"The Sea of Caninsula is extending a warm welcome to Princess Delilah Farthing. She has a few words to say and I ask that all of you listen closely and extend the kindness Caninsula is known for...Princess?" He holds his hand out and I step up to the microphone, my shaking hands resting on the stand in front of me.

"Thank you for your welcome, King Otto. I'd like to extend my gratitude to all of the kingdoms represented here today. I'll make this short and sweet." I smile and there are various chuckles throughout the room. "My father arranged a marriage without my knowledge and did not give me the choice of getting out of it. Since I do not feel comfortable going home knowing that I would be forced to do something I don't want to do, I'm making it known here and now that I will *not* marry King Avaban. I still hope to one day rule Alidonia in a way that is best for my kingdom, and this in no way fits that plan. I ask for peace and neutrality between the kingdoms, that my leaving Alidonia willingly will not cause any disruption, only that I be allowed the freedom to marry who I choose when that time comes." I face one camera in particular and speak to it in hopes my father is watching. "Papa, I love you and I ask that you let this matter drop. Let us be a country of peace and goodwill, even now, amongst each other." I look around at the people watching me with rapt attention and smile at them, the relief that this is almost over nearly buckling my knees. "Thanks so much for your time."

I walk to the side of the room, the flash of cameras blinding, and watch as Luka, Jadon, and Alex from Yuman all show their support. Five other kings whose names all flow together—I really will have to learn who everyone is... I'm ashamed of myself for not knowing—also speak, and at the end, journalists start asking questions.

King Otto holds up his hand and says, "That will be all for now. We appreciate you coming out, but Princess Delilah has traveled a long way and I don't want to exhaust her more. Thank you." He holds up his hand in a salute and the journalists and camera crews pack up and exit the room.

I'm flanked by Jadon and Luka and a few guards as we

walk back to a conference room. King Otto walks in behind us and clears his throat.

"I thought that went as well as can be expected," he says. He looks at his ambassador and the commanding officer of his army. "Any news from Alidonia?"

"It's quiet, Sir. No statement has been made yet."

I already know my father is furious with me. I hope he will cool down and think about this before he says anything.

"I'm hoping he'll be willing to hear me out. Doing this publicly was the only way I knew to ensure a marriage doesn't take place. Thank you so much for your willingness to stand behind me. I pray for peace for all of us." I bow to King Otto and the other kings who have made their way into the room.

"We will hold you to that, Princess Delilah," King Otto says, his tone more serious than before. "You're welcome to stay here as long as you need."

"Thank you so much, but I'll be leaving right away. I don't want to risk any of you and I don't know King Avaban well enough to know what he might do in all of this. I'm embarrassed to say I've been focusing on how my father will react, with very little thought toward Avaban. I wish I didn't have to do this so publicly, but you were all there when the announcement was made. I guess it's only fitting that you're here for this part too."

Each king bows in return and I walk out of there, with Jadon, Eden, and Luka following. The guards check the plane thoroughly and then we board, with one of the guards getting in place to fly the plane instead of Luka.

Jadon looks at me, his shoulders tense and no hint of the easy smile he's had with me before now. All of them are waiting to hear where I want to go and the pressure suddenly seems more than I can stand.

"Can I speak with you for a moment, Jadon?" I swallow hard.

He motions to the back bedroom. "We can talk back there."

I turn and walk to the bedroom with him on my heels. He closes the door behind us and crosses his arms, his eyes calculating.

"Why are you acting like this?" I ask.

"Like what?"

"Like you suddenly don't trust anything that comes out of my mouth?"

He snorts and drops his arms, his hands balling into fists. "When I realized you're after my kingdom." His full lips pucker as he clamps them shut and my heart picks up a few beats. "I'm just trying to figure out how you're playing this. If Avaban was a ruse or if you really do need my help and then will systematically try to take all of us into your control."

My mouth drops and the room feels like it's closing in on me.

"It's no secret I think Alidonia is the greatest place in the world, but it's also no secret that I'm clueless. I've put myself in your hands—how could I possibly be working to bring you down?"

"Time will tell."

I step closer to him and put my hand on his arm. He drops it and our hands join, like they're drawn by invisible magnets. His stare burns into me and he licks his lips, causing my face to flush. He reaches out and touches my face with his other hand, moving so close I can't breathe.

His breath is hot against my face and it sends chills down my spine.

"What do you want from me, Delilah?"

"I would like to go to Farrow, please." It's a whisper, a plea. I'm too short on air to say more than that.

He runs his thumb over my chin and tilts my head back slightly so I'm looking into his eyes and not staring at his mouth.

"My home is yours for as long as you need it..."

I start to thank him and he puts his fingers over my lips, stopping my words.

"The minute I think you're not being honest with me, I will send you back to your father before you can even blink."

I swallow hard and close my eyes, his nearness too much for me. I nod slightly and his hands drop.

"I'll tell the pilot." He walks out of the room and I sag against the door, unsteady and wondering if I'll be able to survive Jadon Safrin.

CHAPTER FIFTEEN

Jadon

Delilah stays in the bedroom for the entirety of the flight, which is a relief. I don't know how I'm going to get anything done with her in the house. The adrenaline rushing through my veins is impossible to ignore.

I almost kissed her. I came this close to dragging my mouth down her neck, feeling her pulse against my lips before claiming her mouth. I watched her like a man starved when she closed her eyes and it took every ounce of strength to back away from her. I rub my temples and stare out the window, not really seeing anything.

"You okay, Jadon?" Eden asks.

"I'm fine."

She mutters something and I turn to look at her. "You're not fine," she says, rolling her eyes. She leans in and lowers her voice. "And I don't see how you will survive with Delilah under your roof."

"She's gotten under his skin," Luka says, pointing at me, but talking to Eden like I'm not right here.

I scowl at both of them. "Keep it down, would you? I said I'm fine and I don't need the two of you weighing in."

Luka laughs. "Dude's horny as a motherfucker and it wouldn't hurt him to have a little one-on-one with Delilah. She wants it as much as he does."

Eden covers her ears and starts chanting nonsense so she doesn't have to listen.

I throw a pillow at him to shut him up, too keyed up to laugh at him like I normally would.

Luka puts his elbows on his knees and looks me in the eye. "Basile will be there when we arrive. If your dick gets you into trouble with this one, he'll be around to talk sense into you. I wish I could see how this all plays out," his grins light up his whole face and I want to punch the fucker, "but I'll have to trust Basile to keep me posted."

"Shut the fuck up," I mutter, just as I hear the door to the bedroom opening. "I mean it. Both of you. You know I'm not like that...I don't know what it is about her."

Eden presses her lips together, still smiling knowingly at me. I hate that they know me so well. Or that I'm this transparent when it comes to Delilah. It just can't happen. Nothing. No getting her out of my system or getting to know her better or whatever nonsense Luka was spouting. I am offering her a refuge for a short time and that is it.

Delilah sits next to me and buckles her seat belt.

"We'll be landing in about twenty minutes," Eden says. "You came out just in time."

"Did I hear you say you were returning to Niaps tomorrow?" Delilah asks.

"We'll see my uncle when he arrives tonight along with our guards, but then yes, we need to get home," Luka answers. "My right hand can cover for me, but I don't like to leave him alone for too long, especially without my uncle there."

"It'll be a shame to see you go so soon," Delilah says, looking at Eden. "I've enjoyed getting to know your family."

"You've surprised me, Delilah," Eden says, her smile genuine. "I know I wasn't too warm when we first met, but I can't help but like you." She shrugs. "Just don't give us any reason not to trust you." She bites her lip but is still smiling so it softens her words. "And don't let Jadon pull any tricks over on you either." She winks and I want to shake her. She laughs when she sees my glare and I shake my head, so ready to be home.

We're quiet the rest of the way and our landing is smooth. When we stand and Delilah tries to get her bag, I take it out of her hands and motion for her to walk ahead of me. She whispers her thanks, flushing when she looks at me, and I ignore the heat rushing through me. It's going to be a long week or month or however the hell long she's planning on staying.

Basile is already into the wine when we step into the dining room, his face ruddy. He barrels into me with a huge hug and I laugh, pounding him on the back. I nearly trip over Star and laugh, patting her on the head. She seems even bigger than when I left.

"That dog pines for you," Basile says. "I heard she just sits at the door waiting for you to return."

I lean down and give her an extra scratch behind the ears and she looks up at me adoringly. I can't help but laugh. "I guess she's grateful I brought her home when I did.

Thank you for coming, Basile. I know you have plenty to do in Niaps, so I'm grateful for your help here."

"And who is this pretty little thing with the icy eyes?" he asks, bowing to Delilah.

"Princess Delilah Farthing," I answer. "Delilah, this is Basile, Luka's uncle and now my advisor." I beam at Basile. I already feel better with him here. "Delilah will be staying here for a while and word cannot get out that she's here. I'm assuming Luka told you the situation."

"He did and I assure you, my team and I will be nothing but discreet. By the god of Niaps, I pray this will not turn into bloodshed for either of our countries," he says, holding his glass up.

"Bloodshed!" Delilah puts her hand over her mouth. "Why do you say that?"

Basile turns to her, his eyes serious now. "Wars have started for less than this." He grins then and it's hard not to feel lighter when he smiles. "But you are in the best hands. Between Niaps and Farrow, and a great many other kingdoms from what I've heard, we are all ready to fight for your rights."

"Thank you. But I only want freedom, not a fight."

Basile nods. "Of course. That is our goal. For now, we should celebrate that we're all together! It's been decades since we've celebrated with the Farthings." He leans in and whispers, "I wasn't able to come to the grand ball, so I missed that...oh, that wasn't really a celebration for you at all though, was it? Pity." He shakes his head and holds out his arm for Delilah to take. "Can I interest you in the most perfect red?" When Delilah nods, he pours wine in a goblet and hands it to her. "The Safrins know how to do this right. I'm going to enjoy my stay here. I hope you will too."

They clink glasses and it seems if Basile says it, the matter is settled.

———

After dinner, we obsessively check the news, emails, and I see Delilah checking her phone every few minutes...for any word from Alidonia. All is still quiet. It's as if they are going on with business as usual.

It's not sitting right with me. They're *too* quiet.

I try to enjoy the last night of Luka and Eden being here, knowing I'll miss them tomorrow once they're back in Niaps. But we're too distracted and anxious to really say much. I walk to the window and look out, Star on my heels, then step back to the piano and look at Delilah for the hundredth time in as many minutes.

"Do you play?" she asks.

"We were all forced to have piano lessons, yes," I say with a grin.

"He's the best of us," Eden pipes up.

"Why are you always outing me these days?" I groan.

"I never knew how much fun it was until now," she says, laughing. "Play something for us. Please," she adds, wagging her eyebrows obnoxiously.

"It's a good thing I love you because you are being—" I leave it hanging and when she starts motioning for me to move to the piano, I give in and sit down. "It obviously means nothing to my siblings that I am the king."

"Probably makes it more fun to boss you around," Delilah says, her eyes lighting up. "I'd love to hear you play."

I turn toward the piano and start playing a song that I've never played for anyone. I've worked on it when no one else is around, the melancholy notes something I've felt to my bones in my aloneness. I start out softly and then build toward the end with a crescendo that takes over the whole room. When the last note rings out, I sit for a moment, still feeling the emotion of the melody. I'd almost forgotten I had an audience when I hear a soft hand clap and Eden stands up and walks over to me, wrapping her arms around my back.

"That was the most beautiful thing I've ever heard," she whispers. She moves back next to Luka and puts her head on his shoulder.

I glance at Delilah, embarrassed that I lost myself in the song and see the tears streaming down her face. She wipes them quickly, her face flushing with the pink that I've come to look forward to.

"I don't know why I'm crying." She laughs, wiping another tear that falls. "That was—" She shakes her head and covers her mouth. "You have a gift."

Now I'm really embarrassed but moved that the music touched her so much. There's a sweetness, a softness about her that I wasn't expecting. I think she's far more naïve than she seemed when I first met her.

"Play something else," she says, coming to stand by me. "Something happier though. That was heartbreaking."

I start an upbeat song and watch her while I play, the candles casting light over her hair and making her face glow.

Luka grabs Eden's hand and they dance around the room, and when the song is over, they make their exit. Basile chooses that moment to go to bed too and it's just Delilah and me. I look up at her and then quickly look away. She takes my breath away.

"What's wrong?" she asks.

"Nothing." I shake my head and smile at her, putting the lid down on the piano.

"Your expression changed. Did I do something wrong?"

"No, no. You're just too beautiful for your own good. I could get lost staring at you," I say it matter-of-factly, as if saying it casually will take away from the depth I feel when looking at her. There's more to her than meets the eye. I wish I had the time to unravel all her secrets.

I stand up and she doesn't move out of the way but stares up at me like she's memorizing my face.

"Did I do something wrong?" My voice is teasing, but my body is tense as I resist touching her.

When she reaches out and touches my face, I flinch slightly and her eyes widen. I lift my hand to hers and hold it there against my face. Her lashes flutter and her eyes close as she leans in and puts her head on my shoulder. We start to sway, the music I played earlier still in our heads as we move.

She feels too good against me, her curves melding into me, closer and tighter, the longer we dance. Soon, my hand is on her waist and I can't tell where she begins and I end. Every muscle is taut, my resolve to stay unaffected, a losing battle.

"Delilah," I whisper when the desire to kiss her takes over every thought.

"Yes," she whispers back and it's all I needed.

I tilt her face back and kiss her with all the pent-up tension I've felt since the day we met. It's fire and ice, lightning and thunder, peace and war, all in one explosive kiss. I savagely explore her mouth and she reciprocates with equal passion. My hand stays at her waist and her cheek, but when she whimpers for more, I can't take it and I bend down to lift her up. Just as her legs are wrapping around my waist, the door flings open.

Delilah's legs drop to the floor and we back away from each other, scorched.

Luka's eyes are panicked, but he doesn't seem to notice our compromised position.

"Alidonia has invaded the Sea of Caninsula. King Otto is dead."

CHAPTER SIXTEEN

Jadon

My God.

I stagger backward and my legs hit the piano bench. I hold onto the piano to steady myself.

"What do you mean? Not Alidonia. No, that can't be true," Delilah says, her voice breaking. "What happened?"

Luka and I both look at Delilah and then each other. Luka's jaw ticks and he looks like he wants to hit something. I step past Delilah and move toward the door.

"Let's talk in my office. Any idea where they're heading next?"

Luka nods and we start walking out.

"Don't you dare leave me out of this. I need to know what is going on as much as you do!" Delilah says, her eyes sending daggers through us both.

"Delilah," I start, but she holds up her hand.

"I need to know," she says quieter this time.

"You must understand that it's really hard to know

whether to trust you right now." I hit the wall with my fist and avoid looking at her.

"You trusted me enough to kiss me senseless a few seconds ago." She looks like she wants to spear my head with a stake right now and I shudder.

"That was a mistake." I avoid looking at her when I say those words because nothing about that felt like a mistake until now. I look at Luka instead. "We're going to my office. We will talk to you in the morning to discuss our next option for you."

"What do you mean? You're treating me like a prisoner now? What—"

I hold up my hand and stalk toward her, getting in her face. "Give me a minute to figure out what's going on. Your father just killed the king, guess who's probably next on his list?" I point to Luka and myself. "And you're sitting here in our house. How do we know you're not in on all of this? The timing is suspect, don't you think?" I'm yelling and Luka pulls me back. I run my hands through my hair, raging. What is she doing to me?

"Jadon, man, back off. Okay? Let's talk. Delilah, you should go to your room and stay there. Jadon and I have some things to discuss and no, you are not a prisoner here, but you're not in on our discussion about this either. Just give us tonight, okay? It's possible we will need to return you to Alidonia tomorrow."

"I'm not going back there, not like this!" she cries.

I clench my fists together and stare at Luka, silently begging him to get me out of here before I explode again.

"You may not have a choice," he says quietly.

He opens the door and motions for her to leave. She reluctantly walks out, her head held fucking high. If I didn't still feel like yelling at her, I'd be damn impressed by her bravado right now. She goes upstairs to her room and I feel a pang in my chest as she walks away.

"I don't want to believe she's part of this," I tell Luka when we step into my office.

"I know you don't, but you're going to have to put your dick aside for now."

I bristle at that and he shrugs.

"I'm not oblivious to what I walked into just now, and I need your brain working at a hundred percent, brother." Luka points at the laptop, tapping at the map. "I think his army is heading here next. I've already arranged two dozen of my troops to come. But we need to come up with a plan for stopping him before he attacks."

"I'll send a few agents to Alidonia."

Luka nods. "I will too. But Jadon...I think there may be a better option. Something that would get the information to us much faster...if we can trust her."

I stare at him and let what he's saying sink in. When it does, I shake my head, holding my hand up and then pounding my desk. "No. No, we can't put her at risk like that. Or risk our own countries, for that matter. I still don't know where she really stands. How can we risk it either way?"

"We'll know one way or the other by the information she gives us. It could be the only way."

"I don't like it. And you heard her, I'm not sure she'd even be agreeable."

"If we promise we'll have protection there too...someone on the inside watching her."

I blow a long breath out. "I'm sure Farthing will have so many guards on her, she won't be able to leave her room without it getting back to him."

Luka leans his head back and stares at the ceiling. "Maybe if she agreed to marry Avaban..."

"What? The fuck, Luka? That's what started all of this in the first place. So she wouldn't have to!"

"I'm not saying she actually marries him—although, if it comes to that, we can still get her out of it later—but her father might trust her more if she acts repentant and agrees to marry him. Maybe it will put a halt to all of this at least momentarily, and we can figure out what they're planning."

I sigh and nod. "I don't like it and neither will she."

"If she's queen material, she'll be willing to sacrifice for the greater good."

I know what he's saying is true, but everything in me screams to protect her, not put her at further risk.

We stay up all night, hashing everything out with Basile and the guards. My ambassador comes at five in the morning and we discuss the strategy of the army. The troops from Niaps arrive and Luka and I have group chats with the monarchies who are at the biggest risk, should Alidonia attack them. Everyone agrees that they will probably strike Farrow next and are sending backup.

"Have you spoken with your father about any of this?" I ask Luka when we've gone over everything until we're blue in the face.

"No."

"I think it'd be a good idea. He seems to get chummy with Farthing at the most opportune times. Find out what he knows. Talk to the guards you've got on him, see if he could be part of this."

Luka nods. "You're right. I've put it off all night, but I know you're right."

I put my hand on his shoulder and squeeze. "You should get some rest. I'll talk to Delilah later this morning and figure out how to best get her home."

"I can't sleep, but I'll take a shower. You should do that too. It'll help."

We go our separate ways and an hour later, I'm reaching for more coffee when Delilah walks into the dining room.

She looks exhausted; her eyes are red-rimmed like she's been crying or up all night. Both probably. It hurts to look at her. The physical draw I feel toward her is still raging through me, especially after that kiss. I feel guilty about the way that I handled things afterward, but I'm still conflicted about her part in all of this.

I man up and do the right thing. "I apologize for how rough I spoke to you last night. It was not my finest moment and I'm ashamed of myself."

I hold a teacup out for her and she takes it, opting for hot water for tea instead of coffee. I wait for her to say something, but she simply goes through the motions of preparing her tea, still not looking at me.

"Delilah?"

When she still doesn't look at me, I set my cup down and turn to face her, while she stares down at her teacup sitting on the marble countertop.

"Talk to me," I whisper.

"That was my first kiss," she says so softly I barely hear her. She looks up at me then and the look in her eyes sends a knife through my heart. "It's true I've not had many opportunities, being sheltered in the castle all these years, but there have been efforts made by different men in the past. I've always managed to avoid it. Last night I didn't want to avoid it, but you made me wish I had."

Damn. Her vulnerability crushes me.

"I feel like such an asshole." I swallow hard and reach out to touch her arm.

She backs up before I can.

"I was trying to say that it was worth it." She swallows hard. "I've decided something." She drops three sugar cubes in her tea and stirs then takes a sip. "I will return to Alidonia and agree to marry Xang. I refuse to be the cause of a war."

"Luka mentioned that being the best option, but I don't like it. I don't like it at all."

"You don't really get a say in my life, though, do you?" Her words are sharp stabs and I feel every single one.

"We have sent guards to Alidonia and can make sure someone is watching you." I put my fist on my forehead and rub the growing headache. "Delilah, give me another day to think about this. I really don't want to put you in danger. I don't trust your father."

"Last night you didn't trust me either. My father might be a lot of things—I'm coming to terms with the fact that I don't know him as well as I thought I did—but he wouldn't put my life in danger."

"I hope you're right."

"I'll try to find out what they're planning next and get word to you when I know."

"I don't want you to put yourself at risk. Please promise me you won't and that you'll watch your back every second," I say, stepping closer to her.

I reach out and take her hand and this time, she allows it. I rub my thumb over her fingers, memorizing the feel of her silky skin against my callused fingers. She closes her eyes and when she opens them again, she stares at me...the first time she's looked at me since coming into the room.

"I can't promise that." Her voice is quiet resolve. "I have already contacted my father to let him know I'm returning. By text and voicemail—I wasn't able to get through—but hopefully it was enough warning to safely fly into the province just outside Alidonia. If you can fly me there, I can arrange the rest of the trip."

I nod in agreement.

She pulls away and walks to the door, leaving her tea behind.

"Delilah—"

She turns and looks at me.

"It was a kiss like no other," I tell her. "I felt that kiss—" I move until I'm in front of her and I don't second-guess myself, I put both hands on her cheeks and lean down until my forehead touches hers. "With everything in me," I whisper. "I don't know what to do with these feelings I'm having for you. I shouldn't even be saying this, but knowing I was your first kiss..." I kiss her cheek, first one side and then the next. "It does something to me. I can't let you go without telling you it meant something to me too."

"Thank you." Her voice skates across my skin and she leans up to kiss my cheek too.

And then she's gone and I feel the gravity of what I've just lost.

CHAPTER SEVENTEEN

Delilah

I practically run back to my room, leaving the clothes Eden let me borrow on the bed. I'm wearing the outfit I escaped in and it sets my nerves on edge, knowing I'm going back into the lion's den.

Home.

Where is home anymore?

If my father is not who I thought, if my home is not a safe place for me...what am I going back to?

I don't know and I don't want to think about it, but it's there, an ever-present nagging in my skull. It's time to do my part, whatever it takes, to preserve our kingdoms.

Ten minutes later, someone knocks on the door. I open it and Jadon is standing there, looking like heaven in a blue suit.

"The plane is ready whenever you are. I will escort you most of—"

"I don't think that's wise," I interrupt. "Let someone

else take me, please. I can't let..." I shake my head when my voice cracks. "I don't want anything to happen to you, Jadon."

"Well, now you know how I feel."

As much as it heats my skin to hear those words, it also fills me with dread. Whatever this is between us is not going anywhere. I don't even recognize the feelings he invokes in me, but I want it with all my heart...which is why the sooner I get out of here, the better.

"I'm ready to go. I won't try to talk you out of coming because I might not know you very well, but I do know you're too stubborn for your own good." I walk past him, enjoying the smirk he gives me. It feels almost like it did in the beginning, when all we had to worry about was someone finding out we'd met at the Cave of Stars. "Just stay alive, okay?"

"As you wish," he says. He puts his arm around my waist as we walk down the hall and I want to move in slow motion to prolong the feeling.

Eden and Luka are in the foyer, waiting to say goodbye. At first, I'm not sure how Eden will react to me, but she steps forward and holds out her arms and I step into them for a hug.

"Please stay safe," she whispers.

I nod, my chest welling with emotion. "I will. You too. Thank you for your kindness to me when I needed it most."

"It was an honor," she says.

I have to back away before I'm a puddle of tears and I nod at Luka without saying anything. He trusts me less than Eden and Jadon do and I don't blame him. The love he has for both of them is evident in everything he does.

The plane ride is quiet and tense. There are three guards flying with us, but they stay in the cockpit, and I don't even see the pilot. Jadon sits next to me. I'm so on edge, even my skin feels prickly, like I'm just waiting for the other shoe to drop. I feel raw from the inside out, lacking sleep and high on distress. It's probably a good thing that Jadon and I don't talk, but knowing this is probably the last chance we'll ever be in the same vicinity together is killing me inside.

I still want to know everything about him. I want to know his sadness, his triumphs, what motivates his kindness, what fuels the rage that hides just under the surface... until someone he cares about is hurt. Does he care about me or is this just who he is with everyone? The things he said today about our kiss...it matters to me. It meant something to me too. But the anger I saw last night when we found out about King Otto...the way that anger turned on me...I don't know how to reconcile the two.

I guess it doesn't matter anymore.

I'm on my way home to marry someone else. A stranger I know even less than Jadon. Someone who filled me with unease within the first minute we met, unlike the man next to me who is *supposed* to be my enemy.

"Delilah," Jadon says quietly and goose bumps pop out across my arms. "We only have these hours left together. It's a long flight—it will feel like forever if you don't relax. Try to quiet your thoughts. I can feel the tension oozing out of you. I'm afraid you're going to explode." He chuckles and I shiver. "What can I do to calm you?"

A few things come to mind. Him kissing me again is at the top of the list. And once I'm imagining his lips on mine, it's all I can think about.

I don't want Avaban to be the first man to defile me. That's what it would be—a defilement.

I turn to him, suddenly more nerve coming over me than I've ever known.

"I don't want to give Avaban any firsts," I tell him. I turn to him, taking his hand in mine.

He swallows hard and blinks, his jaw tense. "What are you saying?" His voice sounds hoarse and he clears his throat.

"I don't know why I trust you, but I do. I'm handing my life to a man I don't know, and I don't want to give him any part of me that matters. Do you understand what I'm saying?"

He tilts his head and bites the inside of his cheek. "I think I do, but I might need you to spell this out for me." He turns so he's facing me and stares at me until I feel the heat rising on my cheeks.

"As I said earlier, you were my first kiss." I lift my head back and stare at the ceiling of the plane. "Why is this so hard to say? I want you to be my first...everything," I whisper.

His pupils dilate and darken, the lust in them making my breath catch in my throat. He doesn't speak for a long time and I start to get restless, afraid he's going to turn me down. But finally, he says, "Are you sure about this? I don't want you to have any regrets—"

I put my fingers over his lips to pause his words and he kisses my fingers. He takes my hand in his and kisses down the inside of my wrist and then stands up. I stand up too, but I'm shaky, and he steadies me first before turning and walking toward the bedroom in the back, my hand in his.

He closes the door behind us and we stand for a moment, just looking at each other. He's right, I do feel like I'm going to explode soon from nerves.

"We don't have to do anything you're not comfortable

with," he starts, looking at me with apprehension. "I don't have any condoms." He looks shy. "I'm clean, and I've never had sex without a condom...but we can do other things."

"I want it all." My voice comes out bolder than I expected and I grin sheepishly, giving a slight shrug when he starts grinning back.

"You do, huh?" he taunts. "I'll pull out then." He presses his lips together. "This is really happening then?"

"I hope so."

His eyes track down my body slowly, as if he's allowing himself to truly see me for the first time. I wish I was wearing something sexier than this black sweatshirt and pants that were meant to hide me in the dark. He doesn't seem to mind, his tongue reaching out to trace his lower lip.

I pull the sweatshirt over my head, wanting to speed this up, and he puts his arm out to stop me when I start to take off my pants.

"Let me," he says. He undoes the button on my pants and slides the zipper down so slowly, my heart starts to gallop out of my chest. When he gets on his knees in front of me, my mouth drops and he lowers my pants until they drop to the floor. He stares at my lacy panties and gives them a tug, lifting his eyes to look at me for a second. "I'll need to keep these." They drop to the floor and he buries his face into me then, his breath skating across my most delicate places.

"Jadon," I whisper.

"Let's pretend there's no one left on this earth but the two of us right here, right now," he says, kissing me in places I'm too embarrassed to think about, but it feels so good I never want him to stop. "I want to make you feel so good you never forget that I was right here." He plants a kiss on the inside of my thigh and I tremble. "Or here." He moves to my center and flicks his tongue across me in a way that makes my knees buckle. He chuckles against me and holds me steady. "Lie back on the bed. I'm going to taste you until you're screaming my name..."

He stands up and gives me a nudge and I fall back on the bed.

"I got ahead of myself." He looks at my bra and grins, his teeth clenching his bottom lip as he undoes the clasp. He takes a deep breath when I toss the bra off of the bed. "You're even more beautiful than I imagined. And I've imagined you every day since we met." His eyes crinkle with his smile and I think he is so gorgeous it makes my chest squeeze.

He bends down and takes my nipple between his teeth, tugging it and then flicking it with his tongue to soothe. He does it again and again, until my back is arching and I'm leaning into his touch, trying to pull his body on top of mine. He insists on taking his time and I want all of him, now. He gives each breast equal attention and when his hands start wandering down my body and land between my legs, I moan.

"Jadon," I cry, more insistent. His fingers move faster as he rubs and flicks, and when they drive into me, my head falls back and I think I've seen heaven. But he's not done, he keeps going until my whole body is trembling, his fingers dipping in and out, faster and faster. I start to feel like I'm losing control and then I really am, my eyes rolling back as I give in to the waves that take over.

"So sweet," he says, kissing down my chest and then to the place his fingers just were. I lean my head up, slightly mortified to see him down there after I just exploded, but he looks up at me like he's right where he wants to be. He starts flicking faster and I'm already so tender, it sends me over the edge again.

I moan his name over and over, not wanting to ever forget the way this feels, the way *he* makes me feel. "Thank you," I cry, going limp.

He wipes his mouth and kisses up my body, until he's leaning over me with a grin I haven't seen on him before. I laugh, covering my eyes with embarrassment and he moves my hands, leaning down to kiss me.

"I should be thanking you," he whispers. "I loved every second of that."

"So did I." I don't even sound like myself. My voice sounds like a sex kitten and I giggle when I think about what we've just done. And I still want more. I unbutton his shirt and he stops me before I pull it off.

"Are you really sure about this?" He has that concerned look on his face again and I frown.

"Do you not want me?"

He's leaning over me again in the next second. "How can you think that? Did I not just show you how much I want you?"

"You're doing me a favor."

He laughs so hard, the sound bounces across the bedroom, and I'm sure they can hear him all the way in the cockpit.

"Oh, sweet Delilah," he rubs against me, his pants still on, but I have little doubt of what I'm feeling, "I want this more than I want my next breath..." He kisses me hard and I lose myself in it, every sensation on overload.

He undoes his pants and pulls them off, his mouth never leaving mine. His fingers reach between my legs again and he smiles when he feels how wet I am.

When I feel his bare skin against me, I groan. "You feel so good," I whisper.

He inches in, just a tiny bit, and my eyes widen.

"We'll take this slowly," he says.

He feels huge and I don't know how this is going to work, but when he starts kissing me again, he's able to go a little deeper each time. It stings and he pauses here and there when he can tell it's too much. But then it starts to feel good again, almost from one second to the next, like magic. I relax and let my hands explore the planes of his back, the muscles in his arms, and when he starts to drive into me faster and faster, I wrap my legs around him and give everything back to him, my body instinctively knowing what to do.

"I could do this with you forever," he says, looking into my eyes. "But ahhh, you feel a little too good." He starts to pull out, but I press him in deeper with my feet and hands.

"I want all of you," I whisper.

"God, you're too good to be true," he says as he spills inside of me.

I stare at him through it, in awe of the way his emotions play out on his face. He's a revelation and I take in every second, every twitch, every groan, putting it to memory. Nothing will compare to him. Ever.

CHAPTER EIGHTEEN

Jadon

"Are you sure you're okay?" I ask when I lie beside her.

I push her hair back and stare in her violet eyes, hoping I'll always remember what she looks like in this moment. It's going to torment me and be my salvation, losing her. I already know this, and yet I'd dive headlong into her again and again, given the chance.

"I'm so good. I'm sore, but in the best way." She tickles my chest with her slow sweep across my skin with her fingertips.

I close my eyes and enjoy the moment, already wanting more of her but trying to quiet my body down. It's hard when just being near her is a craving I can't fill.

"I'll be right back," she says finally, getting up slowly.

The bathroom is just a few steps away and she gets up, letting me enjoy the view of her glorious backside as she walks away. I hear the toilet flush and the shower running and when she opens the door, the light hits her and she looks like walking sunshine. I stand up and her eyes roam over my body, lingering on parts of me that can't be ignored.

She grins. "You didn't get enough?"

"I don't think I could ever get enough of you." I trace circles on her stomach and up to her nipple, covering her breast with my hand and squeezing. "Let's clean up and then I want to kiss you more." I move past her into the bathroom.

"I want to do all of that again," she says.

I turn and her mouth parts, the little seductive princess wrapping me around her finger even more.

"I'm yours." I kiss her lightly. "I'm yours," I whisper again when we step into the shower. *Fuck me, I'm hers. How the hell did this happen?*

There's not much room, but we wash quickly and then I lean her against the wall of the shower and kiss her like a man on fire. I can't get close enough and when she moans into my mouth, her body pressed as tight as she can get, I lift her up and wrap her legs around my waist. She shudders against me when we line up just right and I remind myself to keep taking it slowly.

"Tell me what you want," I say into her mouth.

"I want you every way I can have you. I want to memorize you until I can close my eyes and feel every part of this, years from now when it should be impossible. I need more," she whimpers when I put my fingers between us and tease her. "Please. Mark me. I need to have proof you were here."

"Fuck, Delilah. You're making me crazy." I kiss her hard, until we're both panting and when she reaches down and touches me, I lose my mind. I carry her out of the shower and we fall on the bed, still completely wet.

I make sure she's ready and then slowly fill her again. She doesn't want slow this time, though. She grips my hair in her fists and thrusts back hard, making my head fall back. I roll over and pull her on top of me, teasing her with the tip of my cock until she cries out.

When she's slowing down from her high, she whispers, "More."

It's all I needed to hear and I roll her back over and fill her to the hilt. "I want to stay right here forever. In. The. Air. With. You." With each word, I slide all the way out and then back in, until she's gasping, her whole body shaking. "I don't know if I can let you go," I whisper into her hair so soft that she can't hear me.

I know I can't keep her.

But I also know I won't ever be able to let her go from the grip she's got on me.

Ever.

Nothing has ever felt like this.

"Delilah," I whisper, looking in her eyes again. "You are...everything." I thrust all the way in and twist my hips in a circle, over and over and over. Until my vision goes black and I see stars.

I'd like to say I go easy on her, but every time I try to kiss her and be gentle, things heat up again and she climbs on top of me like a tiger about to pounce. I cannot quench her thirst and I'd like to think it's me, that I'm what she can't get enough of, but part of me knows she's also chasing an escape. Her life changed forever when she ran away, and now she's going back to uncertainty. I want to give her what she needs and she doesn't want to think about anything but this moment.

"What is your favorite way to do this?" she asks when we're catching our breath.

"Have sex?" I say, laughing. "Can you not say the word?"

She flushes and I laugh harder. We've had sex three times now and she's still shy with me.

"What's your favorite way to have sex?" She leans her head up on her elbow and smiles at me, her cheeks red.

"So far, every time with you is my favorite."

She rolls her eyes. "You don't need to feed me lines. Tell me. What position?"

"I'm not feeding you anything. I am starving though. Aren't you?"

"There will be plenty of time to eat...when we're apart." Her voice changes when she says that, and I reach out and touch her face, eager to see her smile again.

"Food, blech." I make a face and my heart feels buoyant when she laughs. "You're much better than food. Sex...it's different with you." I bite the inside of my cheek, not wanting to make this too serious, but wanting her to know I don't usually feel this way. "I think every position we tried would shake heaven and earth."

"Yeah," she whispers, leaning over until her forehead touches mine. "What is that about?"

I tap her heart and then lean down to tweak her nipples because I can't get enough of them. "There's something in here." I tap my heart. "And here." I tap her temple and then mine. "And in here. Between us. Do you feel it or is it just me wanting to believe you feel the way I do?"

She runs her hands through my hair and bends down to kiss me. Her tongue caresses mine and I jolt to life again. "I feel it too. So much. I-I don't know how I will ever le—" Her voice breaks and she kisses me again. I want to hear the rest, but she holds me firmly in her grip and we get lost in each other.

This time when our bodies come together, it aches. It's poignant, the way we move in sync. I hear her call and answer it; she seeks my void and fills it. We are one in the most profound way. Two lost souls who have never wanted anything more than to be loved.

Saying goodbye to her feels like saying goodbye to light.

To hope.

To a future.

The end of life as I've always known it.

CHAPTER NINETEEN

Jadon

The last twenty minutes of our flight, we return to our seats, but this time, my arms are around her and her head is against my chest. Our fingers are entwined and I kiss her hair every few minutes. When she lifts her face to look at me, I kiss her.

When we land, I panic. I turn to face her and grab her face. "I don't know how to do this. This is a terrible idea. Let's turn around, get out of here. It's not too late. I can't lose you."

She's shaking her head even though her lip is clenched in her teeth and tears are welling in her eyes.

"No, Jadon. It has to be like this. You think I could live with myself if I caused more people to die? It's the only way. I don't want to marry Avaban, but if it puts a stop to this, it'll be worth it." A tear drops on my finger and I let out a string of curses that would make my father turn in his grave. "You've given me something that I'll never forget."

She closes her eyes and kisses me one last time. "Thank you," she says when she pulls back.

She undoes her seat belt and stands, wiping her face and straightening her shoulders like she's bracing herself for battle. I stand and wrap my arms around her, hugging her tight against me, and she melts into it for a few seconds, but then pulls away.

"You need to go." Her fingers tease the scruff on my cheeks and brush over my lips. "Goodbye, Jadon. Please be safe."

She backs away and I tug at my hair and lift my hands to the ceiling of the plane, hitting it.

"We'll be doing everything we can to put an end to this," I say as she walks away. "Watch your back every second," my voice raises and she keeps walking. "Dammit, Delilah. I don't want you to go."

She turns as she reaches the exit and one of the guards starts to open the door. She smiles at me, her eyes caressing me the way they have all day.

"It has been the most beautiful day," she whispers, lifting a hand to her lips and kissing it before extending it to me.

And she's gone in the next breath. The guards walk off with her and when they've alerted me that she's reached the car safely, the pilot backs the plane up and gets us out of there before anyone knows I've accompanied the princess.

Back to being alone.

Exhaustion sets in on the way home. I still can't sleep. Everywhere I look, I see her. I go to the bedroom and just stand there, my mind replaying every way I had her.

Eventually, I give in and crawl into the bed, wishing I could rewind this day and start over. I'd savor every second even more than I did. I wouldn't waste any time being so suspicious and cautious. About an hour before we're supposed to land, I fall into a deep sleep and wake up to the pilot announcing that we're landing soon. I scrub my palm over my face feeling like death with crispy burned edges. I shouldn't have let myself fall asleep at all, but my work will be cut out for me as soon as I get off the plane.

I check my email for any surveillance updates from the guards with Delilah, but there is no word. This is torture. I should have insisted she stay.

And be like her father, basically keeping her under lock and key?

At least I would've kept her safe.

And content.

My blood heats at the thought of her writhing under me and I rub my eyelids, unable to get her out of my head. She's awoken a beast within me that I didn't even know was there...I'm reduced to an animalistic need for her. A devoted dog whose heart beats only for their owner.

I wonder if she knows she claimed me from day one.

Later that night, I get word from Lostrand, my inside source in Alidonia, that Delilah has arrived at the castle and so far, there have been no major disruptions.

"I have a friend in the house," he says.

"That friend is one hundred percent trustworthy?" I haven't stopped pacing since I got home and now is no different.

"He despises the Farthings and wants to see the king brought down even more than you and I do."

"But will he also protect Delilah?"

"He will."

"Okay, I trust you, Lostrand. If you see Delilah without cover, can you swear to me that you'll forget everything else and protect her? I don't feel right about sending her back to the wolves."

"I swear to you, I won't let you down, King Jadon. You can count on me."

"Thank you."

I slam the phone down and put my head in my hands. Delilah is our best hope of keeping an all-out war from breaking out, but I'll only be able to hold King Otto's family for so long before they demand justice. And it might only be a matter of time before Farthing goes after all those who were at Delilah's press conference. I hate what this requires of Delilah and am not going to rest until I figure out a way to get her out of there before she has to sacrifice herself to Avaban's will.

She went in not expecting a way out, but I'd rather die than see her marry Avaban.

Or anyone but me.

I slam my hand against the wall repeatedly, the pent-up anger forcing its way out of me. I don't know what I'm thinking.

I will never marry Delilah.

CHAPTER TWENTY

Delilah

I expect to see my father right away, but I'm shocked to see not only Caulder with him but Avaban himself. My blood simmers seeing the three of them together, looking smug as I walk down the long hallway toward them.

They stand there looking like a combination of pious and poisonous with their heads held high and the anger dripping through their veins as they try to intimidate me. I don't know why I've never seen the way Caulder looks at me, like he owns me yet despises me. I avoid looking at my father, not wanting to see the truth. I'm afraid it will crush me and I need to remain strong in all of this.

I get within a few feet of them and stop. My father takes a step forward and then walks the rest of the way, his shoes echoing around the room. I feel the rage before I even look in his eyes and then I feel it in the handprint he slaps across my face, my head jerking to the side with the force of it.

I hold a hand to my cheek and stand steady, my insides quaking, but my will keeping me from showing it.

"How dare you disgrace me like this. I've never been so ashamed of you. I've only asked one thing of you your whole life...you've lived a sheltered life of luxury, wanting for nothing. And you repay me by going against me in this way? Who helped you escape?"

"Marrying this man is the one thing you've asked of me?" I fling my hand toward Xang. "Is that what you're saying? No, Papa. You didn't *ask* that of me. You sprung it on me in front of hundreds of people because you knew how I'd react!"

"Who helped you escape?" The vein on his forehead bulges when he yells and he staggers forward, his hands clasping around my neck.

"Papa!" I whimper. "Please, you're hurting me."

He drops his hands and backs away, his chest heaving. He pulls out a handkerchief and wipes his face. "I can't even look at you right now," he says under his breath. "You sicken me."

My lips tremble, but I am stone otherwise. If I let it, the hurt will bring me to my knees.

"I came home." I look past my father to King Avaban, who stands watching the whole thing with disinterest. I'm nothing more than a pesky flea on one of his dogs. "I'll marry Avaban and we can put the whole thing behind us."

"It's not as simple as that," Caulder says, smiling. "When you let all of those monarchies toss in their alliances, all boundaries went by the wayside. You have waged war with your dramatic behavior. And you'll pay for that."

"This discussion is between my father and me." My

voice is cold and final when I look at Caulder. He bristles, but I'm not the first one to look away.

"You need to watch your place," he mutters under his breath.

"I think you're the one who needs to watch your place, cousin," I spit the words at him, unable to hide how much I hate him in this moment.

It hits its mark and he steps back, his face turning into a splotch of red.

"Now, now," Xang walks toward me, holding a hand out, "let's not discuss wars just yet. We have a wedding to see about."

"I'll need some time to plan it," I cringe when he squeezes my hand.

"I don't think that will be necessary, not after your dramatics," he says under his breath.

"You have six weeks," my father says. "We will need to do damage control and see where things are with the Sea of Caninsula. I hope you don't rest knowing there is blood on your hands," he says, leaning into my face.

"I didn't kill anyone, Papa. This is on *your* hands. I will marry Avaban if, and only *if*, you put a stop to this madness."

"It might be too late," he says.

"Things are going to change around here," I say loudly, making sure Caulder can hear me on the other side of the room. "I will be involved in the discussions between you and our advisors, and Xang, you and I will get married in six weeks *here*, where we will later reside." My voice shakes, but I figure there's a reason they want to marry me off. What's the worst that can happen to me before the wedding? "I'm the next in line and Papa isn't well enough to handle things here without me."

Caulder sputters, talking under his breath, and my father doesn't look much happier. Xang just smiles like it's the best deal he's heard in a long time, and I vow to get to the bottom of his agenda.

"You're not going to be able to run this kingdom on your own," Papa says. "I don't know what fancy ideas you got in your head over the—what, forty-eight hours or so you were away? But I'm not dead yet. Everyone can just back off and let me run this the way I see fit."

I hold back everything I want to throw at him, all the thoughts I have about how awful I think he is, how my view of him has flipped upside down and now I'm siding with the enemy...I keep that to myself and nod.

"Yes, Papa," I say like a trained monkey. I nod at Xang. "It's time to start planning a wedding."

I rush to my room and fall face forward on the bed, the adrenaline in my body nearly causing me to vibrate with nerves. That went better than I expected. It won't be easy to stomach dealing with Avaban when he has my family backing up everything he says, much less marrying him— but I can't think that far ahead right now.

One day at a time.

And for this day, I've experienced all that my mind, body, and soul can deal with.

I lost my virginity.

To the enemy.

And it was the most beautiful thing that's ever happened to me.

I came home to face the father who betrayed me.

He didn't kill me. But he didn't welcome me with open

arms either. It remains to be seen how our relationship will play out. This is uncharted territory. I've never been at odds with him. I hate it.

I want my loving father back, the one who doted on me. But did he ever really love me? Or did he just love the puppet he'd created?

How did I go my whole life without stepping out of place, never rocking the boat? It's as if my taste buds have formed for the first time, my eyes are seeing colors they've never seen, I hear inflections that went unnoticed before... have I really been sleepwalking my entire life?

As horrible as it feels to be home under these conditions, I wouldn't change what I discovered with Jadon for a single second.

My eyes close as I relive the bliss of being underneath him, his body pressing into mine, as he awakened a part of me I would've never known was lying dormant...if it hadn't been for him.

The gratitude I feel for him is staggering.

All at the enemy's hand. An enemy I will dream about every night and keep in my heart for as long as I live.

It makes this hell I'm in now more bearable.

Knowing that if I die tonight, for a few sweet hours with Jadon, I truly lived.

A knock at the door wakes me out of a dream about Jadon, my hands in his long hair as he took me from behind. I gasp when the knock gets louder, coming out of my stupor and sitting up, heart pounding. I sit up and look around. My room is dark, but I'm still wearing my clothes and have no concept of what time it could be.

"Delilah?" Caulder says.

"One minute." I get up and turn on the light, straightening my clothes as I walk to the door.

I open it wide and he stands there, looking past me into the room. He strides in, not waiting for me to invite him.

"Nice of you to show up." He crosses his arms and levels me with a glare I haven't quite seen from him before. "What are you working on, Delilah? I need you to drop the bullshit and level with me."

I rub my head and blink, my head still foggy from sleep. "You'll have to start over. I don't know what you're talking about."

"Why did you come home? You start a war, get a king killed, and come home ready to do what you were asked to do in the first place? Something doesn't add up. Who got to you? And what's their agenda?"

I shiver, the way he's staring at me making me anxious. "No one got to me. I still don't want to marry Avaban, but I will if it means no one else will get hurt. I'm sure you can understand that—can't you? And I didn't get a king killed. King Otto was gracious to me—that shouldn't have cost him his life. Who was responsible for that anyway? You?" I scoff and his eyes narrow. "No, wait, you're not brave enough for that. You're always hiding behind Papa...until I come around and then you want to exert your authority over me." I walk over to him and get in his face, ignoring the tremors in my body, the fear that washes over me when he grabs my arms and shakes me. I keep talking, my teeth rattling. "I'm finally seeing who you really are, Caulder. You've done that all by yourself."

He shoves me and I fly against the wall, my elbow hitting especially hard. I clutch it in my hand and rub out the soreness. It helps distract me enough that I don't hit

Caulder or do something else equally stupid. If I'm going to bring peace to my kingdom, I won't get it by knocking him out the first time he makes me this angry. Nothing will ever be resolved that way.

"I'm watching you," he spits out. "You think because you have a title, you're safe from me, but trust me when I say that you're safe from *no one*. Wake up, little princess. Papa isn't going to save you this time." He smiles and it is so chilling I can't believe he's the same person I've always known. "And I'm just looking for any excuse to murder you in your sleep." He cackles and I back into the corner of the room when he stalks toward me. "One wrong step," he says under his breath, "and I will push you straight off the edge without a moment's hesitation. Got it?"

He puts his hand around my throat and squeezes, the veins on the side of his face popping out. He looks the way my father did earlier when *he* was squeezing my neck. I've been so blind.

"I asked you a question," he spits.

"Got it," I choke out.

"Good." He releases me and I stand taller, trying to regain my composure.

I don't want him to see me cowering in fear ever, but I'm still shaking, so for now, I simply try to quiet my mind.

"Here's how things will go. You will marry Xang in six weeks as you agreed to do. But the two of you will then go to Blorl and reside there. Because of your new position as queen of Blorl, I will be given the reigning crown upon your father's passing...which is only a matter of time. Your father's health is good right now, but one wrong move from you, and I can make that go away."

My eyes widen and I cry out, my fear forgotten as I step forward and hit him in the chest. He barely registers my fists at first but clamps his hands around my wrists like he's handling a pesky child.

"You leave him alone," I yell.

"Keep your commitments and I will." He shrugs and drops my wrists. He laughs coldly and walks to the door. "Goodnight, cousin. Sweet dreams."

I fall back on my bed and huddle into a ball under the covers. I don't recognize my life anymore.

CHAPTER TWENTY-ONE

Jadon

The next morning, I go see Kathryn. She's more subdued than usual when I sit across from her. She studies the chess game and doesn't look at me until I speak.

"How are you feeling today?" I ask.

"The days all bleed into the next. I don't know what day of the week it is most of the time. I'm restless and angry to be locked in here for so long. I'm sorry for what I've done to you, Jadon. But please, don't leave me here forever. Do you think you'll ever feel comfortable around me again...beyond guards and keeping me locked away?"

I stare at her for a few moments, trying to read any motives behind what she's saying. Her expression seems genuine enough, but I can't tell anymore with her.

"You've never apologized to me before," I finally respond. "What exactly are you apologizing *for*?"

"I've had a lot of time to think in isolation. And I have a lot to apologize for." She blinks rapidly and her eyes fill with tears that hover near her bottom lashes for a few long beats before dropping. I stare at them transfixed, not sure where she's going with this. "I don't expect us to be close overnight," she continues with a deep breath, "but I regret how I've taken out your father's indiscretions so long ago against you. As wonderful as he was, he wasn't perfect. He was away for a couple of years at war...and the fact that you were conceived during that time was never your fault. The moment I decided to give him a second chance when we heard about your mother and you, I should've also accepted you."

I'm too shocked to respond. The years of hurt and rejection have done a number on me. Since the day I came into Kathryn's house at six years old, I've been seeking her approval...often to the detriment of my well-being. Something inside of me shut off when she tried to kill me months ago, even while trying to defend her actions in my head.

Instead of acknowledging what she's said—I'll have to deal with that another day; it's too much for today—I ask, "Now that you're feeling more clearheaded—at least I'm assuming you are—can I ask a couple of questions?"

She nods.

"Have you remembered anything else about your time in captivity? Did you ever see anyone besides the two men and woman who held you and Ava?"

She shakes her head. "No, I've gone through it over and over in my mind, trying to even recall the slightest noise that could've been someone else...or conversations I might have overheard and not remembered. But there's nothing. I don't remember ever hearing or seeing another soul." She leans in. "I think the Farthings are behind it though. And most likely that Titus Catano played a part."

I steeple my fingers together and stare at her. She's not

saying anything I haven't already thought, but I'm disappointed that she doesn't have anything more than a gut feeling.

Before I leave, she stands and it's then that I notice how much weight she's lost. Guilt rattles around in my chest and I pause at the door.

"Thank you for what you said. I'll think about it. I honestly don't know if I can ever trust you, but...I'd like to try."

She swallows hard and nods. "I understand."

That evening I call Basile into my office and he comes in with a bottle of wine and two glasses.

"How are you settling into Farrow?" I ask, grinning when he hands me a glass of wine.

"Besides missing Chelsea, our chef and my favorite bedfellow, I'm settling in fine. I do miss the sound of the waves crashing against the cliffs. When all this with Farthing is resolved, I'll need to explore and find the water."

"I didn't realize you were a beach lover."

"I despise sand. But I love hearing it and seeing it...in the distance." He laughs and I join him.

His energy for life is contagious.

"I have a proposal for you." I decide to bring it up when he's on his second glass of wine...knowing him, he's probably way past his second glass, but I'm only counting what I've witnessed.

"Lay it on me."

"I'd like to pay a visit to Titus. Do you think you can get me in?"

His eyebrows lift to the ceiling and he sputters. "I

thought you'd say something like you need help organizing your financials or something else snooze-worthy."

I chuckle. "If only. No, it's time that we get to the bottom of all of this. I think I'll get an idea of whether Titus is involved in the attack on Otto if I talk to him personally. Or if it's Vance working on his own. I need to know what we're dealing with here."

Basile nods solemnly and pours us another glass of red. He clanks my glass before looking at the fire crackling in the fireplace.

"We need to see how far this goes. My concern is what they might have planned next. Farthing is the obvious suspect for Otto since he knows that's where Delilah went, but...I just need to be sure."

"Understood. I can get you in to see Titus, no problem. In the past, the guards couldn't be trusted, but Luka's been working on weeding them out for a long time now. He'll be able to authorize our visit and we'll know fairly soon if we're compromised..."

I nod. "Great. Can we leave first thing in the morning?"

"Yes. One request—"

"Name it."

He grins and I brace myself. "Will there be any time for a little visit with Chelsea?"

I smirk and roll my eyes. "I'm not heartless. Of course. Get me into the jail and you can spend all our time in Niaps with Chelsea if you're that anxious to see her."

He laughs. "I don't even need to see her. As long as I can touch her, I'm happy."

"You're filthy. Who knew?"

"Didn't realize this was news to anyone." He drains his glass and lifts the bottle, his eyes questioning whether I want more. I shake my head and he pours the rest in his glass. "Well, if that's all...I'll call Luka and start working on the guards. We'll need to leave before sunrise to get there during visiting hours. It won't leave us much time to work with."

"Let's leave at 3:00 A.M."

He sighs, his shoulders falling. "I'll need to nap on the plane so I have enough stamina for Chelsea."

"TMI." I'm grinning though, hard not to with Basile around.

The sky is an inky black and blue when we roll down the tarmac before the sun rises the next morning. Basile looks half asleep and he's snoring before we're even in the air for five minutes. I barely slept again last night, thoughts of Kathryn's apology, how I might best get the truth out of Catano, and Delilah all at war for prominent space in my head. I eventually doze off myself and wake up hours later when the pilot says we're about to land.

Basile cracks an eye open at me and I yawn, rubbing a hand over my entire face.

"You look beat. You're sleeping some aren't you, son?" he asks.

"Not enough, but I do feel better after that nap."

He nods. "We must keep you healthy and your head free of the fog. I have to say though, even at your worst, you handle things more calmly than anyone I've ever seen. Natural born leader..." He leans his head back against the seat as we bump into our landing.

"Thank you. I don't always feel calm, especially right now."

"Keep trusting your gut. I'm here because I trust your

gut and so does Luka. We're all sort of following your wisdom here. And I don't believe we're the only kingdom doing so."

I feel the pressure behind what he's saying, but it also helps to know I can only do my best...the rest will have to fall into place.

"Thank you, Basile. I appreciate your input."

———

Luka is waiting in the car with his driver, and Elias, his right hand.

"Only one car?" Basile frowns.

I clear my throat. "Would it be possible to stop by the house? Basile needed to—" I leave it hanging so Basile can take the conversation in whatever direction he wants.

Luka shakes his head. "Chelsea isn't with us anymore, Uncle."

"*What?* Where is she?"

"I don't know. She quit a couple of days ago...and without any notice. Left us in such a lurch that Brienne has been cooking." He makes a face. "And I wouldn't wish that on my worst enemy."

I laugh...until I see the look on Basile's face. I put my hand on his shoulder and squeeze. "You okay?"

"She's been with our family for such a long time. What reason did she give for leaving?"

"She didn't even tell us directly that she was leaving. She left after breakfast a couple of days ago right after she told Brienne she wouldn't be back."

"What the fuck?"

"Wish I knew. I'm sorry—I know you were...rather attached...to Chelsea. And I wish I had more details to give you, but we've got our hands full with everything else, right?"

Basile glances out the window, his expression unreadable. Finally, he says, "Right. No, I don't expect you to keep tabs on the employees who quit...I just expected more out of her."

"I agree. I did too," Luka says. He looks at me, suddenly all business. "We'll have to be quick about this. For the most part, I've cleaned house in regards to those guarding my father, but you never know when one might defect. My friend Plars will let us in and guard you when you talk to my father."

"Are you going in with me?"

"If you're comfortable with that."

I nod and then enjoy the view of the ocean the rest of the way to the prison. Basile is silent.

The prison is an ancient stone building out on an island. Basile stays with the car, while a boat takes Luka and me to the island. We're admitted through the staff entrance to avoid attention. After we're searched for weapons, we walk down the long, grey hallway to see Titus. He's kept in a private area, and when the room we're to meet in is unlocked and we step inside, I'm shocked by how nice everything is. It makes me wonder how nice his cell is.

"He's not suffering much," I mutter under my breath.

"He's been transferred to solitary a few times and that looks drastically different than this wing," Luka says.

We sit and wait for less than five minutes before the door is unlocked again and Titus Catano comes in, his hands cuffed in front of him. The guard locks Titus's cuffs to the table before he sits down. He regards his son first, silently, and then he locks eyes with me. The hatred in his eyes doesn't surprise me, although I would've thought he'd taper it down some while he's in prison, in hopes that Luka will show mercy on him during the next trial. He doesn't seem to care and the wave of rage he brings into the room is unsettling.

"Something serious must've gone down for Neil Safrin's son to deem me worthy a visit," he says, his lip curling. "Hello, son." He gives a slight nod to his son. "How does it feel to be sleeping with the enemy in more ways than one."

"Well, every night I get in bed with Eden is the best night of my life, so I'm not suffering there," Luka responds, his jaw ticking. "But I also don't mind having Jadon for an ally. Not even for a second," he adds under his breath. "He's got more integrity in his whole body than you have in your little finger."

Titus scoffs as he gives me the side-eye, trying to size me up and shrink me down all at once. "I don't have anything better to do, but I still don't want the two of you wasting my time. What do you want?"

"You're already in prison, so it would serve you to be honest for once in your life," Luka says. "I'm asking for you to tell the truth."

Titus adopts a bored expression and sinks back into his seat like a teenager slouching at school. The almighty King Titus doesn't look so powerful anymore.

"Go on," he says.

"Were you behind the kidnapping of my sister and step-mother?" I ask.

"No, but I know who was."

I lean forward, my heart picking up. "And?"

"And what?"

"*Who was it?*" Luka yells.

"Get me out of here and maybe I'll tell you." He laughs. He lazily looks us over and Luka looks close to pounding the smirk off of his father's face.

"For once in your life, can you have a little decency? What could you possibly have against Jadon—your vendetta was against his father. Jadon has done nothing to you. Who was behind this and do you swear it wasn't you?"

"Jadon is guilty by association. I will never befriend a Safrin king, never." Titus shrugs and rattles his cuffs. "Now, is that all?"

"How deep does your alliance with Alidonia go?" I ask.

"It's as deep an alliance as my hatred for you," he says simply. He throws his head back and laughs and Luka slams his fist on the table.

"Then if we find out Farthing is behind Jadon's murder attempt, we will be placing blame on you as well." Luka stands up and walks to the door and knocks for it to be opened. "We're wasting our time, Jadon. My father wants to rot in here."

I lean down and get in Catano's face. "It's a shame. You've aged so much in here. You used to be almost as handsome as your son. Now you look like a shell of that man. Old, shriveled up. Hate will do that to a person. I hope you're as miserable in here as you fucking deserve." I grin when he snarls at me and stand up straight.

The guard lets us out and Luka slams his hand against the wall. He turns to the guard and his lip curls as he corners him. "You let me know every guest my father has, every questionable conversation he has, every time he fucking pisses wrong. Am I clear? This is a matter of life and death."

"Yes, sir."

Luka backs off, somewhat mollified, and we continue down the hall. As we go out the same door we came in, the sound of an incoming boat gets louder.

"How many people come in through this entrance to see my father?"

"No one has but you since I've worked here," the guard says. "I'll look at the log."

Luka motions for me to step in the alcove just out of view as we watch the boat dock and a tall, imposing figure gets out.

When he gets closer, I'm glad we're hidden because I'd be tempted to strike now, before it's time. He goes inside and Luka and I look at each other.

"That's all the fucking confirmation I needed," I tell him. "What could Caulder Farthing possibly want with your father if they're not working together?"

CHAPTER TWENTY-TWO

Jadon

Basile and I fly back to Farrow after having dinner with Luka and Eden. All of us are troubled by Caulder showing up at the prison. As much as Luka distrusts his father, to know he outright lied to him yet again, does a number on him. It's a constant boulder going up to guard your heart when you realize your parents are not who you thought they were. There's something innate in us that wants to believe in our parents at all costs. I think about my conversation with Kathryn and wonder if I'm crazy to believe her apology.

Luka apologized again and again as he said goodbye and I tried to assure him just as many times that I do not hold him responsible for his father's sins.

Basile and I sit across from each other and I put my hand over my glass when he tries to pour a second glass of wine.

"Suit yourself," he says.

"We have to get her out of there." My teeth are gritted and I look out the window without seeing anything at all.

"I assume you're talking about the beautiful princess," Basile says dryly. "Jadon, you are one of the wisest kings I've been around; it would be a shame to see you lose your head over a woman."

"Too late."

It's the middle of the night when we get home and I don't stop to calculate the time difference to Ava. I send her a picture of Caulder.

Did you ever see this man when you were kidnapped?

Ava: No, but I know they weren't working alone. Who is that?

Nephew to Vance Farthing. He paid Titus Catano a visit today.

Ava: Oh shit. Is that proof enough that he was also behind Father's murder?

It's proof enough for me. I know in my gut that he's behind the attempt on my life. What I don't know is if the king is behind this or if Caulder is working on his own.

I pause for a moment when the clock clangs four times. Star looks up at me from the foot of the bed and then nestles deeper into the covers. She's taken to sleeping on the bed with me and I can't say I mind it.

What are you doing awake?

Ava: You needed me.

I put my head in my hands and exhale the stress of the day.

I love you. We can talk again tomorrow. Sleep. I don't want you worrying about any of this.

Ava: I always worry about you. It's hard not being with you right now.

I would be a wreck if you were. The thought that you're safe and having fun—you are still having fun, right? Gentry is treating you well?

Ava: He treats me like a queen. :) The kind of queen I WANT to be.

Nothing could make me happier. Night, little one. I love you.

Ava: Love you.

Sleep is hard to come by, but I get a little bit after talking with Ava. She has a way of calming me. I miss her every day, but knowing she's safe is everything. When she was missing, I lived in a constant nightmare.

Pretty much how I feel now with Delilah across the kingdoms in enemy territory. I wonder if she has any idea of how dangerous Caulder is. And I'm not going to rest until I know if Vance is calling the shots or if it's Caulder...because if it's Caulder, I'm a lot more concerned for Delilah. With Vance, I at least think he's going to fight for his life and hers...

Caulder is a wild card who might stop at nothing to become king.

Holy shit. This just gets worse.

I call for Basile to come to the office and when he sits down, he looks more exhausted than I do.

"You okay?" I ask.

He shrugs.

"I've never seen you without your—" I wave my hand toward him "—devil-may-care attitude...what's going on?"

"I can't reach Chelsea. I don't know if she thought I was never coming back or if I didn't call enough...I *have* been terrible about keeping in touch...but surely she knows I haven't stopped lo—" He stops and looks at me with wide eyes. He holds out his hands and shakes them. "Enough of that. There's a good reason I am still single. Women fuck with your mind," he says, sneering. "I was good to her and she just up and disappears." He gets up and walks to the window, looking desolate. "What did you need to see me about?"

"Well, I think you should definitely find her, put your mind at ease. She's welcome to come here, if you're missing her this much."

He waves his hand. "I don't need to think about her right now. We have more important matters to tend to."

I chuckle and he groans. "You've got it bad, don't you?"

"About as bad as you do for that white-haired princess. We're a mess."

"I'm worried about her. The guard on her doesn't have access to her full-time and it's driving me crazy not knowing what's going on. She's silent...not that I expected her to reach out, but..."

"You hoped," Basile finishes for me.

"I hoped." I sigh and smooth a few papers on my desk just to keep my hands busy. "I've decided to go to the Sea of Caninsula today. I received a message earlier that King Shua is wanting to strike over his father's death. There's been an outcry over Otto and I need to see what I can do to temper that...as you know, my heart is always for peace. But it's only a matter of time before it's beyond that. And I'd like to get Delilah out before that happens..."

"If you get Delilah out now, there's sure to be a war. Who will they hit next? We have to be ready," Basile says.

"I agree. Which is why at least fifty kings will be meeting with me later this evening in Caninsula. We'll be discussing strategy and a timeline. Can I trust you to take care of things here while I'm gone?"

"I swear on all that is holy, you can trust me." He turns toward me and places his hand on his heart. "It's an honor to serve you, King Jadon."

I grin at his formality and stand up, pounding him on the back. "Thank you, Basile. With you, I don't feel so alone."

I sleep on the flight to the Sea of Caninsula, dreaming about Delilah once again. She's riding me, her hair brushing against my chest as her mouth parts and she whispers my name over and over. I wake up shaking and hard as a rock. And troubled. Would I even know if something happened to her? I can't keep doing this for much longer. I should've never let her go. I have to think of an alternative for her, something that won't sink her in danger even deeper. Until then, I can only hope she is holding her own.

King Shua and his sister, Solvang, meet with me first, extending their arms in welcome.

"Your father would be so proud of you," I tell Shua. He's not even twenty-three yet and has such a heavy burden overnight since King Otto died.

"My father always drilled peace into us. Peace, peace, peace," Shua says through a clenched jaw. "He was a good man. We thought he would live forever..." Shua laughs, but it's pained, hollow. "I never thought I'd be king. We're a kingdom of stillness, of *alhoni-osha*—love is first—but this has turned us upside down. Our people want justice."

Solvang reaches out and takes her brother's hand. Her brown eyes are sorrowful and it hurts to see the two of them suffering. Her father reached out to me on more than one occasion, asking me to give thought to a marriage between us, but I always refused an arranged marriage. She's beautiful, but there have never been sparks between the two of us.

I tell them about seeing the former king Titus in his disgraced state and that Caulder paid him a visit. Shua shoots up from the table and starts cursing in his language. I can only make out a few of the words, he spews them out so quickly.

"We have to strike now, show Alidonia that they cannot defeat us. We may be small, but we are mighty—you'll see how mighty tonight when all the dignitaries arrive. I've been working overtime to get everyone here...even some you might not expect."

"It would have to be well-planned out. I—" I look at Solvang and hope that she doesn't have any romantic attachment toward *me*, because this might backfire if she does. "I don't believe Delilah has anything to do with her family's madness. I-I'd want to get her out of there before any of this takes place."

"You have fallen for her," Solvang whispers. She smiles faintly, but her eyes fill with tears. I'm unsure if it has anything to do with me or is strictly about her father. "I will go." She nods resolutely. "I will go to her."

"No, no, I didn't mean that. You can't go there—that

would be disastrous!" I reach out and take her hand. "We'll find another way. I just wanted you to know I can't jump into an immediate war without considering her."

Shua's lip curls and he glares at me. "You're thinking of your dick at a time like this? Our father is dead!" he yells. "He died saving Delilah." He tugs Solvang's shoulder and her hand drops from mine. "You will not risk yourself for her."

"I need to see for myself if she is worthy of King Jadon's love and our protection. Our father thought she was worth saving...I will find out if he was right." Her voice is steel and lace, beauty and torment.

Oh God, what have I done?

The meeting with monarchies—some that I've never met, others that I've known my whole life—stretches into the next day. By the time we get up from our chairs, stretching and exhausted beyond belief, very little feels resolved. We've agreed to get our armies ready, and they've entrusted me to lead them in saying when we will strike.

We will definitely strike, it's only a matter of timing.

I can only hope and pray that Delilah will be safely tucked away when that time comes, preferably in Farrow. It feels far-fetched at this moment, but miracles have been known to happen.

Shit, who am I kidding, this is a clusterfuck and the two of us are at the epicenter.

CHAPTER TWENTY-THREE

Delilah

Three weeks later...

I spend my days staring vacantly at dress samples, sampling meals and cake like I have nothing better to do than plan my wedding to a man I despise. It's more evident than ever that my role in this family has always been a façade. What I interpreted as adoration from my father was a master pulling my strings. What I thought was easy camaraderie between me and my cousin was simply him biding his time until he could undermine me and take over the kingdom.

What else have I been wrong about?

I look at the castle with new eyes. My view of Alidonia has even changed. The ocean looks stormy instead of enticing, the cliffs haunt me instead of pulling me in.

I feel like I have shed a part of me that I can never get back, and it is like a raw wound constantly exposed. I long for the quiet simplicity of Farrow, the dark wood of the Safrin estate that felt like a warm hug, the calm Jadon brought every time we were together...until he touched me and calm was the last thing he made me feel. Even now, when I think of his touch, I feel the heat rush through my body.

How can I miss someone I know so little? Someone I spent so few days with...

I wander around the castle aimlessly. My dad and I avoid each other. He might have allowed me back into his household, but I don't think I'll ever regain his trust again. And vice versa.

And Avaban. My nose curls in disgust just thinking about him. He sleeps the day away and then comes searching for me when he wakes up, scratching his crotch, his breath reeking of alcohol and sleep. He gets a kick out of annoying me and Caulder eggs him on, loving having someone in the house who belittles me more than he does.

I hear them in the parlor and scurry past the door, not wanting to get stuck in a conversation with either of them. I'm supposed to meet with a designer this afternoon, so I at least have an excuse for getting away.

"Delilah," Avaban calls.

I roll my eyes and walk backward until I'm in the doorway again.

"Come here," he says.

"I'm busy."

He frowns and laughs at the same time, the sound like fingernails against a chalkboard. My contempt for him grows every day.

"I said *come here*—you think you can continue this stick-up-your-ass behavior for much longer?" He grins and what some would consider a handsome face actually looks hideous to me. "Just wait until I get you in Blorl," he elbows Caulder and Caulder smirks at me, "you'll learn to be grateful...among other things."

"Trying to plan this wedding." I probably say that ten times a day; it's at least been a good excuse. "I'm supposed to finalize a dress today."

He waves a hand at me and walks to the bar, pouring a shot for him and Caulder. He lifts it up to me and downs it. "It's not about the wedding, it's about the wedding night." He laughs at himself and I walk away before I have to listen to him for another second.

My father walks down the hallway toward the living room and I turn in the other direction. Once again, he's missed Avaban at his worst. I wonder if he already knows exactly who Avaban is. Didn't take me two seconds to figure it out, and my father isn't stupid.

"Delilah," my father says.

I turn around, troubled by how weak his voice sounds. "Are you okay, Papa?"

He puts a hand on his throat and then drops it. "Not feeling the best today, but I'm fine. How are the wedding plans coming? Everything on schedule?"

"We should be ready to go in three weeks. I just have to find a dress." I don't know why I haven't been able to settle on a dress. I've seen the most spectacular gowns imaginable. I think that's the problem. I don't want to waste anything spectacular on Xang Avaban. "I'm supposed to look at a new designer today."

Papa nods and clasps his hands together. "Good. Let me know if I can help with anything. I—" A pained look shoots across his eyes and I take a step toward him. He turns and walks the other direction before I get any closer. He's taken great pains to avoid me as much as possible. I haven't tried to cross the divide between us myself either—I'm still so angry at his betrayal...so confused about who he even is. I'm waking up—or maybe growing up—and seeing a man who is a stranger...and that terrifies me.

I stare after him, looking for any signs that he might be getting sick again. He's still so frail; it wouldn't take much to send him into a downward spiral. I take a deep breath and go to the library, where I'm supposed to meet the designer this afternoon. I settle deep into the coziest chair...it's too hard to be considered cozy, but it's the closest thing to it in this house. I find a book and read a few pages before it drops across my chest and I give in to sleep.

I feel the hair on my neck stand on end and I open my eyes, screaming when there's a face in front of mine.

She clamps a hand over my mouth, her eyes wide, and shakes her head. "I'm sorry. I didn't mean to startle you. I'm here with the dresses."

She motions toward a pile of dresses on the loveseat and I nod slightly. She drops her hand and steps back, assessing me with shrewd eyes. She's beautiful. Tall with radiant brown skin, her large eyes sweep over me. She clenches her lips together and appears to be trying to read my mind with the way she's studying me. I sit up and drop my feet to the floor, trying to tame my hair.

It's uncomfortably quiet and I stare back at her, unsettled. "You look familiar," I finally say.

She shakes her head and looks around the room, for what? Someone to pop out? I stand up, ready to go out the door and send her away if she doesn't stop acting so weird.

"Wait," she whispers. "I'm sorry. You're very beautiful."

I can't place her accent, but her words are lilting and melodic. "So are you."

She steps closer and still doesn't lift her voice beyond

the whisper. "Is there a place we can go that we're sure isn't being recorded?"

I pause, unsure of what to make of her, whether I should trust her or not. "My room," I whisper back.

She nods and steps back. I walk to the door and she picks up the dresses, following closely behind. When we reach my room, I shut the door behind us and put my hand on my hips.

"You're sure it's safe in here?"

"I've thrown away all the recording devices I've been able to find. It's probably safer in the bathroom." I go in there and she follows me, waiting until I turn on the water before she starts talking.

"I cut off my dreads so I'd be less recognizable." She pulls off her long black wig and her hair is trimmed close to her scalp.

I gasp. "Princess Solvang!"

She lowers her head.

We've never met, but I should've recognized her beautiful face even without her usual elaborate braids. She looks beautiful either way, but I'm sad if she did anything to alter her appearance for me.

"Why did you put yourself at risk?" I ask. "I'm so sorry about your father. I can't tell—"

She freezes and the look she gives me—I'm not sure if she's here to help or here to kill me.

"I had to know for myself." That's all she says and I wait for her to elaborate, but she doesn't.

The longer she stares at me, the more uncomfortable we both get.

"Shall I show you the dresses?" she finally asks.

"I really don't care what I wear to this wedding. The uglier, the better, honestly."

She grins at that. "I didn't bring anything ugly, but we can work on that."

"Why are you really here?"

"Do you love him?" she asks. She steps closer and she's so tall, I have to crane my neck to look up at her when we're standing like this.

"Who?" But somehow, I know who she's talking about. I flush even as I say it, and then notice the pink in her cheeks too. "Do *you* love him?"

"It's impossible not to love him," she says. "But he doesn't love me. My father tried many times to make my wishes come true, to marry us off...there's nothing I've wanted more since meeting him as a teenager."

"There's something about him," I whisper. "He's perfect, isn't he. And it isn't just that he's the most beautiful man I've ever seen—he's that for sure—but it's more than that. It's the depth behind his eyes, his relentless pursuit to do the right thing, his bravery in the face of danger..."

She smiles and it's welcoming, it's impossible to resist smiling back. "So yes, then."

I laugh and sit down on the edge of the tub, glad that the running water can drown out the pounding of my heart. "It's too soon for love. And crazy. I barely know him."

"Well, he loves you."

My mouth drops open. "How do you know?"

"He's willing to risk everything for you."

"I came here because I do love him," I whisper. "If I leave, he could be killed."

"If you stay, everyone who matters will be killed, you included. Get out now, while you can."

"It's not that easy. I'm not willing to risk Jadon's life." I grin. "That is who we're talking about, isn't it?"

She laughs and it's the prettiest sound. I reach out and

take her hand, tears forming in my eyes. She sobers and squeezes my hand.

"I don't know you, but I know you must love him a lot to come all this way. Especially after what happened to your father." A tear drips down my nose and into my mouth. "Jadon deserves someone like you. He'll forget about me. You should go to him, tell him I'm fine, and find a way to make him happy."

She sits next to me and sighs, her arm going around my shoulder. "I don't think that's going to work."

CHAPTER TWENTY-FOUR

Jadon

I haven't heard from Solvang since I saw her in Caninsula. One of my guards has confirmed she's in Alidonia. She's ignoring my calls and hasn't responded to a single text. Shua is furious that she's gone and calls me every day, threatening to go there himself. I manage to convince him that we have to bide our time. The moment will present itself and we will act swiftly when it does.

I see pictures here and there of Delilah and I study them like a man starving. She looks okay, besides the dark shadows under her eyes. When Solvang has been there a week and there's still no word, I reach the end of my patience.

It takes negotiations and a lot of planning, but I leave Basile with instructions on a few upcoming meetings, and I take off for the border of Alidonia with a dozen guards. The army at home is instructed not to breathe a word about me being anywhere but Farrow. There's a small town on the outskirts of Alidonia, a little too close for comfort if I can't stay hidden, but close enough that I rest a little easier at night, knowing I can reach Delilah in far less time than from Farrow. I talk to the team I have watching her, but they don't know as much as I'd like. Her wedding is in two weeks, best I can tell, and if I have to stay here until then, I will.

She will not be marrying Xang Avaban. Not as long as I'm breathing.

I'm also here to prepare for what is sure to be a war once I take Delilah. I hope to God she comes willingly. I don't let myself think otherwise. I didn't misread the look in her eyes on that plane. I know she went back as a sacrifice and I can't let her do that for me or anyone else.

I stay in a secluded area, in an old furnished house that Basile was able to rent for me. Quincie deals with the owner and I'm able to move in with a few clothes and little else. Well, except for Star. The dog and I are so attached at the hip, I couldn't bear to leave her, not knowing how long I'd be gone. She's trained exceptionally well in a short amount of time, so at least I know someone has my back should I run into trouble.

With the help of a few of the guards, we set up the security feed, the cameras filling an entire room. Those who aren't working with me here, go into Alidonia and are able to get closer to the castle. We've been working with Alex from Yuman and Luka, they've sent several troops as well, and as far as I know, the Farthings aren't aware of it...yet.

After I've slept a few hours—a full night's rest a distant memory pretty much since I met Delilah—I try calling Solvang again. Instead of letting it go, I call her three times in a row and when she answers the third time, I stutter my hello.

"I didn't expect you to answer."

"Is that why you've called incessantly?"

"So you *are* getting my calls..."

She laughs. "I've been busy."

"Okay. Any word about Delilah? Were you able to see her? Did anyone suspect it was you?"

"I've seen Delilah every day for the past week. She's asked me to stay on until the wedding."

I rub my hand over my mouth and sit down. "What?"

"I stepped on the balcony to take your call."

"You're at the Farthing castle right now?"

"Yes."

"What the fuck!" I yell into the phone and then pull the phone back. "How the hell have you managed to stay hidden?"

"I'm disguised fairly well, and I haven't left Delilah's quarters since I came. She eats in her room and hasn't been able to ke—" She clears her throat and pauses.

"What? She hasn't been able to what?"

"Jadon," she whispers into the phone, "I should go. But listen to me, you have to get her out of here. She's insisting on marrying Avaban because she doesn't want anyone else to get hurt, but from what my brother is telling me, this war is happening with or without her. Get her out, but don't do it until you have a fail-safe plan. There's more at stake in this than you realize. Be very sure before you strike."

"What do you me—" The words are barely out and the line goes dead. "Solvang!" I stare at it to see if I'm imagining it, but she's gone. "Fuck!"

A few minutes later, she texts.

Solvang: Next time I'll call you. It's safer this way.

Very little is accomplished. I stare at the screens, sometimes twenty hours at a time. A new camera is installed on the periphery of the Farthing grounds, the side that is closest to Delilah's bedroom. When she walks out onto the balcony, my heart collapses inside my chest. I search my mind to think of a plan, anything to get her out of here. Short of storming through the castle with an army behind me, I'm coming up short.

Alex calls me on day four of my stakeout. Luka knows him better than I do, but he's always seemed like a likable guy. There's the family history with him and Gentry being brothers, but since they've put it aside, it hasn't been a problem for me.

"I used to date a girl in Alidonia." This is the way he starts the conversation.

"Okay..."

"She got in touch with me recently. She says her brother is one of the guards in the palace and no one is happy with the way Farthing is running his kingdom. Rumor has it he's under Caulder's thumb, poor health and all that. Her brother has wondered if—well, he's more than wondered... I'd say he's fairly certain..."

"Spit it out," I try to laugh to sound less impatient, but I don't fool Alex.

He laughs and groans. "I'm sorry. I'll be out with it. He thinks the king's sick again and that maybe Caulder has something to do with this relapse."

"Shit..."

"Yeah. Luka and I have been talking about all of this— and he told me about you guys seeing Caulder at the prison. I want you to know you have my support whenever you choose to invade. We're ready here. But...he also mentioned your...attachment to the princess..."

"You could say that..." I've given up trying to pretend otherwise.

"Well, I just wanted to offer my services. Yuman has always stayed out of most of the kingdoms' problems. I'd wager a guess that I am nowhere on the Farthings' radar. I could go meet with the guard who works there, see if he can help me get to Delilah..."

"And then what?"

"You be ready to hit Alidonia hard...once we know she's out of there."

"I really only want to get the person responsible for any harm that's coming to Delilah. You think Caulder is the brains behind all of this?"

"From what I'm gathering, back in the day, Vance was a lot more aggressive in his risks, but no one believes he's capable of that now. His mind isn't what it used to be, and from the sounds of it, his health is failing every day."

I freeze, seeing Delilah on one of the screens, her hair blowing in the breeze. I can't see her expression from here, I can only make out that it's her. I wonder if she realizes the danger she's in.

"Find out about Caulder. There needs to be no doubt whatsoever. Just to be clear, I don't want a war."

"Got it. I think you'll need to talk King Shua out of it though. He's also a friend of mine and he's not thinking clearly."

I curse into my fist and watch as Solvang walks out onto the balcony next to Delilah. Fear grips its vines around my mind as I stare at the two of them. I knew Shua wasn't quite thinking clearly already, but what are Solvang's intentions?

CHAPTER TWENTY-FIVE

Jadon

Two days later, Alex sends me a recording of his conversation with the guard. At the end, the guard says something so chilling, I break out into a sweat despite the crisp night air.

"I found the poison Caulder is using on the king."

"How do you know it's Caulder?" Alex asks.

"I've been keeping a closer eye on him like you asked. Saw him pour something into his food and then take the tray in to the king. When he came out, he went to his room and had a garbage bag that he took to the dumpster on the far end of the grounds. I emptied the contents when he left, and there was quite a cocktail of poison in there. It's surprising Vance isn't in a coma already...but I suspect he's going to up the doses each day...or less often maybe. Just enough to make it a gradual slide."

Alex stops the recording and I stop pacing.

"We have to take it to the authorities," I tell him. "Caulder needs to be arrested—"

"You've seen how this shit plays out when royalty is involved. I think we have enough proof, but I also can see loopholes. I don't want Caulder to get away with this."

"I don't either, but Vance's life is on the line. Listen, are you able to get to Delilah? Tell her what you've discovered... let her know we'll help both her and her father get out of there."

"You really want to help Vance? After all he's done to your family?"

"I can't exactly fight a man who's being poisoned...what kind of fight is that?"

"You're a better man than me. If Vance has done half the things I've heard, he doesn't deserve your grace."

"No man deserves to die that way." I think about Catano in his prison cell and wouldn't mind seeing Vance in prison, but not being slowly poisoned to death. "What do you know about Avaban?"

"Not much. He rarely leaves the estate and he and Caulder are thick as thieves. That's about all I know."

"Okay, let me know when you've talked to Delilah. When are you leaving?"

"I'll go tomorrow. Just wanted to talk it over with you first."

"Thank you. Make sure to take enough guards."

"Will do."

The next time I call Solvang, she answers on the first ring.

"I said I'd call you," she sputters.

"If you're looking out for Delilah and no one else knows you're there, what does it matter if she knows I'm calling?"

There's a long pause.

"Let me talk to her, dammit."

"Now is not a good time."

"Tell me why I should trust you, Solvang. Give me one good reason."

"Because I'm here with the woman you love, and you're not. I wouldn't mess with me if I were you." Her voice sends a chill down my spine.

"You so much as hurt a hair on her head and I will make you pay. Do you understand me?"

"It's nice to know how little I matter to you." She sounds like a different person. "I hear you loud and clear. But who's to say you'll ever catch me?"

She hangs up and I'm left to imagine the worst possible scenarios. I'm packing a bag when Quincie comes in.

"We're going to Alidonia," I tell him. "I can't wait to see who might come through for me. If we're going to get Delilah out, it'll have to be me."

"But King Alex might get her out tomorrow without anyone being the wiser," he argues.

"Tomorrow could be too late."

I make several phone calls. Basile first, then Luka...and I call Alex when we're in the air, just a few minutes from landing. Everyone has tried to talk me out of it so far, but I won't get peace until I see for myself that she's okay.

"Something's come up. I'm about to land in Alidonia and I'm going in tonight."

"Are you sure that's a good idea?

"It's a terrible idea, but I'm going anyway."

"Well, I'm actually already here. I decided to get here early to visit my friend." I hear giggling in the background and roll my eyes. Alex is a notorious ladies' man. "She won't mind if I head out unexpectedly. Let me go instead."

"It's almost nine o'clock at night—what will your excuse be for knocking on the door?"

"I won't knock on the door. I have my climbing gear with me." He laughs and I groan. "Well, do you have a better idea?" he demands.

"No, I don't." I roll my neck, and it makes a foreboding crack. "Just don't get caught."

He doesn't say anything.

"Alex!"

"Sorry, I was just getting a goodbye kiss. You think I'd get caught? You really don't know me well, do you?" He laughs again. "I'll call you as soon as I know more."

"Get them out of there," I yell, but he's already gone.

I toss the phone across the plane and put my head in my hands. This has got to be the craziest thing I've ever done.

We go to my guards' headquarters, a dingy building not far from the Farthing estate. It sits next to a business complex and the surrounding parking lots are empty, save a few cars in front of the building.

Quincie unlocks the door and we go in, not bothering to knock when we enter the last door at the end of the hall. Two guards jump up and then double over with relief when they see that it's us.

"You nearly made me shit a brick!" Sal says, pounding Quincie on the back. "King, beg pardon."

Palza, the other guard, doesn't say a word, just holds his hand to his chest and smiles weakly before nodding his acknowledgment and sitting back down to face the screens.

I laugh and reach out to shake Sal's hand. "I'm sorry we didn't give you any warning. This wasn't a planned visit." I point to the screen that faces the window and tap it. "We'll be seeing a guy scaling this wall sometime tonight if everything goes as expected."

Sal's eyes widen. "Anyone we know?"

"Only the king of Yuman," I mutter.

I'm still not sure how he expects to get around the guards, but he seemed quite sure of himself.

Two hours later, I see a shadow on the wall and lean in closer.

"It's him," Quincie says.

Alex flings something on the wall and in the next minute is scaling the wall in record time.

"Fucking show-off," I laugh. "What the hell is he anyway?"

"If he gets the princess, he's a fucking superhero."

I'd prefer to be the one saving Delilah, but I don't give a shit which of us gets her out of there. Alex reaches the balcony and swings a leg over before jumping down. It takes him a few minutes, but he finally gets the door open and disappears inside.

One minute.

Two.

Five.

When we hit the ten-minute mark, I am about to explode. *Where the fuck are they?*

Approximately twelve minutes and thirty seconds after going into Delilah's room, he steps out, holding...

"That's not her," I say softly. *"That's not her!* What the fuck is he doing?"

He has Princess Solvang in a fierce grip, a rope holding the two of them together, and he scales down the wall nearly as fast holding her as he did alone.

CHAPTER TWENTY-SIX

Delilah

I'm exhausted. The stress level is at an all-time high right now. Keeping things at a manageable distance with the three men who look at me like I'm their target practice takes work. I stay in my room most of the time and Solvang has been a nice distraction the past couple of days. She's funny and helps the days go by faster. I bring food to her throughout the day and we pour over bridal websites, ordering ugly party favors and getting ideas for center-pieces, the more hideous, the better. It's weird having a built-in friend that I still don't know very well, but I think we're both lonely enough that it's working. From what she's told me, she's surrounded by men at all times too.

I stretch out across the bed, swiping from one picture to the next and hardly able to keep my eyes open. The next thing I know, Solvang is placing a blanket over me and moves my laptop, typing away while I give in to sleep.

I hear a shriek and sit up, heart racing. Solvang is

leaning over me and someone is gripping her arm. She looks at me with an intensity that scares me and I back away, rubbing my eyes, still foggy.

"She was going to hurt you," the man behind her says.

I look at him closer, expecting to see one of our guards who doesn't know Solvang has been staying here, but it's—is that really Alex Forbrush?

"King Alex?" I rub my eyes again.

The king of Yuman is such a good-looking man, there are few who can compare. He has a face that is impossible to forget. Jadon is the *only* man who has ever made me weak in the knees, but I can appreciate how Alex must affect a lot of women.

"Is that really you? What are doing here?"

Solvang wiggles, trying to get out of his grasp and he tightens his hold on her. A large knife drops from her hand. She shoots him a murderous glare and I stand up, holding out my hands.

"This is Princess Solvang, from Caninsula? She's been helping me. You can let go of her. She must have heard you coming..."

Alex grits his teeth and leans into Solvang's ear as he mutters angrily, "She was about to murder you in your sleep...if I hadn't shown up when I did..."

I stare at Solvang and she looks away, her shoulders dropping.

"I wouldn't have been able to go through with it," she says.

She holds her head higher, as if daring me to argue with her, but her eyes betray her. Sorrow and underlying rage.

I've been so eager for a friend that I haven't seen the way she despises me.

It hurts, but I'm used to being betrayed. And why

wouldn't she hate me? I don't know why I trusted that she'd want to help me anyway. I sit back on the bed and stare up at them, feeling lost.

"You won't get another chance to test that theory," Alex says.

He starts tying her to my bed and I jump up again.

"What are you doing?"

"You're coming with me, and she'll be found like this... tomorrow, if she's lucky. Let your cousin deal with her. He's known for poisoning whoever gets in his way." His eyes narrow on Solvang. "You're working for him, aren't you?"

"I'm not." She shakes her head. "My father is dead because of her. I had unfinished business. I didn't plan on getting...attached at all." She looks at me then. "Please, Delilah. Believe me, I wouldn't have killed you."

I hold up my hand. "Stop. Talking."

Her mouth drops and she closes it quickly.

Alex continues tightening the rope and Solvang stops fighting him.

"What did you mean about Caulder poisoning someone?"

"I have reason to believe he's been poisoning your father. A guard of Jadon's saw him pour powder into your father's food and later checked the bag Caulder tried to dispose of..."

I stand up and start pacing. My dad has seemed off again for days now. "Why didn't the guard stop Caulder?"

"You're the priority. Jadon is in Alidonia and wants you out of here before hell breaks loose."

I shake my head frantically. "No. I can't leave my father! Knowing he'll be murdered as soon as I'm gone? There's no way I can leave now. If you try to take me, I will scream at the top of my lungs and it won't matter which kingdom you rule over, you'll be a dead man."

"Delilah, come on," Alex steps away from Solvang, walking toward me.

"I mean it, Alex. Take care of Solvang, or let Jadon deal with her however he sees fit. I'll deal with my cousin."

"Jadon won't like this."

"It's not up to him."

"How will we know you're safe?"

"You were able to scale the wall to my bedroom. Seems like you can figure it out."

I turn my back to him and try to quell the fear in my gut. I don't have any idea what I'll do, but I don't want Alex to know that. I need them out of my room so I can think. And it's crucial that I get my dad out of here.

I turn around. "You need to leave. A guard usually walks by in five minutes and I don't want anyone getting hurt..."

Alex drags Solvang to the door and opens it. "We have cameras on you. If you could step on the balcony regularly to let us know you're okay, it would probably set Jadon's mind at ease. If anything will after this," he adds, shaking his head.

I get a warm feeling in my chest that Jadon is looking out for me, that he didn't just wash his hands of me when we said goodbye.

I nod and walk to the door, putting my hand on Solvang's shoulder. "I know you came with the wrong intentions and for all I know, you would've killed me tonight had Alex not stepped in at the right time, but...your presence here the past few days has helped me at a time when I felt so alone. Thank you for that. I'm so grateful for the sacrifice your father made for me, he was truly a good man, and I will forever be sorry that my family is responsible for his death." I back away, my hand dropping by my side. "But if you come near me again, I will slit your throat without batting an eye."

Her lips press together, tears forming in her eyes. She nods and blinks and a tear rolls down her cheek. "Fair enough," she whispers.

I watch as Alex secures her to him with the rope and grabs the other rope that he used to get up here. He crawls over the edge and Solvang holds onto him for dear life. She whimpers and buries her head in his neck and I feel a small sense of satisfaction that she's afraid.

I lie awake for hours, the sense of dread building. Part of me hopes Jadon will scale the wall next and force me to get out of here. But no, I have to make sure Caulder doesn't win...and Jadon never shows his face.

I need to find out if what Alex said is true, if Caulder has been poisoning my father.

It's impossible to know who to trust anymore and sad that my family is probably at the bottom of the list.

The next morning, I stumble into the kitchen hours before I normally do. The men shouldn't be around for a while, but our chef, David, is already at work preparing breakfast.

"I'd like to be the one to deliver my father meals from now on," I tell him.

"Your cousin has been in charge of that." He frowns.

"I've just been made aware of that, and I'd like to be the one to do it from now on," I repeat. "My father has been getting worse each day, and I'd rather not blame *you* for that, so I suggest you let me see you prepare his meals and then I'll be the one to deliver it."

He looks appalled that I would suggest anything suspect coming from his kitchen, but it could all be an act. For all I know, he could have been in Caulder's pocket for a long time.

"I assure you, I use all the best ingredients and nothing is ever spoiled. Your father is in no danger from my food!" he says hotly.

I grin and raise my eyebrows. "Let's keep it that way, shall we?"

I can tell he wants to argue the merits of his cooking, but he swallows it down and nods. "Yes, Princess Delilah."

"What time does Caulder usually eat?"

He looks at the clock over the stove. "In an hour."

"I'd like to take my father's meal to him at least half an hour before Caulder shows up each day. Can you make that happen?"

"Of course." He shrugs.

"Excellent."

He prepares a tray with a beautiful plate of food and when it is exactly how he wants it, he lifts it for me to take.

"Here you go. I hope it is to your liking."

I beam at him and he stares at me, blinking fast.

"It's perfect."

Relieved, David returns a lopsided grin and lets out a long breath.

Delilah 1; Caulder 0.

My father is still sleeping when I knock on his door. I peek in and he lifts his head and looks at me blankly.

"Papa?"

I rush to him, setting the tray on his bedside table before placing my hand on his forehead. His face is pallid and clammy.

"I'm not sure I can eat," he croaks. He tries to sit up and leans back on his pillows, sagging deeper into them.

"David made you healthy things today," I tell him. "When did you start feeling worse?"

"I haven't felt right for a few days."

"What have you been eating?"

"Mostly soup. Caulder brings oatmeal in the morning, but soups the rest of the time."

My face feels hot at the mention of Caulder. "Do you usually eat it all?"

He gives me a small grin. "Every now and then I throw it out so I don't have to hear Caulder griping at me."

I put my hand on the wall, my relief nearly knocking me over. Maybe the effects of whatever he's been given aren't very bad because he's not eaten enough of it yet. I should've known if Caulder was capable of this, he wouldn't wait for me to get out before moving forward with his plan for Papa. Why didn't I act then? I put my hand over my heart and try to calm myself; it feels like it's going to pound out of my skin.

He clears his throat. "How's the wedding planning coming?"

I take a deep breath and an idea begins forming in the back of my mind. It's crazy, but it just might work.

"It's going well. I was wondering...how would you feel about our wedding being televised? I think it would put a positive message out there to all the kingdoms, that we stand united?" I'm talking nonsense, but my father perks up, his cheeks even flushing a bit when he smiles.

"That's a wonderful idea!" He motions for me to come closer and he takes my hand. "I'm so happy you've come around to this marriage, Delilah. It's for the best. I just—"

He coughs and it rattles his chest. I grab his water and hold it for him to have a sip when he slows down. I study him carefully, confused by his symptoms. He looks like he did right before things got really bad. Has it been poisoning all this time?

My god.

I start shaking, my insides quaking until it shows on the outside too. I spill water on my father and hurry to wipe it off. "I'm sorry, Papa. What were you going to say?"

"I want to be at your wedding more than anything. Just one more week..."

"You're not going anywhere. You'll be feeling better in time for the wedding. Don't worry."

I help feed him and even though we don't talk much, it's the best time I've had with him in so long. Almost like old times.

Before I knew who he really was.

CHAPTER TWENTY-SEVEN

Jadon

"What is this?" I yell when I see Alex at the appointed meeting place.

Alex is steadying Solvang and has a hold on the rope around her, tugging on it as they walk toward us. She stumbles behind him and he tightens his grip. He holds up his thumb, motioning toward Solvang.

"She was about to kill Delilah when I walked in."

"What?" I stare at Solvang, the girl I've always considered a friend. "Do you want to explain to me what the hell you're thinking? Murder? Who are you?" I get in her face. "Your father would be devastated by this," I say it quietly, but she flinches like I'm still yelling.

"My father isn't alive to be devastated...because of her." She closes her eyes for a second, then stares at the ceiling, anything to avoid eye contact with me. "I wouldn't have gone through with it. I-I grew fond of her in spite of everything. I don't think she meant for any of this to happen. But

I don't think she deserves you either...that's what I really planned on stopping." The tears start falling in earnest then and her nose drips. She tries to reach her nose to wipe it, but she's bound too tightly to Alex. "I know you don't feel the same about me, but I—"

"What, you think *you* deserve me?" I laugh. "Give me a fucking break. You don't get a vote in what I deserve. You lost that right when you lied to my fucking face. I trusted you..."

"You're willing to throw away your respect, your dignity, all the people who are following your leadership... all for that pint-sized fairy? She's weak, Jadon. She let me into her trust within minutes—you can't trust someone like that who doesn't see danger coming straight for her."

"I think that's all the more reason *to* trust her—the fact that she believes in the good in people, whether they deserve it or not." I hold up a hand and turn around, walking away from her. "I can't look at you." I give Alex a withering look and force myself not to hit him. "Tell me why you left her there to rot and saved this traitor."

I hear Solvang crying and rub my eyes. I'm fucking exhausted and all the meanness is coming out of me.

"She refused to come, Jadon. I told her about Caulder poisoning her father and she wouldn't leave him." Alex puts a hand on my shoulder and grips it.

I count to ten and shake him off. "She's in that castle with a murderer and you decided to save this one? You need to both get out of my sight. Lock her away. I don't need to hear the details, just please take care of it, Alex. I thank you for your trouble tonight. Next time, I'll know to take care of things myself."

Alex starts to say something and stops, pulling Solvang with him. I hear a car start up and know that I should see to it myself that Solvang is behind bars, but I let it go.

I drive back to the little brick building and go straight for the camera room. Delilah is standing out on the balcony and I take a deep breath, reassured that at least for now, she's safe.

I stare at her until my sight blurs.

Of course she won't leave her father. The girl knows loyalty, that's for damn sure. Her father is willing to toss her to that trash Avaban, and yet the minute she finds out her father's health is compromised again, she's there to protect him. If only everyone had someone in their corner like that.

It reminds me of Ava and Eden's love for me, my love for them, and my heart softens toward Delilah even more. If I can't get her out of the house without her father, I'll just have to drag Vance out of there too.

The entirety of the kingdoms will know I've lost my mind if I save Vance Farthing.

The next day, I talk to Paquin, my guard stationed at Delilah's house.

"She won't leave her dad's side," he says.

I can actually see Paquin outside. He knows where the cameras are and he looks directly into one as he talks to me.

"Has anyone besides Delilah, Caulder, and Xang been in to see Vance?"

"No. Caulder and Xang have left Vance alone today. They talked about golfing."

"I'll put an additional tail on them if they leave. Stay on Delilah."

"Will do."

I talk to Quincie and have him arrange guards to follow Caulder and Xang's every move while they're out of the castle.

"Do whatever you can to keep them gone as long as possible," I tell Quincie.

"I can do whatever I want?" Quincie grins.

"Within reason, absolutely."

He rubs his hands together and takes off while I turn back to the screens. I haven't seen Delilah yet this morning and it has me uneasy. I don't relax until I see Caulder and Xang pull out of the garage, their car creeping away from the castle.

I tell Paquin to create a diversion and I head to the Farthing castle myself. My blood is pumping. I'm going to see her today...hopefully, I can be more convincing than Alex.

I'm almost to the house, already over the gate and next to the gardens on the south side, when my phone vibrates. I turn it on but don't say a word.

"Caulder's coming back!" Paquin yells. "And Delilah is gone. The butler said she left five minutes ago. I don't know how she got past me, but she's not in her room. Nothing is showing on the cameras. My diversion must've helped her get out without being noticed. *Shit!*" He fumbles with something and curses again. "The camera near the back exit is busted."

I didn't see her leaving, so it must've been the minutes between my run here and climbing over the gate. I curse violently, hanging up the phone and bending over to catch my breath.

I stay hidden in the trees and when it gets too hot to stand any longer, I walk back to the guard station. Quincie is back and we exchange a wordless look while we sit in front of the screens.

"I'm gonna get another shower," I say after we've sat for an hour with no movement. "If she comes back, pound on the door."

———

I've showered and am putting clean clothes on when Quincie pounds on the door.

"She's back. And Caulder and Xang just left."

I hustle back to the grounds and wait a while to make sure I don't see any guards outside. I throw the rope up until it hooks over the stone and crawl up as fast as I can, leaping over the balcony. She's standing in the doorway and her eyes widen when she sees me walk toward her.

"This is becoming a habit, visitors invading my space... who knew we needed a moat?" She opens the door to let me in and I turn to her, wanting to take her in my arms and hold her tight.

She walks to the opposite side of the room and turns to face me, her body language screaming distance.

"Are you okay?" I finally ask.

"About as well as can be expected," she says quietly. "How are you?"

"I've had better days."

She nods, her smile faint but somehow making me instantly lighter. "Yeah, me too."

"It's good to see you."

Something shifts across her face and her shoulders relax. "It's good to see you too."

"You're being so agreeable." I laugh softly and she does too. "God, I haven't stopped thinking about us, Delilah. You have invaded every part of my mind and body..." I stalk toward her, only stopping when I'm touching her. My hand snakes through her hair and I pull her face up, bending down until my lips are touching hers. Only then do I feel like I can fucking think straight.

She kisses me back and I get lost in her, my hands exploring her face and hair and back and thighs. When it gets heated and I pull her leg over my hip to get more friction, she pulls away, breathing hard.

"I can't leave with you, Jadon," she says. She skirts past me and I turn and try to catch her, but she slips just out of my reach.

"What if I could get your father out too—would you consider it then?"

She turns and looks at me, her eyes bright. I could drown in her and be a happy man.

"You'd do that for me?" she asks. "I know he hasn't been the best father to me, but I can't sit by and watch him being poisoned by Caulder."

"I would move heaven and earth for you, Delilah. If you haven't noticed, I'm hopeless where you're concerned. There's nothing I wouldn't—"

She reaches out and takes my hand. "Will you trust me? Let me do this my way?"

"As long as it doesn't mean you are marrying Avaban."

She puts her hand on my lips and shakes her head. "Trusting me means not questioning what I do from here on. Okay?" She grins and pulls me to the bed. "My father is sleeping. The others aren't due back for hours. No one will bother us. I don't know if I remember how good you felt... maybe you could remind me?"

I laugh against her skin, my nose dragging across her collarbone. "I'd be happy to remind you. I'd rather be reminding you somewhere far away from here, but...I can't say no to you. I'd like to just urge you to remember that if I'm found here, I'll be hung for trespassing."

She arches into my mouth when my teeth tug on her nipple under her shirt. "Didn't seem to scare you off from climbing my wall. Let's make it worth your time."

"I'll climb your wall all right," I say and she giggles, making me smile. I pull her short skirt down and she pulls her shirt over her head, standing in front of me with the most beautiful lace barely covering her. I motion to her bra. "Take it off." When she does and then steps out of her lacy panties, I grin. "This is definitely worth my time."

We're both sweating hard after venting all our frustration and lust on each other. We lie facing one another, my hands unable to stop exploring her body even now, after I've touched every inch of her.

"Was it as good as you remembered?" I ask, leaning forward to kiss her nose.

"The next time will probably be better." She laughs when I frown. "Only because this time was even better than the last."

She curls up into my neck, her arms wrapping around me and I feel complete.

"Do you think you would've felt the same if we hadn't met at the Cave of Stars first?" I ask.

"I haven't made any declarations about what I'm feeling," she says, trying to stay straight-faced. I glare at her and she laughs.

"Always so sassy." I jab at her side, tickling her until she dives under the covers to be quieter. "The way you were chanting, 'Never stop, never stop,' just now sure felt like a declaration."

"Fine. I do like you quite a bit." She ducks under the covers again and I jolt in shock and then bliss when she wraps her mouth around my cock. "I like you very, very much," she says against my skin.

Later, we whisper about everything and nothing.

"Don't fall asleep," she whispers when I get quiet.

It's almost dawn and I have to go before the sun rises.

"Please, can't I talk you into coming with me? I'm not too proud to beg."

She puts her hands on my cheeks and pulls my mouth to hers. "Trust me," she whispers again.

I lean my head against hers and sigh, the weight of leaving her here almost more than I can take.

"Please don't make me regret this." I kiss her one more time and get up, putting my clothes on and not looking at her again.

If I see her staring up at me from that bed, I'll never leave.

CHAPTER TWENTY-EIGHT

Jadon

She asked me for more solid proof on Caulder and the poisoning, and also to find the connection to Titus. I've come to a dead end about the men who kidnapped my sister and Kathryn, but I'm still looking for the answers there too. This is what motivates me for hours after I leave her. Quincie is on it too and he yells when he sees something in one of the files he's hacked from Caulder's email.

Paquin swears that finding proof about the poison will be easy.

"I've found something..." Quincie expands the screen and it's an email dated a month before my father was killed.

My breath hitches when I read the email addressed to what we know is Titus Catano's email. After sitting through the hearing, I could quote a handful of Titus's secret emails and recorded conversations. This is one I've never seen.

. . .

It's time for one certain dynasty to come to an end. I would be glad to accept your offer. I have a contact in Farrow who will take care of the brakes.

Consider it done.

By tomorrow, we should be free of that self-righteous prick forever and then we can move on to the next in line. Only a matter of time before they're wiped out.

In return, I expect you to stand by me when I take over the Farthing monarchy.

As always, it's good doing business with you.

From one stepping stone to another and forever grateful,
Caulder

My hands are trembling, but I'm excited and *livid*. I slam my hand on the table several times, anything to get some of this pent-up energy out.

"Forward that to every dignitary, as well as the police forces of every kingdom." I look at the time and the wedding will be happening this time tomorrow. "Do you think they'll arrest Caulder before the wedding?" I laugh as I look at the clock again and then slam my hand down again. "Why couldn't she get out of there? What if there's *not* enough time...we still need the proof about him poisoning V—"

Quincie puts his hand on my shoulder and I tense. "Relax. We're bringing him down. I'm forwarding now, look." He systematically forwards the letter to a mass email and leans back with his hands behind his head when it sends. "Done. And I'll just print this and take it to the police now. You stay here and try to—" he points at me and waves his finger, "chill."

"I won't be able to *chill* until we're home in Farrow."

With Delilah by my side.

It's a restless night. Star paces next to me, sensing my unease. I watch the news and the house fanatically, waiting for that moment when the cops will tear down that driveway to the castle and carry Caulder off in cuffs...but it never happens.

I can't eat. I can't function. I feel like I'm about to explode.

Trust me, she said.

Trust that she'll get out of this on her own? Trust that I'll get her out of this even if it's after she's married?

I can't fucking trust anything right now.

I groan and put my head in my hands, trying desperately not to lose my grip now when we're so close to everything coming together. I feel my pup's wet nose pushing into my hand and I sigh, reaching around her neck and hugging her. My heart rate calms long enough to think about a few options, in case whatever she comes up with doesn't work.

I've already moved on to how I'll kidnap her from Blorl if Caulder isn't arrested, if the wedding happens, and Xang whisks her out of here. It'll be a lot harder, but at least in Blorl, she'd be safe from Caulder.

Trust her. I might be able to trust her, but I don't trust anyone around her. That's the problem. And I'm not sure she is able to protect herself.

Solvang's words come back to me about Delilah being weak, and I have to shut those thoughts out of my head or I'll storm into that palace and be gunned down during the wedding.

If it meant her not marrying that bastard, I'd be willing to risk it...

CHAPTER TWENTY-NINE

Delilah

I take the package out of the bag I've hidden in the back of my closet and stare at it for a while before walking through the motions. I can't think too much about what I'm doing and when I wait the allotted time and stare at the result blankly, it's as if I'm watching it happen to someone else.

This isn't my life.

I'm not about to marry Avaban tomorrow night.

My family isn't this mess that I'm ashamed is my blood.

I don't love Jadon Safrin.

Denial, denial, denial. It's a pretty little word that I immerse my head in to get through the day.

I wrap my surprise in a fancy box and tie a huge bow around it, not allowing myself a moment to *feel*. That would be disastrous. Once I get through tomorrow night, I'll allow myself to think about everything.

All this numbing works for the time being. Caulder knocks on my door in the afternoon to remind me of a meeting with the family lawyer. He walks with me to the study and the lawyer is already there waiting with Avaban.

"I don't want to do this without Papa." I look around and when no one responds, I walk back to the door. "I'll go get him."

"That's not necessary, Delilah. You know he's not been feeling well," Caulder says.

I stare at him long enough to make him fidget and walk out the door. Papa is sitting in a chair by the window when I walk in.

"The lawyer is here. We're signing the prenup and I thought you should be there to make sure everything goes as it should."

"I didn't realize that was today." He frowns. "Of course. I'll walk with you."

"You seem better than yesterday."

He nods. "I've felt a little better each day since you've been coming to eat with me. That pretty face cheers me up."

This is the sweet dad I've always seen. Now I realize our relationship has consisted of shallow conversations such as this one, so I'll have to make sure I don't rock the boat again until I have to.

Avaban is impatient when we walk in, looking at his watch like we've really inconvenienced him, but I smile at the lawyer and make sure Papa is comfortable before I sit down.

A stack of papers is placed in front of me, and I scan through it, ignoring the heavy sighs and agitation with me taking my time. I pause at the part that states I must ensure that I'm a virgin, wondering how they are planning on proving that one and smile to myself.

I sign the documents and hand them to Avaban to sign.

"Looks like we're official," he says.

"Not yet." I smile.

———

That evening I eat in my father's room, and he's feeling well enough to feed himself. I can't believe the difference in him in such a short amount of time.

"You look so much better," I say when he finishes everything on his plate.

"I feel like a new man. God knew I needed to be healthy enough to see my baby girl get married."

My lips feel pinched as I smile and I pick up our trays so my face doesn't give me away. I set them outside the door and David is the one to pick them up and carry them back to the kitchen.

"Should I read to you for a little while?" I ask.

My father nods and folds his hands together.

I pick up the book next to his bed and go to the last place we left off, getting situated on the loveseat by him. I read for a couple of hours until Papa's head droops to his chest. I put my hand on his shoulder and give him the slightest shake.

"Can I help you to bed, Papa?"

He murmurs something and stands up, a little unsteady, but he makes it to the bed with no trouble and pulls the covers up to his neck.

"Thank you, Delilah," he whispers.

"Goodnight, Papa."

I leave his room and shut the door, my thoughts bittersweet. An era is ending. This will be my last night in this home. I'll leave this castle and who knows—I might never come back.

I hear voices in Caulder's room and slow down, leaning in to hear better.

"I thought he was going to be bedridden by now...what if he starts suspecting?"

I take my phone out of my pocket and start recording.

"This up and down...back and forth—he's gonna know you're poisoning him," Avaban says.

"Stop worrying so much. How would he come to that conclusion? We have to make it look like he's sick. He's had good days and bad days, right?" Caulder chuckles and then I hear both of them step closer to the door. I jump when it sounds like they're crashing into the door.

It's quiet for a few moments and then I hear a moan. My eyes widen. What...

Another moan and fumbling against the door.

"Ahh, yes," Caulder groans. "Yes. You're going to miss this..."

"Not for long," Avaban laughs, "I'll be back before you know it. Alone."

My heart thumps harder.

I listen for a bit longer, but it's quiet except for the growing moans and I really don't want to hear the rest.

I rub my eyes and wish I could scrub my ears and brain and all remembrance of what I just heard. I don't know what all of this means, but I just got all the proof I need.

I'm wired when I get to my room, but I know there's nothing I can do about this tonight. I compose an email to Jadon with the recording attached. I'll send it tomorrow afternoon, right before the wedding.

Getting ready is a solitary affair. Only select officials and a few distant family members are invited. It's another example of what a sheltered existence I've lived that I don't even have a single friend attending. Why have I never realized how strange this is? Was it always my father or Caulder that kept me isolated? I've never even had a personal maid since my mother died, with the exception of that woman who helped me the night of the ball...Darcy. I haven't seen her since—she must've only been sent to help me into my mother's gown and then was probably thrown out the minute I escaped.

I don't take much time with my hair and my makeup is simple, what I'd normally do for any day. I put on the over-the-top dress that I disappear in and laugh at my reflection. I look like a balloon of lace and tulle and ruffles. The gown is ridiculous. I don't bother with a veil. I want everyone to see the contempt on my face when I look at Xang Avaban tonight.

I walk to the chapel alone. I'm a little surprised Papa didn't show up to force me to the altar, but they seem sure that I'll show up. I guess I *have* been pretty predictable my whole life. Besides my disappearing act the night of the engagement, I've never stepped out of line, and since coming home, I've given them no reason to think I'm not going through with the wedding.

My father is at the door of the chapel and his eyes widen when he sees me. "Oh, hello. You look...lovely."

I loop my arm through his and then pat it. "Now, now, Papa, no lying allowed on my wedding day. I know I look like a clown." I smile up at him and he frowns. "It was intentional." I wink.

"Delilah...I really hope you're not going to try and—" he starts.

"Oh, I'm not trying anything…" I lean up and kiss his cheek. "Is everyone here?"

"I believe so."

"Let's get me married then!"

His Adam's apple bobs and he looks relieved. The music starts playing and the doors open with a flourish. The small chapel is only half full and I'm a little disappointed there isn't more of an audience to see this dress, but then I spot the cameras and I look directly into one, smiling wide.

I'm handed over to Xang too soon and it physically hurts to have to put my arm through his, but I do it and we walk the rest of the way to the altar where we kneel. The minister says a few things and prays over us and then we stand up and face each other to say our vows.

Xang opens his mouth to speak and I hold up my hand. "I'd like to go first, if that's okay."

He's so stunned he just nods dumbly and I grin at him, further catching him off guard.

Underneath my bouquet, I pull out a paper I've sealed with a pretty stamp and tucked between the huge petals. I walk over to Papa, holding it out for him to take. He does and wipes a bead of sweat forming on his brow. Then I walk back to Xang and pull out a package that seems too big to hide underneath the bouquet, but it fit perfectly. Our guests laugh at the cleverness, but Xang looks as serious as I've ever seen him.

I look at Papa. "Why don't you open yours first…"

He undoes the seal and holds up a copy of what appears to be the prenup. Except on the front page, it says the prenup was never valid. My dad frowns and then starts flipping through page after page, going pale when he sees what I've circled. He looks up at me and stands up, shaking the papers.

"Why don't you open yours now," I tell Avaban.

Papa pauses to see what Avaban has and when Avaban holds up the contents, there's an audible gasp. He studies it, not sure what he's seeing at first.

I point at it and whisper, "It's a positive pregnancy test." His nose curls in disgust and he throws it on the ground with a shudder.

I look around at everyone else. "The baby's not Xang's."

I start laughing hysterically and when my dad and Caulder grab my arms, guards start walking toward us.

"Let me go. You'll want to hear what else I have to say," I say loud enough for my voice to echo through the chapel. "I'm carrying Jadon Safrin's baby, and therefore, I will not be marrying Xang Avaban today or ever. Our agreement stopped holding validity when I lost my virginity and—" I pull one last thing out of my bouquet—my phone. I push play and put the phone in the microphone so everyone can hear the recording of Avaban and Caulder.

Caulder tries to rip the phone away from me and the guards hold him back. They surround Avaban and my father and once I have room, I pull the ribbons on my dress, making the pile of ruffles fall to the ground in a heap. I have a sleek dress on underneath and shoes made for running, and as soon as I step around the huge mound of material, that's exactly what I do.

CHAPTER THIRTY

Jadon

I don't know what to do but watch the wedding unfold. There are too many guards to get on the grounds today. Kidnapping her just isn't an option...for now anyway. I'm sitting, watching the screens like a man lost in self-pity. I let the whiskey drain down my throat and pour another shot, sick that she's actually going through with this.

I'm surprised by her wedding dress choice, but even though it's the last thing I'd have expected her to wear, she still looks like a goddess.

My goddess.

I sling back the shot and pour another, a little bit dripping down the side of the glass.

She looks like she might fall over under the weight of that elaborate gown, but fuck me, she's so pretty. I'm picturing her out of that dress, the way she looked on her bed in the moonlight, her pale skin luminous and so soft.

Quincie turns up the sound and I give my head a good shake to snap me out of this.

"What the fuck?" he says.

"What? What happened?"

"Did you see that? She pulled two things out of her bouquet, or maybe that dress? That's a fucking huge dress, what does she have hidden in that thing?" He laughs.

"Shhh, what is she saying?"

"I didn't catch it, but Xang is holding—wait, he just threw it down!" Quincie tries to zoom in on whatever he dropped, but I'm too busy watching Xang's face. He looks enraged.

"Oh shit, what is she doing?" I say under my breath.

I hear her then, as clear as day, when she says, *"The baby's not Xang's."* All the blood rushes to my head and I lean in watching her as close as I can get. And when I hear her say my name, I nearly fall to my knees.

"I'm carrying Jadon Safrin's baby, and therefore, I will not be marrying Xang Avaban today or ever."

Everything else is a blur. I see her gown collapse and watch her take off running, but I'm out the door, stumbling toward the castle before I see anything else.

I watch for her along the way, knowing in the back of my mind she probably couldn't meet me this fast, but when I reach the edge of the Farthing grounds and still haven't seen her, I'm surprised. I climb over the gate and am surrounded instantly.

A dozen guards are on me, pulling me up to my feet and knocking me down in the next second. I'm punched in the face and in the stomach, the knees, over and over until everything is a big ache and I'm not even sure where they're hitting because everything hurts. I don't stop punching and kicking, although I'm stalled a bit when I'm repeatedly stabbed. I manage to knock at least six to the ground but more keep coming. I'm dragged in the grass and behind the castle, my eyes barely open enough to make out where we're going, but I feel when the grass changes to stone and I'm taken underground, down steep stairs, where it feels damp and cold, the water seeping through the stone and chilling the air. Stone turns to dirt and the clanging of metal makes me jump before I'm dumped into a cell and the bars lock me in.

I lean over and struggle to stay alert, the vision of Delilah running out of that chapel in white, the last thing I see.

I rise and fall into consciousness like a wave I can't quite catch. One minute I feel myself surfacing above water, only to sink to the bottom for an indeterminable time. I gasp for air and I try to swim to the light, but when I open my eyes, there is only darkness.

It's quiet except for the chatter of rats close-by, and I pound my hand on the dirt when one gets too close. Delilah was running to me, I know she was. I hope to God she got out of there safely. I pace the floor, dripping blood all over the dirt, and rattle the bars, yelling until I'm hoarse. I have a knife wound in my lower back and a couple in my legs. I rip up my shirt to make a tourniquet, focusing on the wound bleeding the most.

I pass out again and dream that she's forced to marry Avaban anyway. It's the rattle of the cage that wakes me up and I try to keep my eyes open long enough to see who stands over me, on the other side of the bars.

"It's me, boss," Quincie whispers. "It's the middle of the

night and the night guard took a break. I knocked out the second one. I'll figure out a way to get you out of here. I'm not sure we can trust any of the guards. Paquin has disappeared...Avaban and Caulder have been arrested, but the guards are on you nonstop. I'm not sure what to think."

"Stay on Delilah," I croak. I lean over and cough up blood.

"I'm so sorry, King. I let you down."

"Does Luka know what's happened?"

"He's on his way."

"Watch Delilah...don't worry about me. I'm afraid for her."

"Yes, sir. I swear I will."

"Quincie?"

"Yes, sir?"

"If something happens to me, make sure Delilah is taken to Farrow...make sure she's taken care of...her and the baby."

"Nothing's going to happen to you," he says, his voice breaking.

I sit up, trying to keep my wits together and stay awake. I have to come up with a plan. I crawl to the edge of the bars and rattle them until my fists feel twice their size. Sleep comes again as hard as I try to fight it, and this time when I see Delilah, she's screaming and bloody and I thrash around on the ground, banging into the walls and getting dirt in my wounds. I'm a raw, exposed nerve and the pain is so great that I don't know whether I'm alive or if I've already died.

CHAPTER THIRTY-ONE

Jadon

"He's still alive?"

"I think so. He yelled for most of the night and then quieted down the past hour or so. He's still talking in his sleep. I think he's dreaming of the princess. He keeps yelling her name."

"Don't let the king hear you say that. He's torn apart the first floor of the castle, all on his own."

"Has he lost it? I thought he was sick again."

"Apparently he was being poisoned by the nephew. Bastard can't keep any of his family members happy." The guard laughs and it sounds like he's slapped hard. "Ow, what was that for?"

"Don't be talking about the king like that if you want to stay alive. What are you thinking? There are ears everywhere around here, man!"

"Okay, okay. I like a little drama, but this is a bit much for me, know what I'm saying? I like to get home to the *missus, have a little port before bed...staying up all night watching a dungeon is not my idea of a good—"*

"Did I not say to shut up?"

"You're pissy tonight."

"It's been a long time since we've had anyone in the dungeon. It makes me anxious."

"Fair enough."

"Hey, did you hear that?"

I rattle the bars and listen as the guards pause and step closer. One of them comes around the corner and shines a light in my face. I put my hand over my eyes and he lowers the light.

"Could I have some water?" I ask.

"Uh, we don't have any water for you. Sorry," the one who's ready for his daily port says.

"Would you mind getting some? I won't trouble you for anything else," I add.

"What's he saying?" the other one asks.

"He wants water," the first one whispers.

"He doesn't get anything out of us. Nothing. Don't go near him. We're to stay as far from him as possible. King says he's not to be trusted."

They walk away and I strain to hear what they'll say, but they're quiet, and they don't come back.

The hours stretch, perhaps feeling more prolonged because every cell in me is aching to get out and find Delilah, but the injuries are also distracting and making every second an agony.

I don't hear any soldiers talking, no guards gossiping outside the door. Everything is still, too still.

My stomach gave up growling a while ago, the gnarling sounds a mere flutter now. If I tried to eat, it would just come up anyway. I tell myself to shove the hunger away.

I dream and wake and it all feels the same, each hell is as bad as the next, except in the dreams, sometimes I see Delilah's face and that is mostly better...until I see her father dragging her away from me, hear her screams, see Caulder squeezing her throat until his handprints are huge red marks on her neck. In those moments, I pray to wake, and when I do, I pray that none of this is real. That she got away and is safe from the evil clutches of her family. I don't know who to blame for this, if it was Caulder who caught me before I could get to Delilah, or if it was Vance. It doesn't really matter, I think they both wanted me dead. *Where is Delilah, and who is she with?*

"Jadon, wake up." My cheeks are slapped, lightly at first and then harder. "Wake up!"

I feel something wet on my face and I reach out blindly, grabbing a wrist.

"There you are. Come on. Let's get you out of here. Star, back up, girl. Let him breathe."

Star's tail thumps loudly against the bar.

"Luka?"

He flashes a light over me and cringes when he gets a better look.

"Yep, it's me, brother. You look half-dead. You still in there?" He taps my head and grins, already giving me a hard time.

"You're not going to let me live this down, are you?" I

groan, laughing and then coughing as he helps me sit up. I wince, rubbing my ribs.

"And why should I? Even the great Jadon Safrin needs a knight in shining armor to save him now and then…"

"It would be you," I mutter. He helps me stand and one of his guards gets on the other side, helping me balance. "Thank you. I'm really glad to see all of you."

They help me up the stone steps and when the sunlight hits my face, I duck, the brightness shooting pain directly behind my eyes. Star walks as close to me as she can get, which is difficult since Luka is already doing the same.

"Watch your step," Luka says, as we step over two bodies. "These guys weren't so lucky."

"Where's Delilah?"

"Uh," he starts and then falters. The dread builds in my gut.

"Tell me."

"Vance took her. We haven't been able to find her yet, but I have people searching the castle for information. Everyone cleared out of there after the wedding and whoever didn't, we took care of…they'll find something."

I sag into Luka and he carries most of my weight the rest of the way. A helicopter is on the Farthing grounds, propeller whirling.

"How long was I down there?"

"Three days."

His answer hits me like a hard slap to the face.

"*Fuck*. Delilah could be anywhere by now."

We fly to one of the Safrin safe houses where my wounds are tended by one of our family doctors. I start out with broth and work my way up to toast by later in the evening. The next day, we fly back to Farrow.

I argue with our family doctor about taking meds. He's

waiting for me when I get off the plane and insists I go straight to bed. My ribs are bandaged and I got stitches in my chest at the safe house. He looks over my other bruises and frowns.

"I'd like you to take something tonight. Mainly so you can sleep through the night. Knowing you, you haven't slept a straight night through in months now."

I look at him sheepishly. "I could use the rest, but it's not good timing. There's someone I have to find."

"You're not going to find anyone if you're dead." His mouth is a flat line of disapproval.

"True," I chuckle, "I guess one night of sleep can only help."

The rest does help and when I wake up the next morning, feeling better than I've felt in weeks despite being banged up, I think about calling my doctor to thank him for forcing me to rest.

But the sight that greets me in the dining room makes me forget everything for the moment.

Ava and Gentry are sitting at the table, eating breakfast. When Ava sees me walk into the room, she jumps up and runs to me, hugging me and then apologizing when she remembers I'm hurt.

Eden and Luka walk in and they hug me too and Gentry gets up to join the fun. Star growls when she can't get to me and Gentry laughs, backing up enough to let her in.

"Am I dead? What is going on here? What are you all doing here? Any word?" I ask Luka.

He shakes his head and I feel myself deflate.

"We were so worried about you!" Ava says, helping me to a chair like I'm an invalid.

I kiss her forehead and laugh when she stares into my

eyes like she's trying to read my mind. "What are you doing?"

"Just making sure you're of sound mind," she says. "Do you feel like you were drugged?"

"Not until I got home. What—"

"Well, you know what happened to me and Mother... just making sure you're not dealing with the same. You might not even be aware of it." She shrugs.

"I was mostly left alone in the cell. I don't think they knew what to do with me. It wasn't as high tech as your whole ordeal was...but you've made a good point. I should do a scan today to make sure."

"How's Mother?" Ava asks quietly.

"We had an interesting conversation before I left. She apologized."

Both Eden and Ava stare at me in shock. I take a few spoonfuls of scrambled eggs and slather my toast with peanut butter, honey, and gheirdan. When the flavors hit my taste buds, I groan, my eyes closing.

"I missed food."

"Tell us about the apology," Ava says.

"It was...surprising. She might just be desperate to get out of that house, but she apologized for everything...said she should've accepted me long ago."

"Wow." Ava lets out a shaky breath. "That must have been—are you okay?"

I grin at her and pat her hand. "I'm fine. I learned a long time ago not to get my hopes up about Kathryn. Time will tell if she meant what she said. With all the conflict with the Farthings, I don't really have time to get to the bottom of it. I have to find Delilah."

"Eden said you fell for her." Ava grins and she and Eden share a look.

I frown at Eden and she just smiles. "I never said that... well, except to her." Everyone laughs and I start coughing when I laugh too.

"She must feel something for you too, since she's *having your baby*!" Ava yells the last three words, throwing her hands up and pumping her fist. "It is about time I'm an auntie!"

"Oh, you heard about that." I beam at her and then quickly sober, the realization of where everything stands too dire to be happy about anything. "I have to make sure she's okay. Her father—I don't know what he'll do to her...and honestly—there's no way to know it's true until we find her. She could've been doing all of that for show. It was a good one," I add. "I need to know if it's true, but more importantly, we need to get her out of her father's control. I believe he's capable of anything."

"I thought it was more the cousin...Caulder? What about Titus?" Gentry frowns.

"All I know is Caulder and Titus are both in prison and she's still missing...I've never trusted her father. But who knows? Nothing would surprise me now. I need to find her so we can get to the bottom of all of this."

Gentry nods. "We'll find her." He looks half asleep, and Ava reaches out and brushes his hair back with her fingers. He smiles at her with adoration.

"Love looks good on the two of you," I tell them.

Ava grins. "It'll look good on you too. Get well and we'll figure out where your girl is."

"I'm still not positive we can trust her," Eden says. "But I *really* like her."

"Why don't we pay Mother a visit and ask her about Caulder—or if she remembers anything else." Ava frowns at me. "Did you already?"

"I haven't lately, no."

"Okay, finish eating and then we'll go ask her a few things."

"Yes, ma'am," I tease Ava, poking her in the side.

She shrugs. "I figure I have bossing rights until the day I die...I don't see anyone else telling you what to do."

We all laugh and I have the thought that everything would be right in the world...if Delilah were here. My house is full of the people I love. She should be here too.

CHAPTER THIRTY-TWO

Delilah

I was so close to freedom.

So close to getting back to Jadon.

The justice, seeing the color drain out of Caulder's face when he heard his sins exposed on live television, the triumph, seeing the look on my father's face when he heard I was pregnant with Jadon's child.

I thought I'd covered all the bases.

I should've known it couldn't be that easy.

I didn't believe it myself when I realized I was pregnant; Solvang was the first to mention it when I kept saying how tired I was.

"You're acting like my cousin did when she was first with child," she said, laughing. "Good thing you're getting married soon, you can still cover it up if you are."

I hadn't responded to that, although I did stare at her in shock and hoped she just thought it was because I wasn't used to talking so freely about sex with a stranger.

But the first chance I got, I left and put my wig on in the car, buying several tests at the pharmacy furthest from the house. I took the test and stared at it the whole time, amazed by how quickly it said positive.

I laughed and cried and laughed some more. Then panicked and cried and laughed and panicked.

Jadon's baby.

If I didn't do one thing right again for the rest of my life, knowing I am carrying Jadon's baby feels like the most perfect thing I've ever done. It would still feel that way if I weren't terrified of losing this baby.

I've been in a secluded room, who knows where, waiting to face my fate.

I've underestimated my father.

And now that he knows he underestimated *me*, he's not going easy on me anymore.

He was on me before I could reach the car as I ran out of the chapel, his hand squeezing my neck and a gun digging in my back. All the guards surrounded Caulder and Avaban and didn't seem to notice that my father was leading me to the landing, either that or they chose to ignore it and let my father punish me as he saw fit. The plane was ready to take off, with a pilot on board who didn't acknowledge that my father had a gun to my back.

Once on the plane, he blindfolded me and cuffed me to the chair in the front of the plane. He didn't say a word, but I heard every sigh, every flick of his hand as he tapped faster and faster on the window. His rage was palpable.

I fell asleep while we were flying and then was tossed in a car and driven for about an hour. I was led inside and cuffed to a metal bed then left alone for what seemed like forever.

I fell asleep again and when I woke up, the blindfold was off.

All I've seen so far are white walls, white sheets...it's very sterile.

I put my hands over my stomach and pray to the gods of all the kingdoms. *Lord, please let this baby live.*

I start to drift off again, the feel of Jadon's hands on me all I can think about. I close my eyes and feel his chest against my back, his legs entwined with mine as we fell asleep. I thought I would be by his side by the time this night was over, lying like spoons in that way that is so comforting, but I'm alone again...only this time, I know I'm not really alone.

I have his baby growing inside of me and that is everything.

I smile against my pillow. My father thinks he can beat me in this, that I will cave the first moment he exerts his authority on me, but now that I know I'm pregnant, the mother of all dragons is rising up in me.

I will watch my father burn before bowing down.

Out of the flames, the diamond is born.

Out of the ashes, fear is buried and life rises up.

I laugh out loud and it sounds loud in the empty room, but it fills me up. I shiver and get lower under the covers, resting for now so I'll be ready to fight later.

When I wake up next, I stretch, my arms flailing over my head. My hand hits the metal headboard and I flinch, but then it clatters to the floor and I sit up, looking back to see what happened. One of the posts is on the floor and I look down the hollowed metal. There's something on one side of the bottom, a little two-inch strip of metal and I try to squeeze my hand down there to get it out. I have to get out of bed and pull the bed away from the wall, which takes more strength than I have for the first five minutes. It's heavy. Tired and a little dizzy, I give up moving the whole bed and just go to the corner where the post fell off. I put it back on and stare at the strip of metal. It's pointy and sharp. *Could it hurt someone?* I prick my finger and blood forms immediately. Okay, this could be useful. I bend down to pick up the metal post and see something on the wall that catches my eye. Tiny slashes.

Curious now, I put all my strength in moving just that one corner of the bed and when I get it back far enough, I drop the metal and rub my fingers over the wall. In tiny print, someone has etched into the wall. It's a white wall and the etching is not very deep, so I have to get closer to make out what it says. I get on the floor and lean as close as I can get.

It says: Help me.

And then in smaller marks, it says: Kathryn Safrin was kidnapped and held here.

Underneath that are the lines and I realize it was the length of time...or at least the length of time she was able to etch in. I count each line and there are twenty-six.

Kathryn Safrin was held here for twenty-six days? I sit on the floor, shaking. How far will my father go to get what he wants? How many sins has he committed against the Safrins? Against countless other people?

When I start shivering uncontrollably, I get up and try to get the bed back to where it was, holding the metal piece close as I crawl under the covers. Is my father leaving me here to die or does he have some sort of other torture in mind for me?

My stomach growls. Once the shaking stops and I'm warmed up, I get up again and start pounding on the door.

"Papa!" I yell.

"Papa...I need to talk to you."

"Papa! I'm hungry."

"I'm sorry, Papa. I don't know what I was thinking. None of it was true about the baby. I just wanted to get out of marrying Xang. It's true he's having a fling with Caulder though." I laugh, thinking about them in prison. Maybe they can be in the cell together at least...that's one way to see if a relationship is going to work.

I cackle for a while over that.

It's silent.

"I'm sorry. Please let me out of here. I'll do whatever you want."

The door cracks open and my father steps in.

CHAPTER THIRTY-THREE

Jadon

Kathryn hugs Ava and Eden and then looks at me, her smile timid. There's an awkward moment for everyone as she looks at my bruised face but doesn't say anything.

"It's good to see all of you," she says.

It's the nicest she's been while in solitude—really the nicest she's *ever* been to me, including her apology the last time—and I appreciate the fact that she's trying.

"How are you feeling, Mother?" Ava asks.

"I'm feeling more myself every day. I think I've been back to normal for a long time, but it took a while." She glances at me out of the corner of her eye and I look down at the table, picking up a chess piece and rolling it around in my hand. "While we're all here together, I'd like to say something. I told Jadon the last time he was here, but I would like to apologize to all of you. I've never been fair to your brother, never treated him with the love and compassion he deserved. There's a reason I'm in here, and I will regret my choices for the rest of my life. I'd rather die myself than see any hurt come to you, Jadon. I want all of you to know that. And I'm okay if I stay in here forever. I don't deserve your trust."

We all stare at her and Eden is the first to respond.

"Thank you, Mother. I don't know what to say to all that just yet, but I, for one, am glad to hear that you're finally acknowledging how awful you've been to Jadon. He's our family, he's the king of this monarchy...and he's not going anywhere." Her eyes fill with tears when she says the last part. "Although, he sure gave us a huge scare over the past few days."

"I can see something has been going on." Kathryn reaches out and touches my face, just under a cut. My heart quickens, that steady craving for a mother's love still tucked away inside. "What happened?"

"Caulder Farthing and—"

"Caulder?" She makes a face. "Who is he in relation to Vance?"

"You've never heard of Caulder?" Ava asks.

"I don't think so."

Ava opens her phone and pulls up the picture of Caulder I sent to her. When Kathryn sees it, she pales and her hand shakes.

"Kathryn?"

"I saw him...he came to the place." She looks at Ava with wild eyes, the fear in her voice undeniable. "He was there. Where we were kept."

"You're sure?" Ava asks. "Because I never saw him, not once."

Kathryn nods, pointing at the picture. She puts a hand to her throat and then her head drops into her hands as she weeps. Kathryn is a lot of things, but she is not overly dramatic. Unused to this display from her, Ava and Eden gather around her, rubbing her back and trying to soothe her.

"He's evil," she whispers over and over. She rocks back and forth and when Eden finally wraps her arms around her, she quietens and the shaking eventually stops.

"I'm sorry to bring up bad memories, but did he ever say anything to you?" I ask. "Do you know what he was planning?"

"It was all about bringing an end to your reign," she says quietly. "He has a...brutal temperament. He was the one who started my brainwashing, and when I wouldn't cooperate at first, he—" she sobs into Eden's shoulder again, "—is he the one who did this to you?"

"He's played a hand in all of it. I hardly know where he begins and Vance ends. The two of them are still a puzzle to me, and add Titus Catano to the mix, and we have a clusterfuck of huge proportion." I put a hand through my hair and tug. "Do you remember anything about the place? Anything at all that you may have forgotten to tell me?" I look at Kathryn and then Ava. They both look at me, deep in thought. "We know it wasn't that far from Yuman. But if there's a sound you remember, a smell...any details on the walls or the furniture..."

"The bedroom I was in was so stark. There was a metal bed. I remember the metal was oddly heavy for a piece of furniture. And it was a metal we don't have here in Farrow. Not foolproof though—one of the posts fell off."

"Can you describe it?"

"It had square posts and was so heavy. Underneath the white paint, it was the color of pewter..."

"Okay. Anything else?"

"I remember when I was let go, I thought I smelled a paper mill nearby."

"I didn't know what that smell was," Ava says, crinkling her nose. "It smelled awful."

I lean forward. "You haven't said anything about that before now.

"I don't think you would've ever smelled one, Ava," Kathryn adds. "Paper mills are a thing of the past, and it probably wasn't that at all, but that's what it smelled like."

"We'll look into this. This is really helpful, Kathryn. Anything else at all?"

She shakes her head sadly and reaches out her hand for me to take. "I want to help, Jadon. Anything at all."

I nod and squeeze her hand before standing up. "Thank you. I'll let you all visit while I discuss this with our team."

I hustle back to the house and Luka and Gentry are deep in discussion in my office, looking at a screen that shows the Farthing grounds.

"Anything new?"

"The team who's been scouring the house should be here within the hour," Gentry says. "I spoke with Alex and he asked that I let you know he's willing to do whatever he can to help. He's got King Shua on his back about throwing Solvang in prison, so it sounds like that's something that will have to be dealt with shortly."

I groan. "I miss King Otto. These kids of his are turning out to be a huge problem. We have a pause on the war with the Farthings...I don't want to wage war with the Ottos in the meantime. Ask Alex to do his best to keep the peace until we can figure this out with Delilah."

Gentry nods. "Will do."

"You getting along better with your brother these days?" I ask. I rub the lines between my brows. Thinking about Alex gives me a perpetual scowl.

"Alex is an arrogant bastard, but he's pretty cool too," Gentry says. "Why do you ask?"

"I'm furious at him for not getting Delilah out of the castle when he had the chance...but I went to get her and the same thing happened, so I have to stop blaming him."

Gentry laughs. "No, he could stand a few people giving him shit. The guy's been handed the silver platter all his life. Could be knocked down a peg or two and still be just fine."

I laugh and pound Gentry on the back. "Thank you for bringing my sister to see me. She knows how to cheer my spirits."

"Wouldn't think of trying to contain her. She found out you were hurt and would've murdered me if I didn't bring her right away."

I chuckle and stop when my ribs protest. "Kathryn and Ava said something about the place they were kept. I'd like to look into it. Kathryn said it smelled like a paper mill when she left the place. Do you know of anything like that... you know where Ava was found...anything in the hundred-mile radius that could fit?"

"The Sulphur Springs!" He slams his hand on the table. "Not too far from where I grew up. We didn't usually go there because of the smell...there were nicer springs closer. But yeah, wouldn't be far from Yuman..."

I nod. "We'll need to get a team there right away, see if we can find this compound. Maybe it will lead us straight to Delilah."

CHAPTER THIRTY-FOUR

Jadon

The team arrives, looking a bit haggard but happy with their results. They found Caulder's stash of poisoning supplies in a locked safe in his room. They torched the safe and managed to save the evidence. They also brought all the computers they could find and a team immediately combs those in search of clues on where Delilah could be.

A drone flies over the Sulphur Springs and we all watch from various locations. Gentry offered to go to his parents' house, so he'd be close if we found anything, but I ended up getting over myself and asking Alex to watch from Yuman...that's still close enough that a team could reach her quickly, if Delilah is found there. It's unlikely she'd be in the same place Ava and Kathryn were, but I don't know of any other options just yet. We'll be searching their computers to find out if it leads us to the Farthing safe houses. There's never been even a hint of the whereabouts of any one of their safe houses over the years, so I'm not counting on finding it, at least not as soon as I'd like.

Luka is staying a little longer, but he has been running the daily meetings with the monarchies I've dealt with before now. Everyone keeps griping at me to slow down and let my body heal, but I'm too antsy to be still for too long. I do let Luka do what he can though, and Basile has tended to me almost as much as my sisters. He's still mourning over Chelsea's disappearance, and I hear him telling Ava that he regrets not telling her how he really felt.

I don't want to live with that regret. I hope against all hope for another chance to let Delilah know what she's done to me, the way she's wrecked my heart beyond all repair. How I don't want to be sane or whole or even breathing...if it means a life without her in it.

Could she really be carrying my child? In the quiet moments between barely cognizant and sleep, I allow myself to entertain the possibility. The thought of a child with Delilah squeezes my heart so tight, it hurts. It's not wise to get my hopes up, but they're still way, way up. To the ceiling, up.

I want this baby as much as I want Delilah.

Mid-afternoon, I get a call from Alex. He sounds more excited than I've ever heard him.

"Are you watching the feed? I think we found a possible place," he says.

"I'd just stepped away...one sec, let me get back to my office." I hurry and Luka is already at the door, ready to walk out.

"I was just coming to get you. Come look at this."

"Alex, I'm putting you on speakerphone. You there still?"

"I'm here."

Luka and I walk to the screens and there's a building tucked between trees. Luka points to it. "This isn't on any of the city plans. I think we should send a team in."

"I've got a team on standby, you say the word and we're going in," Alex says.

"Consider this the word," I tell him. "Let me know as soon as you know something."

"Done," he says and hangs up.

———

I watch the screen obsessively and nearly pull out my hair while we wait. And wait. And wait.

"Why is it taking so long?"

We saw the group of a dozen men surround the building and then work their way inside at least half an hour ago. But all is quiet.

I call Alex. "Why is it so quiet?"

"I haven't been able to get through since they entered the building. My guess is they lost all service. It's probably a dead zone, right?"

We both see it at the same time and I yell, while Alex lets out a long string of curses. Luka hits the table next to me and I stare at the screen in shock. The building explodes into a pile of smoke and the fire catches onto the trees, instantly spreading, multiplying with every second.

"Fuck me," I whisper.

Silently, I plead with the gods of all the kingdoms.

Please don't let Delilah have been there.

Please.

I bury my head in my hands and feel like my world has just ended.

It takes me a while to remember Alex and when I do, I feel worse. "Alex, I'm so sorry about your men."

"They went in knowing something like this could happen," his voice breaks. "I just hope she wasn't there."

But the likelihood that she was seems even stronger now, like her father wasn't willing for either of them to live if it meant all their truths would come to light.

CHAPTER THIRTY-FIVE

Delilah

"Where are we going?" I ask, racing to keep up with my father as we run through the woods.

My father ignores me then takes out a device and pushes a button. He yanks my arm harder and I try to run faster. A few seconds later, I hear an explosion that sends me to my knees.

The slap I feel across my face stuns me and I reel back, staring up at my father. A stranger. He doesn't even look like the same man in this moment; his eyes are crazed and he's practically spitting at me.

"Get up. We don't have time for this." He pulls me up and drags me through the trees until we come to a clearing.

He's been moving faster than I would've thought him capable of a few days ago. Was he ever sick? I don't know anything anymore. The world has tilted upside down and I'm trying to crawl back up to center, blindfolded.

A plane waits for us and I'd like to believe my father's

urgency in getting us out of the building was because I said I'd do whatever he wanted, and maybe that was part of it, but I have the worst feeling that maybe we were close to being found. He's too rattled. And that explosion...what if someone *was* close? What if it was Jadon? Oh god. It didn't sound like something anyone could survive. I put my head in my hands and try not to think about that...everything I can to push away the thought that he could've been in that explosion. I can't allow myself to go there.

We've been on a plane for a couple of hours. He won't talk to me, won't tell me where we're going...his anger is consuming him. Now, I'm beginning to see the strain in his body, the sweat along his brow, and his face is red...

"Are you feeling okay, Papa?"

"I need to think!" he yells.

I clamp my mouth shut. Closing my eyes, I force myself to calm down, thinking instead about the baby I'm carrying. It should fill me with more fear that I'm bringing a baby into this chaos, but instead, it brings me comfort.

I keep my eyes closed the rest of the flight, imagining a child with Jadon's black hair and the bluest eyes, running around and twirling in a field of flowers.

When we arrive at our safe house on the south side of Shlovak, it's late afternoon. The staff is there already, hurriedly moving about the house, getting everything in tip-top shape. They scuttle to the door when we walk in, the butler and his small staff lowering their heads in respect. I want to tell them not to bother, but I don't say a word.

My father gives a jerky nod of acknowledgment and we

are led to the dining room where a few things have been prepared.

"Surely you had enough time to do better than this," my father snaps.

In the past, I would have stared at him and said, "Papa!" in admonishment if he ever spoke to our staff like that, but this time I woodenly place a few pieces of fruit and cheese on my plate, hoping my smile to the man who shakily sets out a small platter of sandwiches is thanks enough. I grab a sandwich and smile at the man again; he just stares at me with wide eyes.

A plate clatters and my father points at a woman who has just walked into the room. "What is she doing here?" he barks and the other three staff members stop and stare.

"This is Lydia," the butler says. "She came to help us prepare."

"I've given strict instruction that there are no women allowed on my staff. *Ever*," he spits out. "Leave." He points at the woman. "*Now*."

"I'm so sorry, sir. We needed the extra hands to be ready in time and Lydia is more than cap—"

My father lifts his hand and the man stops. "See her out and then you are free to go as well. We will make do with the two left here." He nods to the two men who haven't said a word since we got here and they nod back.

The butler and Lydia leave the room quickly and I stare at my father, waiting to see what he'll do next. Part of me wonders if he's lost his mind with the poisoning, but no...I think this must've been somewhere in him all along. Maybe my challenging him is forcing his sins to the light, but more than likely, my opinions still don't weigh in on his behavior. His walls are closing in, with or without me.

"Sit down, Delilah. Eat. We need to figure out our next

move." He points at the table and I sit down, warily watching him take the seat across from me.

I don't have much of an appetite, but once I start eating the cheese and a bite of the sandwich, some of it comes back.

The men still lingering clear the room and come back in with wine. I shake my head and ask for water and one of them returns with a jug.

"I think there's a way for us to salvage this," Papa finally says, eventually going into a long explanation of how we'll go about it.

I'm so tired, my eyes have a will of their own, and I wake up to him pounding on the table.

"*Listen!* You've wanted to be part of things for so long, and now that you finally have the chance, you're drooling on your arm like a disgusting animal. Sit up, wipe your face, and listen."

My eyes well with tears, but I wipe my mouth and make sure there's not a tear in sight when I look at my father.

"Have you always been this terrible?" I ask.

"You must know by now that no one is all good or all bad, dear. Even your precious Jadon, who you allowed to defile your body—and your name—is human...and a sub-par one at that."

"At least he hasn't been hiding who he truly is from his daughter her whole life. He lives honestly."

Papa laughs and tilts the wine glass back, swallowing the rest of the contents. "You are so naïve. Always have been. Your brother was always one step ahead of you. While you were playing with dolls and combing your hair, he was talking war strategies. Even Caulder, fool as he was, was always more capable than you'll ever be."

"Have you ever wondered if Omar's drowning wasn't

really an accident? We were all there together, but Caulder was closer to him in the water that day. What if Caulder has systematically been trying to kill all of us off so he could become king?"

His face darkens. I can tell he's going through the events of that day again, the way I have over and over through the years.

"I think perhaps he's played us all," he finally says.

"Except *I'm* the one who realized it. Maybe I am capable of something." I sigh. It doesn't feel any better to know the truth. "Why did you pretend to love me? Why not just show me who you really were from day one?"

"But I do love you. I've always loved you. And it was much easier to keep you occupied if we played nice." He laughs, wiping his mouth with his hand. "It was also nice having a woman's touch when I was sick," he admits. "You remind me of your mother, how caring you are when you're taking care of someone."

"Were you really sick though, or was Caulder just poisoning you this whole time?" I throw my napkin on the table, disgusted by the whole conversation. "You know what, don't bother answering. I can't believe how long I worried about you, how devastated I was that you were sick...whether you were sick or poisoned doesn't matter... our kingdom would've been better off if you hadn't survived."

He slams his glass down, the look in his eyes making me want to crawl under the table, but I don't back down.

"You need to watch your step, Princess. I'll let your insolence slide since we're having this overdue heart-to-heart. We'll have to work together, you know." He pours more wine in his glass and lifts it, pointing at me with his index finger. "I didn't know Caulder was poisoning me until recently," he says quietly. "Have to say I'm fucking impressed. He was trying to kill me the same way we took out King Forbrush...it was really quite clever. And it was supposed to be the young King Safrin next...through his stepmother. The fact that he wanted my position made him clumsy, but that's the kind of person we need on the throne. Someone who will fight for Alidonia and the other kingdoms at all costs."

Now I am crying and I don't bother to hide it because he wouldn't think any less of me than he already does. I'm already the scum on the bottom of his shoe.

"Why? Why would you kill King Forbrush? Or Jadon?"

"The same reason I helped Titus kill Jadon's father..." He finishes his second glass of wine and pours another. "I don't just want to rule Alidonia, Delilah. I want all of the kingdoms to bow down to me, King Farthing of all."

"You disgust me," I spit out. I push away from the table, standing on shaky feet, and walk to the door.

"I'll refresh you on the plan tomorrow, after you've slept...you'll learn to love me again, Delilah. Your mother did, and so will you. Sometimes the worst of us has to come to light before we can move on and truly learn what love is. I see the worst in you, and I still love you." He looks at me almost fondly, reminding me of the years he looked at me just like this.

I shiver and walk out the door, as he yells louder. I put my hand on my ears and run down the hall, trying to wipe out the sound of his voice.

CHAPTER THIRTY-SIX

Jadon

Ten of Alex's men were killed in the explosion. I attend their celebration of life, my mind full of Delilah and the possibility that she was also in that fire. I can't—won't—accept that until it's proven, but my heart is sick.

I walk through the services in a fog, say conciliatory things to Alex and beg his forgiveness for my harshness in Alidonia, to which he's gracious to say there's nothing to forgive, and I get on my plane back to Farrow feeling emptier than ever. My phone sits on my lap and I check it relentlessly, silently begging her to reach out to me. Say even one word to let me know she's okay. But it mocks me with silence.

Gentry stayed in Yuman to be with Alex and the family, but Ava is still in Farrow when I get home. She hugs me tight when I come in the door, her face sorrowful.

"We don't know if she was in the explosion," she whispers. "Don't let your mind go there yet…okay?"

I nod, not able to form any words right now. I pinch my eyes with my fingertips and then lean back, patting her shoulder.

"I'm glad you're here."

"Me too. It's been really quiet without you and Eden though...and Gentry. Basile has been moping around—what is up with him?"

"Chelsea has disappeared on him. Do you have any idea where she might be?"

Ava's eyes widen. "No clue. Aw, that's so sad. They were cute...in a really disgusting, groping kind of way. I seemed to always catch them at the most inopportune times." She crinkles her nose as if remembering a particular scene and then shudders.

I smile and put my arm around her shoulder. "Have you eaten yet?"

"No. I missed dinner and hoped you'd get home so I wouldn't have to eat by myself."

We raid the kitchen, pulling out leftover chicken and cheese and bread. I open a bottle of wine and we eat standing next to the kitchen island like we used to when she was little. Except then, she'd sit on the kitchen counter and I'd stand nearby to make sure she wouldn't fall.

"What if my chance at love is over?" I ask, staring into my glass. "I don't want anyone but her, Ava. To think she might not be alive—I don't want a world without her in it. Even if she ends up wanting nothing to do with me, I want to know she's—"

She puts her hand on my shoulder. "Jadon, please don't give up hope yet. I have to believe that a woman who had the guts to tell the kingdoms on live TV that she's pregnant with her father's biggest enemy can survive *anything*."

I chuckle into my hand and then it turns into a ragged

sound. "God, I can't believe she did that," my voice breaks. "That gorgeous little lunatic."

"You've always had a weakness for lunatics." Ava winks.

I tweak her nose and take a huge bite of chicken. "You're right about that."

All of the kingdoms are in a state of uproar over the disappearance of King Farthing and his daughter. Every time I turn on the news, someone is talking about it, surmising over their theories. It isn't common knowledge about the explosion at the compound or that we suspected the Farthings were there, so that theory isn't on the table, but no one has seen them since Delilah's public declaration. Since she mentioned being pregnant with my baby, I've had reporters camped out around the property, eager to get the full scoop. If I weren't so devastated over the possibility of her dying in that explosion, I'd get a bigger kick out of how she staged that wedding, but as it is, I'm going to lose my mind if I don't find out something about her soon.

My guards have said there's nothing left to investigate at the compound or I would've been there by now, and they're still pouring over the laptops found at the Farthing estate. While I'm staring out the window, lost in thought, Quincie comes barreling into my office.

I glance up, surprised.

"I'm, uh, sorry, sir. I think it's important—"

"What's going on?" I stand up and move to the side of the desk.

He sets a laptop on my desk and motions for me to come closer.

"Take a look at this folder I found. It's coded, but we

were able to break through and figure out where the Farthings' safe houses are. Well, at least two of them."

I stare closely at the email and the way the numbers are turning into letters rapidly as we watch.

"Okay, maybe three now." He grins. He taps the screen and another window opens up. "This is a map of the first two. The third would be," he takes a closer look and taps on the map, "right about here, I think."

"How soon can we take a team to each place?"

"I have several teams ready." He stands up and stretches his neck and I cringe at the loud cracks that explode out of him. He shrugs sheepishly when he sees my expression. "Didn't know if you'd want everyone to split up or if you personally want to go to each one."

"I'd like drones to go to each location first, so we don't have another Sulphur Springs situation."

Quincie nods gravely.

It takes hours for the footage to start coming in. I have to get up and stretch periodically, my knees creaking from all the hours of sitting in front of the screen. After watching every minute fleck of movement, we all conclude that they're not at either of the two locations, and the problem with the third location is that it's hard to get a drone close enough to detect movement without being seen.

"Where are they?" I repeat over and over.

My eyes hurt from staring so hard at the screens and yet I can't tear myself away, certain that as soon as I do, she'll show up on the screen.

I force myself to eat a little bit and absentmindedly

scratch Star behind the ears when she comes and sadly places her head on my knees.

"I know you need to walk, but I can't right now. Sorry, girl."

Basile knocks on the door and tries to get her to go out with him, but she won't leave my side.

"Why don't you get some fresh air? Even five minutes will help." He motions for me to get up.

I stand and Star turns around and around, prancing with excitement. I groan but smile at her. "Okay, okay. Five minutes." I point at Basile. "Don't take your eyes off of the screens."

"Yes, sir." He grins and steps aside so Star and I can walk through the door.

Star's nails click-clack against the floor and she keeps looking up at me like she can't believe her good fortune. We step outside and she takes off running in the grass then falls over and rolls around in it. If she were human, she'd be cackling with pleasure, and I smile in spite of myself. The breeze rustles the collar of my shirt and my hair blows into my face. I pull it back, securing it with my fist.

How does life keep moving, nature continues performing, and people do their everyday tasks, without a thought of Delilah Farthing's disappearance? It doesn't seem possible when every heartbeat, every measured breath I take, consists of a wish, a prayer that she's alive, that she's unharmed, and that our baby will survive this. Star runs up to me and barks, finding a ball that we've left in the yard for her. She nudges the ball toward my feet and I throw it, watching her bound after it. I feel hollowed out, but I go through the motions, tossing it a dozen times, two dozen times, until she's panting and stretches out at my feet.

"You ready to take a nap?"

She nearly knocks me over when she stands and gets on her hind feet, her front paws on my shoulder.

"Oh, now, you're breaking the rules," I tell her and she gives my face one lick. I wrap my arms around her and hug her, feeling pathetic when I nearly cry. What would my kingdom say if they knew a fucking dog and a woman have finally made me crack?

"Come on, let's get back inside. We have a princess to find. I can't waste time getting sappy out here."

She jumps down and we're walking back when Quincie meets me outside, his movements as quick as I've seen them.

"I've found a fourth safe house!" His voice barrels across the yard. We move hurriedly to one another, so he doesn't have to yell. "And I didn't find you right away, so I went ahead and sent a drone there too."

"Good. Where is it?"

"It's surprisingly close to the Cave of Stars...in that region."

We hurry inside and Basile jumps up when I come into the room, pointing at the highest screen.

"I just saw movement," he says.

"Quincie, can you move this feed to the central screen?"

Quincie does a few quick taps on his device and the center screen fills with the fourth drone's feed. A woman walks outside and hurries down the path, looking behind her every few seconds. It's not Delilah, but the fact that anyone is at the house means they could be there, or they will be soon. Quincie zooms in closer to the house and there are several people inside, and a table of food. He keeps zooming and there he is, the king himself.

"Let's go," I tell Quincie. I message the commander who is standing by waiting for word from me. *We're ready*. Basile holds onto Star so she won't follow me as we walk out of the office and I don't bother taking anything with me as I make my way to our landing strip.

The troops are filing onto planes out in the fields beyond our land, and I get on my own, greeting the pilot and the team on my flight. I message Luka, Eden, Gentry, and Ava in a group text as we take off.

I love all of you. If Delilah is alive, I think I've found her location. I'm leaving now with a few troops. My will is up-to-date, should anything happen to me. Everything is covered except for that dog who has wormed her way into my heart. Make sure she's looked after. :)

Ava: You're gonna be in such deep shit with me if you die. And you're already in deep shit for this message...although I'm really glad you let us know what's going on. I'm right upstairs so... I guess we've officially become one of those families who only stare at their phones. I LOVE YOU. COME BACK TO US. And bring that girl with you. We need to see if I approve or not.

Eden: What Ava said, only more. Because she got to see you this morning and I didn't, so I'm already missing you. Love you, Jadon. We need you...don't you dare let anything bad happen.

Luka: Watch your back. I wish I'd known in time to be there with you. Love you, brother.

Gentry: Wait! Are you still here? TAKE ME WITH YOU.

I lean my head back and smile...and hope to God that I can bring Delilah back to my family with both of us in one piece.

CHAPTER THIRTY-SEVEN

Jadon

Before we land, I put on one of the bulletproof vests kept on the plane for emergency situations. A few of my most trusted soldiers who flew with me do the same. We've talked strategy as much as possible with as little as we know of the area. We've studied maps and scrolled through the feed, doing our best to get familiar with the terrain, but some of it will take being on the ground to really know.

It takes an hour to reach the house, and we circle it, keeping watch for about twenty minutes before invading. The soldiers go in before me and when they come out holding onto a woman who is trembling, I tell them to let her go.

"Thank you." She's crying so hard she clutches her stomach. "The king is not here. I tried to tell the soldiers, but they did not believe me. He left maybe three hours ago."

"Do you know where he was going? Was he alone?"

"No, the king threw me out of the house—he didn't want a woman here. I only came back once they were gone to clean the house."

I shake my head and kick at the dirt around me.

"There was a woman with him."

My nose flares as I stop breathing for a few seconds.

"I am worried for the woman. She is not safe with him. He shot one of the staff here, a new guy—I didn't find out his name. There is still some blood left."

I turn and stalk toward her and she looks terrified. "I won't hurt you, I swear it." I hold my hands up and don't get too close. "There was a woman with him? Was it Princess Delilah?"

"I think so. She looked different than the pictures I have seen of her. Very weak."

"Did she look wounded in any way?"

"No, just so tired."

She's alive. I rub a hand over my face, feeling the relief drain through my body like water running through a desert.

When the soldiers come out of the house, I direct my attention to them. "Did you find anything?"

"They weren't here long and didn't leave anything behind, but the blood splatters from that kill she was talking about. Most of it's cleaned up."

"Where is he taking her?" I turn to the woman. "Do you know of any other safe houses? Do you work at those too?"

"No, I only clean this one. I don't know..."

"Who else was here?"

"I can take you to them, if you'd like."

I send a team to go with her and step inside the safe house, hoping to find something they missed.

Half an hour later, I'm still looking, but there is nothing. No sign Delilah was even here.

The soldiers come back and confirm from the men they spoke with that it *was* Delilah. No word about where they were heading next.

When I board the plane, I'm defeated but still feeling better than when I got here. *She's alive.* There's still hope.

When I arrive back in Farrow, I think I'll go crazy if I have to sit for another minute, but I position myself in front of the screens, watching for any sign of Delilah and her father at their other safe houses. Quincie hasn't found another, so it seems to just be the four locations.

"Why don't you take a break, Quincie...get some rest?"

"You need it more than I do," he says. He points at Star, who hasn't left my side since I got home. "At least take her for a walk. She's antsy."

I don't say anything. Star's head is on my feet and she seems content to me.

Ava and Gentry knock on the office door, and Ava runs over, hugging me hard.

"Good thing you listened," she says. "Next time, you'll have the girl."

"She's alive," I whisper. "So at least we know that now."

Gentry puts his arm on my shoulder and squeezes. "You look exhausted."

"Yeah, it's been a while since I really slept."

"You should go to bed," Ava says. "So you'll be ready to take off at the drop of a hat the next time word comes in."

"I know you're right, but..." I scratch my arm and frown. "Where's Basile?"

"Funny story." Ava grins.

"I could use a funny story."

I pull out a bottle of scotch and pour us each a glass.

"Chelsea showed up here after you left today. You'd have thought you were watching an old soap opera. He stared at her, and she ran and jumped into his arms, sobbing."

"He was able to hold her up?" I ask, shocked. Basile isn't the tallest man in the world and I've heard Chelsea makes up for his lack.

"Like a champ," Ava beams. "And she's bawling the whole time telling him that she's sorry she was so mad at him for leaving."

"Hold up, where are they now?"

Gentry scrunches up his face. "If you listen really closely, you can probably tell."

Ava shudders. "It's like I'm in Niaps catching them in the kitchen all over again." She makes a face and I snort. "Anyway, I think we'll have a new resident in Farrow...for at least as long as Basile stays."

"I'm looking forward to meeting this woman. Any friend of Basile's is a friend of mine."

I pick up the glass and swirl the liquid, watching it in the candlelight.

"You'll get your happy ending too, Jadon. I know you will." Ava clanks her glass to mine and Gentry joins in.

"At this point, I just need to know she's safe."

"No, don't settle for safe. Settle for her being by your side *forever*," Ava sings.

I roll my eyes. "Since when are you the romantic?"

"Since I got my own love story...try it, you'll like it."

I groan and shake my head at Gentry. "What have you done to my sister? She's such a sap now."

He chuckles and I drain my glass, pouring another.

Ava and Gentry exchange a look and I scowl at both of them. I don't need their pity right now or ever.

"I have a bit of paperwork to go through." I get up and walk to my desk. Quincie walks back in and I point at him. "Quincie was just going to bed too."

Quincie's eyes narrow and he shrugs. "The night watch is due in five minutes. I'll leave then."

"Good." I dismiss everyone, at least in my mind, and pretty soon, it's just me and the night watch. It feels like old times, when I was a guard trying to prove to my father that I was capable of running an army, should he ever need my help.

I wonder, not for the first time, what my father would've done if Kathryn were being held against her will and cringe when I realize that's exactly what is happening. *Tomorrow,* I tell myself, *tomorrow I will free her and let the chips fall where they may.*

I let the last drops of liquid rest on my tongue for a few extra seconds before swallowing and put the cap on the decanter. I need to have a clear mind tomorrow.

My phone vibrates, shaking so hard it nearly falls off my desk. It's one o'clock in the morning, so I don't hesitate to answer it.

"Yes?"

"This is Commander Moss, reporting from Alidonia."

"Hello, Commander. Anything new to report?"

"Yes, King. They've returned," he says. "The king and his daughter are back in Alidonia. Their plane landed a few minutes ago on the castle grounds. I confirmed it was them before calling you."

"Thank you. I will be there with our men as soon as I can. Don't do anything until I get there...unless they attempt to flee, and then do everything in your power to save Delilah. No shots fired near her, am I understood?"

"Yes, King. You have my word."

"Thank you, Commander. I'll be on my way shortly."

CHAPTER THIRTY-EIGHT

Delilah

I throw up in a bag that I found on the plane, not quite to my bedroom yet. I threw up on the plane and knew I probably wasn't done for the night. The nausea has just started over the past couple of days. I'm hoping it's a good sign that I'm feeling this awful. I wipe my mouth with the back of my hand and lean against the wall.

I think of my mother and wish I had her with me right now. For so many reasons. I don't think my father ever would've stooped to this level if it wasn't for losing her and then my brother. But I'd also love to talk to her about Jadon...about my feelings for him, and about this baby. I'd give anything for her to tell me it's all going to be all right.

I slide down the wall when I feel another wave of nausea hit and lean over the bag, but nothing comes.

Exhaustion like I've never known washes over me and I'm not certain I can even get up to reach my bed.

We've been moving around so quickly, my father paranoid by every sound and fearful of every employee. He's lost what little sanity he had left and went on a rampage at the safe house, shooting the man who dared try to talk sense into him. That was the first wave of nausea I had, when I saw the man's jaw busted wide open, a hole left gaping in his face, and the blood flying everywhere while he lay in a growing puddle of it.

I don't think my father intended on us coming back to the castle so soon, but he seemed shaken by what he'd done, clutching his heart and talking faster and faster. I pretended to be asleep on the plane in hopes that he'd forget I existed for a while, but when I had to throw up, my father started ranting about the pregnancy and how I've disgraced him.

I couldn't get here fast enough then, anything to have a little distance from him. I don't know what to expect out of him.

He yells down the hall and I don't look back to see if he sees me.

"Where is everyone? We've been robbed! We can't even trust our staff anymore—they've taken the computers and left…" I hear his footsteps getting farther away. "I'm sure every valuable is gone…"

I force myself to get up so I won't be here when he comes back. If our staff is gone, I should be able to escape…

But then I hear someone talking with my father. It must be one of the guards because it doesn't sound like any of our house staff.

I'll figure a way out tomorrow, I promise myself, as I make it to my feet and shuffle the rest of the way to my room.

I take a shower and feel somewhat human again, especially after brushing my teeth. When I crawl into my bed, I look at the window and remember the joy I felt seeing

Jadon climbing over the balcony railing. If he could do it before...there's hope he can do it again. I fall asleep, comforted that he's been in this bed with me before. He's loved me and held me and slept with me here. And he visits me in my dreams too, his kiss on my forehead feeling almost real.

I feel much better after a good night's rest. I can't believe I was able to sleep after everything that's happened, but I'm grateful I had a reprieve from my father and woke up feeling human again. I take another quick shower and get dressed slowly, afraid of what I'll find when I leave my bedroom. My stomach is not taking no for an answer though —food is calling.

I don't hear anything until I'm close to the dining room and then it sounds like my father talking to our chef. I'm tempted to turn around and go back to my room, but no, I'm afraid I'll start throwing up again if I don't eat something.

My father is sitting in his usual spot at the table with an array of breakfast food surrounding him. He looks up from sipping his coffee and smiles warmly at me.

"Come sit. David will bring your food out right away."

My brain hurts from the mental whiplash.

I sit down and David is back within minutes, lifting the lid off of a prepared plate. I stare at it for a long time and my father sighs.

"What's wrong?"

"After finding out you were poisoned and knew it, I don't trust any food that I don't see prepared."

He scowls at me and takes a bite of the eggs on his plate

then hands me the plate. "Here, eat mine if you're so untrusting."

My eyes narrow on him as I watch him chew. "How about you take a bite of this first and then I'll eat it?"

He sets down his plate and takes a large bite off of my plate, chewing with exaggerated motions. I watch him for a few minutes and nothing seems to happen, so I take a few bites myself. And then I'm too hungry to be cautious and eat everything.

"You need to put on your best dress. We have reporters coming soon." He reaches out and pats my hand and it catches me off guard. Nothing feels normal right now, but his sweetness after not experiencing it in so long throws me off most. "I've decided to make the most of this baby," he says, his voice low. "That can all change, depending on you and the way you handle yourself with the reporters. If you don't do exactly as I say, there will be consequences. If you cooperate, I'll let you and the baby live and you'll raise the child as a Farthing." He smiles and nods. "First, you'll have to take back your statement about Safrin being the father, but that shouldn't be hard to do." He waves his hand. "You just follow my lead." He chuckles. "I couldn't have planned all of this better myself, really. It's like you've set me up to be even more believable, despite your best attempts to do the worst by me."

I swallow hard and my hands fist the napkin in my lap.

"Are you clear on what I'm asking you to do?"

"Yes, Papa."

"Good. Now, go put on a nicer dress, and put some makeup on. You look like death warmed over."

When I walk out of my room again, with a beautiful gown that flows to my ankles and my face fully made up, I try to steady my hands. I shake my arms for a few seconds and rub my hands together. I've only taken a few steps when the doorbell rings and the house seems to fill instantly. I'm shocked when I reach the end of the hall and the foyer is full of cameras and people milling about. My father directs them to the living room and they all follow like sheep.

I wait until some of the setting up is done and see my father looking for me. He motions for me to step inside and I do, moving until I'm by his side. He looks excited, like he's shed a few years just in the past hour. I didn't realize how much it charges him to pull off the ultimate scheme.

Before I know it, we're ready to start and my father and I move to the table that's been set up for us. I sink into the seat, grateful that I don't have to stand for this. My father clears his throat and the room silences instantly; it must be nice to have that much authority.

"Thank you for coming today. I know you have a lot of questions, so we'll get started. We only have an hour, so let's not waste any time," my father says. "I'd like to start out by thanking my daughter, who saved my life. If it weren't for her, I'd be dead by now, poisoned by my nephew, Caulder Farthing and the former King Avaban. I know all of you heard her announcement at the would-be wedding, that she's pregnant, but as she'll tell you herself, she was grasping for anything to get her out of marrying Avaban." His expression is grave even while chuckling and the rest of the room titters in response.

I feel a wave of nausea and close my eyes, trying to will it away. I jump when I feel his hand on mine and open my eyes.

"It will take time to get over the transgressions against

us, but let me assure you, we are ready to rebuild and make this kingdom better than it's ever been. I've been sick—or poisoned, should I say—for so long, that I feel like a man awakening with a new purpose in life. I might even take a new wife!"

My eyes widen as he hits his fist on the table and beams. *A new wife? What is he doing?*

"I will let Delilah answer any questions you might have, but go easy on her, she's been through quite a traumatic experience..."

I turn and look at him. *Are you done yet?* My hands are shaking and I pull them into my lap, knocking off my father's hand in the process.

The questions start flying and one rings out over the others. "Why did you claim to be pregnant with Jadon Safrin's baby?"

I stare at the reporter in the back, a man with owl eyes behind black glasses. Swallowing hard, I try to formulate a sentence in my head before saying it out loud. Everyone in the room stares at me. My father puts his hand on my back and squeezes my shoulder.

"It's okay," he says for the benefit of the room.

"What better way to stop a wedding than to claim to be pregnant with my father's enemy?"

The room fills to a dull roar as the questions come in earnest now.

"But why claim to be pregnant at all?"

"When did you realize your father was being poisoned?"

I put a hand over my chest and take a deep breath.

"I wasn't sure my father would want to believe the truth about the poisoning at first. My cousin was his most trusted confidante, and it was a hard blow for both of us to realize

Caulder was capable of such an atrocity. I was afraid I'd still have to marry Avaban, even though I suspected he was in on the poisoning..."

That seems to appease them for a second.

There's a shuffling in the back of the room when the doors open and someone walks in.

"Why did your father flee with you and lock me in the Farthing dungeon?"

The crowd parts and Jadon walks in, looking like a beautiful god with his long black hair and pale blue eyes. Everyone gasps, including me.

I bite the inside of my cheek and feel my courage rising, just knowing I have one person in the room who will fight for me.

"Because he knew it was only a matter of time before you exposed his sins." I look around the room. I feel the heat rise in my face and I grip the table, taking a steadying breath. "My father is guilty of killing King Forbrush and helped in the killing of King Neil Safrin. He threatened to kill my child today if I didn't do exactly as he said."

My father stands up, pounding the table again, but this time the veins in his forehead are popping in rage. "Capture him," he yells, pointing at Jadon and then me. "My daughter is full of lies. It brings me such pain to do this, but," he lowers his head, "I denounce you from the kingdom of Alidonia."

I stand up next to him and my arms are pinned back by the guards behind me.

"I have proof of what Lady Delilah is saying...all the proof you'll need is being forwarded to your devices," Jadon says. "The monarchies have joined together and have been combing the Farthing computer systems for days. If you'll take a minute to read the documents, you'll see I'm telling the truth."

The reporters look at their devices and there's a crescendo of murmuring as they read the contents.

"There was a thread with not only Caulder and Titus Catano, but also with Vance here," Jadon says, his eyes drinking me in, even as he's speaking to the crowd. "They tried to cover it up and Vance made a valiant attempt to pin it all on Caulder, even going so far as to agree to the poisoning with his butler, so long as the butler would give him a tonic afterward to offset most of the effects. The latter we have on a video that will play after you've read the documents." He looks at the guards behind me. "I suggest you let her go...unless you want to go down with the king."

They drop my arms quickly and I rub my wrists.

I turn to my father, my lips trembling. "I never knew you, did I? Never knew what you were really capable of..."

The color has drained out of my father's face and he staggers back, holding onto his heart.

CHAPTER THIRTY-NINE

Jadon

Everyone stares at Farthing as he starts shaking. A few guards run to him, ever loyal, and I step closer.

Delilah holds up a hand. "Don't bother. He's faking."

The guards reluctantly pull back and Farthing continues to shake and then goes still. One of the guards starts to check him out again, but Delilah shakes her head.

"I'm telling you. He's fine. And I can confirm the things Jadon is saying, and then some. My father and cousin have had a hand in killing countless people, King Forbrush of Yuman being one of them, along with an attempt on Jadon's life...just this week, he's admitted this..." She pauses to look at me and the sorrow in her face is haunting. "He confessed to his part in Neil Safrin's death, and he killed one of our staff members at our safe house just yesterday."

She has everyone's attention now, and out of the corner of my eye, I see Vance start to move. "Don't let him try to escape," I tell my guards.

Three of my guards step out from behind me and block Vance from going anywhere. Farthing's guards stay close, but with the news Delilah just dropped, they're edging closer to her now, which is how it should be. Their loyalty to their king *better* shift to their princess quickly because he's about to be overthrown.

Once the reporters and police have read the documents I've sent, some scanning over other's shoulders to see the proof, a few officers gather around Vance. He opens his eyes when there's a handful standing over him and two on either side take hold of his arms and lift him until he's standing. If looks could kill, I would be barreled down by now, but the look he gives his daughter is pure evil. I step between the two of them, trying to be a buffer. I don't want her to suffer one more second under his thumb.

"This is a setup," he shouts. He tries to fight off the guards and Delilah shakes her head, her lips clinched together.

"Notice how he's able to stand just fine. I told you, he's a liar, and it's time all of the kingdoms knew it. I'm just sorry it took me this long to realize it," she says.

Her head is held high, but I'm close enough to see the way her hands are shaking.

"Is it true you were never pregnant?" someone calls out.

She looks at me and I take hold of her hand, my other arm going around her shoulder.

"This news conference is over. Please see your way out immediately. We need to give the princess time to process everything." I nod at the guards and they escort the fallen king outside and into the police car. At least a dozen cars surround him, should he try to escape.

The questions keep coming, but I give Delilah a slight tug and we walk down the parted crowd of people and out the double doors. The hallway has an overflow of people and a guard follows us, telling them it's time to go. We keep going—I'm in a part of the Farthing house I've never been before, so once we're past all the people, I pause and let her lead the way.

She loops her fingers through mine and pulls me into a closet off of the kitchen. She turns to me and leans her head on my chest. I hold her tighter, my fingers getting lost in her hair.

"As soon as they're gone, can we get out of here?" she says, lifting her eyes up to mine.

I rub my nose against hers, my lips barely brushing her mouth. "Yes. Where would you like to go?"

"I'd like to show you what I love about Alidonia. I haven't gotten to do that yet. It's probably a crazy time for that right now..." She tilts her head back.

"I think the craziest is past us. It'll probably be a madhouse for a while, yes, but I think the threat of war is over. At least I hope it will be...once everyone is on the same page about what your father and cousin have done. You pull out that black wig again and I think we can get away with going just about anywhere."

I feel her lips lift under mine right before I kiss her hard. She makes me want to yell her name across the world, my knees weak even when she makes me feel like I can do anything. Her touch is powerful and I lean into it like the hungry bastard I am.

I reach down and put a hand on her stomach while we're kissing and she pulls back. "We haven't talked about this yet."

"I'm sorry I didn't tell you in person. I wasn't sure what to do and just knew I had to pull out all the stops if I stood a chance at getting out of that stupid marriage."

"I'm so glad you found a way to let me know. I would've never given up looking for you no matter what, but thinking about our child…it's given me so much hope."

Her fingers trace my cheeks and her smile softens. "Are you really okay with this? It's not the proper way for any king to go about starting a family…"

"I couldn't be happier to have this baby with you," I tell her, hoping she sees the sincerity in my eyes. "I love you. Nothing about us has ever been proper." I can't fight the grin that's taking over my face.

She laughs and the sound nearly brings me to my knees. "I love you too. I didn't imagine telling you for the first time in a dark closet, but…"

I cut off her laugh with a searing kiss and we don't say anything out loud again for a long time. I lose myself in her and it feels like I am *home*.

CHAPTER FORTY

Jadon

We stand at the top of a cliff, the ocean below us and the wind creating havoc as it casts waves against the rocks. We've spent the morning exploring the caves nearby and then climbed to the top of the mountain behind the Farthing castle. As we're looking at the valleys to the side of the ocean, Delilah points out the field of wildflowers on a cliff below us.

"Wildflowers look for any chance to survive," she whispers. "Look there. It's dry all around, but in those crevices, the flowers have found the tiniest amount of dirt and are blooming. They remind me of us and all we've been through to get to this moment."

I lift her hand to my mouth and kiss the inside of her palm.

We haven't talked about the future besides excitement about the baby, but it's lying there under the surface, steadily stirring in my chest. I don't want to add to the multitude of decisions she has to make, but I know it's only a matter of time before we'll have to get to it.

First being, where will we raise this baby?

But, for now, and last night when we managed to sneak out of the closet and get to her bedroom after the crowd had left, I've tried to focus only on loving her. That's the easiest part. It's everything else that feels complicated.

Standing on the cliff, I let the love drive me. I look at her with her hair whipping across her face, her eyes watering with the fierce wind, and when she smiles at me, I don't let anything stop me. I get down on my knees and stare up at her with all the love I feel for her.

Her mouth parts and she steadies her hand on my shoulder like she's afraid she might fall.

"I've been carrying something around with me since a few days after we got off the plane that day. I knew I'd never be able to even think about anyone but you for the rest of my life...it's been burning a hole in my chest since." I reach into my pocket and hold up a small velvet bag. She bites her bottom lip as it trembles and I smile up at her, slowly pulling the strings to open it. I pull out the ring and hold it up to her and she gives it a fleeting glance, her eyes brightening before staring at me again. "Most kings give their queen a family heirloom, but I decided to have one made specifically for you." I lean in, my voice shaking a little. "It's from the Cave of Stars. I think I knew the moment I saw you that we were destined for an explosive love affair." We both laugh and I kiss her fingers one by one. "I want more than that. I want the everyday. I want the hell. I want the bliss. I want everything that means you are by my side. I don't need anything more than your love for the rest of my life." My eyes blur when she gets down on her knees before me, our hands moving to each other's faces. "Will you marry me?" I whisper.

"I will gladly marry you," she whispers back. She pulls my face to hers and we kiss and kiss and kiss, our tears mingling together. A bolt of thunder crashes nearby and I'm not sure if it's my heart or a force of nature.

When we finally part, I hold the ring up and slide it on her finger. It shoots out a kaleidoscope of colors when the light hits it just so.

"Wow." She turns her hand and then stares at me in wonder. "Only a king would get tarmagalcite." She smiles and then starts laughing, her hands winding through my hair.

"We'll have to figure out the logistics of this. You'll be named queen."

She leans back, sitting on her feet and I stretch out next to her. It's getting cool up here, but she doesn't seem to mind, so I get comfortable.

"We can spend the coldest Farrow days in Alidonia and the hottest Alidonia days in Farrow...what do you think?" She turns to me and shivers.

I stand up and pull my hand out for her to take. When she stands up, I wrap my arms around her and nuzzle into her neck. "I like the sound of that."

We make our way down the mountain just as it begins to rain. We start to run when we get closer to the castle and she's laughing so hard, she slips in the grass. I catch her before she falls and she looks so beautiful, I have to kiss her.

"My queen," I skate kisses across her face until she's breathless, "always my queen."

She pulls me as close as she can possibly get, our clothes soaked, and I lean down and pick her up, running until we're under cover. We make it past the foyer and she points to the door.

"In there, it's closer."

I kick open the library door and it slams behind me. I set her down and watch as she unbuttons her blouse and lets it fall to the floor in a wet heap. I start unbuttoning mine and we begin the seductive dance of this love that will take a lifetime and then some to fully play out.

"What do you think of all this gold?" she asks as we lie on the plush rug on the library floor. A big blanket covers us and a fire crackles nearby.

"Not even a little attached." I don't tell her I've never really cared for gold...I don't want to be rude when her whole castle is outfitted in it.

Her head is on my chest and she leans up and grins. "I think I know what I want to do first as queen, besides figuring out some gesture of goodwill to those families my father has..." She doesn't finish her sentence, but I know what she's thinking. The families of the people her father killed weigh heavily on her. "Uh...that will be first...*but*," she leans up and her eyes dance in the firelight, "I think this gold could be put to good use elsewhere. We could feed a lot of people, *house* a lot of people with the amount of gold covering these walls. I've heard about what you've done for the people of Farrow...is it true that you've created housing for *everyone*?"

I nod and her fingers draw circles across my chest. I squeeze her tighter against me.

"I'd love to do the same for my kingdom. No one should be homeless or hungry."

"I'll do whatever I can to help you." I lean my head back against the pillow and stare into the fire.

Pretty soon I'll have to make sure everything is settled with the rest of the kingdoms, that no one is still on the rampage after Vance's capture. Solvang is still in jail and I'm sure that won't last forever, but I don't want to think about it now. With Delilah by my side, nothing is impossible. There's nothing we can't solve together.

CHAPTER FORTY-ONE

Delilah

We've spent the past two weeks exploring the countryside in Alidonia and setting a plan in action for renovating the castle. Workers have already begun removing the gold. One thing I've learned quickly about Jadon is that when he knows there's a need for something, he doesn't waste time making sure it's taken care of...he moves heaven and earth to get things done. I grow more and more in awe of him every day.

I have been crowned the Queen of Alidonia and it feels so odd to be in charge of anything concerning Alidonia. My father and cousin kept such a tight grip on things that I'm at a strong disadvantage. And since I don't trust any of the men Papa had working for him, I am still in need of a court. It helps that I trust the kings I've gotten to know from the other kingdoms...Jadon, of course, but also Luka, Alex, and even Shua has welcomed me now that my father is out of the picture. They all flew in for my coronation, along with

Basile and Luka's right hand and brother-in-law, Elias. Jadon's sisters came and Elias's wife, Mara. Solvang has apologized for her manipulation, but I didn't allow her to attend the coronation or the party a few days later. My trust will only extend so far.

I wish I could've had more time with Eden and Ava one-on-one, but the little time we had together was sweet. We danced the night away at the party and they watched me like eager hawks every time I was near Jadon. I think we'll be just fine...I'm hopeful with a little time, we can grow close. I'd love nothing more than that. My life has lacked with the absence of women in it. I can already tell how special Jadon's sisters are; the way they love Jadon alone makes me love them.

Basile has decided to stay with me until we can form a court. Jadon will come back and forth and help as much as he can, but until we can get things running smoothly here, we'll have to be apart some of the time. Unfortunately, as much as we've tried not to think about it, he can't put it off any longer...he has to leave today.

"I'll be back in a few days," he says, stepping away from the plane for one more kiss. "God, I hate to leave you. Are you sure you can't come with me and we'll both be back in a few days?"

"I don't feel right leaving so soon. Everyone is still shaken about my father. I don't want them to think I'm bailing on them as soon as I'm crowned."

He rubs my stomach and I sink into his arms, groaning. "Don't make it harder," I whisper.

He kisses my cheeks and one last lingering kiss on my lips before pulling away. "I love you. This won't be long. I just need to tie a few things up at home and I'll be back. We're needed more here than in Farrow."

"Okay. Good. Hurry back. I love you so much, Jadon." I smile against his mouth and when he pulls away, I lift my fingers to my lips, trying to keep from crying.

I watch his plane take off and wish I'd said yes to going with him.

Basile and I interview all the leaders of the senate and there are a few who stand out.

"How will we know who we can trust?" I ask him after we've talked with fifteen candidates.

"Gut instinct and then time," he says.

Chelsea pops her head in the door and I smile. She arrived when Basile did and I like the two of them so much. They can't keep their hands off one another, which gets somewhat awkward at times, but Chelsea has a constant smile and the woman can cook like no other.

"I thought you might like a few appetizers before dinner," she says. "Have to feed that baby."

"I can't resist any food right now." I laugh. "I'll be showing long before it's time at this rate."

"You're so tiny, you can afford a little extra," Chelsea says.

We finish up with business over dinner and Lostrand, one of the guards Jadon left behind, stands watch at the door when an explosion rattles the house. It's hard to tell how far away it was, but he rushes to me and Basile covers Chelsea.

"Stay down," Lostrand yells, running out to see the extent of the damage.

Another explosion goes off and I jump, huddling under the table. That sounded closer and I don't wait for anyone to tell me what to do, I get to my feet and open the dining room door.

"We need to get underground. Come on." I motion for Basile and Chelsea to get up and follow me. We reach the hallway and another explosion goes off upstairs.

"Can we reach the plane?" Basile says.

"I think it's best if we go underground. Papa would think of the plane first," I say under my breath. Part of me expects to see him around any corner, but that's impossible...he's locked up.

"You think your father is behind this?" Basile asks as we take an alternate route to the stairs leading below. Every time we get close, another explosion goes off.

"I'm sure of it. I don't think the house will be standing when he's done with it. Let's get to the water and wait this out there."

We change course and reach the door leading out of the kitchen. The house rattles and we make it outside just in time, the kitchen going up in flames the moment we step into the garden. Tears are running down my face, but I don't stop running until I reach the water. Looking back at the house I grew up in, the house that has everything my mother ever gave me, the house that I'd hoped to turn into something worthwhile to my people, explodes into one huge burst of flames. Thank the gods of all the kingdoms that I got some of the gold out.

Basile and Chelsea stand on either side of me, each holding my hand as we stare at the ruins before us.

I pray a silent prayer for Lostrand, certain he didn't make it out of there. I press my lips together as a new wave of sadness washes over me.

Fire trucks roar down the drive and the hoses start gushing water as rapidly as the men are able, but it's too late. Across the city, other explosions are going off, until the sky is black with smoke and the air full of fumes. We walk further down the beach where the air is clearer and my phone rings.

Jadon is on the screen and his face is pure panic.

"I just heard. You're safe?" Frantic. He runs a hand over his face. "Baby, I don't know what I'd do if I lost you," his voice breaks. "We have to get you out of there."

I nod, unable to speak.

"Are you able to reach a plane?"

"We weren't able to get to it," I tell him. "We can go back, but I don't think it's safe."

"No, stay where you are. I'll see who can get there the fastest," he says. "Keep your tracker on your phone just in case you have to move quickly."

"Okay," I whisper.

"I love you. I'll try to get help there within the hour, but it might be a little longer than that."

"I'll be all right," I tell him. "No one has been able to kill us yet, and not for lack of trying…"

Horror flashes across his face, but he smiles. "That's the spirit."

We hang up and keep walking further down the beach. I can't keep looking at the castle. It's too heartbreaking to see it destroyed.

We're sitting on the beach when a helicopter lands in the sand not far from us. King Alex waves from the cockpit, a grim smile on his face.

"That wasn't even half an hour," I say as he helps me on.

"I stayed a few days after the party. All that dancing did me in." He smirks, but I don't buy his nonchalance.

"I don't remember ever being so happy to see you, Alex," Basile says when he gets on.

Alex just laughs and waves at Chelsea.

"There's more to you than meets the eye, Alex." I lean my head against the back of the seat and do my best to avoid the nausea that rises up when we take off.

"I'll do whatever I can to keep fooling everyone," Alex teases.

We're quiet the rest of the way. I wrap my arms around my stomach, close to tears every time I think about what could've happened to my baby today.

When I see the snowcapped mountains in Farrow, the sun setting over the water, and that beautiful dark castle in the middle of the deep green fir trees...knowing Jadon is waiting for me...it feels more like home than Alidonia ever did.

CHAPTER FORTY-TWO

Jadon

I get a phone call right before Delilah is due to arrive and when I see the name flash across the screen, I don't hesitate to answer.

"Lostrand? Is that really you?"

He's breathing hard on the phone and sounds grim. "It's me. I wanted you to know I have the guys locked up here who set the fire, idiots still panting after Vance Farthing. Still eager to do his bidding. Bastards." He coughs for a few seconds and can barely speak. "I nearly died in that fire, but I'll be damned if I let Farthing win. I just handed over three of his men to our guards to let them deal with the situation. I've looked everywhere for Delilah...tried to call her before I called you, but I didn't get through. Please tell me she got out safely."

"She's safe, and she's due here any minute."

He exhales a long rasp of air and starts coughing again. "Thank God."

"You should get looked at—that cough doesn't sound good."

"Soon as I'm back in Farrow, I'll get checked out. If Delilah's on her way, there's nothing keeping me here."

"Thank you for your service. I'm so grateful you caught the bastards."

We hang up and I rub my hands together, trying to calm my nerves before I see my fiancée.

She collapses into my arms, hanging on for dear life. I lean back to get a better look and her eyes appear calm despite the war I know must be raging within.

"Lostrand caught the men responsible for this...they were working for your father."

She sags into me and we walk toward the house. I reach out and give Alex my free hand. "I can't thank you enough for getting her out of there."

I grin at Basile and Chelsea. Basile claps me on the back and squeezes.

"It was my pleasure. I needed to make up for the last time," Alex says, shooting me a dark look.

I pause and put my hand on his shoulder, Delilah coming to a stop with me. "No, it means everything. Thank you." I look at Delilah. "You know I'm never going to be able to leave you again, right?"

She sighs and her lips tremble when she smiles. She still hasn't spoken a word and just as I'm starting to get concerned, she whispers, "I'm counting on that."

Star bolts out of the house when the door opens, her agony at being left behind forgotten when she sees Delilah with me. Delilah bends down and Star licks her face, glancing up at me proudly. We both laugh and I motion for Star to give Delilah some space. She trots next to us as we walk inside and I look down at them both with content-ment, my relief overwhelming, to have this day ending with Delilah here and not across the kingdoms.

We hang out briefly in the dining room, everyone lingering to make sure Delilah is okay. I try to get some food in her, but she's too exhausted to eat much. Before we go upstairs, I stop by our surveillance room.

"Do you want to see?" I almost don't want her to say yes, afraid it will set her back to see the destruction of her home.

"Show me," she says softly.

I open the door and the screen of the castle is a blaze of color as the flames lick whatever is left. It seems her father decided once his truths were unlocked, he would no longer hold any loyalty to his kingdom.

"I need to go back soon. Maybe the day after tomor-row...to see what is left to rebuild." Her stoic face physically hurts my heart; the weight I know she's carrying, but she refuses to let it break her. "I'm glad the fire was stopped before it destroyed the rest of Alidonia. What my father meant for evil, we will turn and use it for good." She gives me a shaky smile. "At least we got some of the gold out." She starts laughing and it turns a shade hysterical. I laugh along with her, just happy to see her smiling. "That's probably what set my father off in the first place."

She turns away from the screen, her hands clasping behind my neck as she leans in for a kiss.

"What he can never realize...because he doesn't know

the true meaning of love or selflessness...is that there's nothing there that I needed anyway. This," she kisses me again, "is what's important." She puts our hands on her stomach. "Raising this baby in a loving home...I'm excited to learn what that's really like."

Our kiss gets heated and she pushes me against the door, leaning on her tiptoes to get as close as she can. I bend down and pick her up, opening the door and stalking up the stairs as fast as I can. When we reach my quarters, I set her down in front of the bed and she takes a look around. I've imagined her here a thousand times, but it's the first time I'll ever make love to her in my room.

"You look like you belong here." I unbutton her blouse and smile when I feel her heartbeat quicken underneath my fingertips. She starts unbuttoning my shirt and our clothes fall in rapid speed after that.

"Can I interrupt this for a quick shower?" She pulls me toward the bathroom and I follow eagerly.

"Do you want company?" I grin as I turn the water on for her.

She steps in and looks back at me expectantly. I'm quick to follow and position us under the water. She closes her eyes and when I put my hands in her hair and start washing it for her, she groans.

"That feels so good." Her hair feels like silk when I rinse it and she takes a deep breath, her shoulders relaxing more. "Jadon?"

"Hmm?"

She turns and looks at me, her violet eyes bright. "How soon can we get married?"

"As soon as you want." I laugh and kiss away the goose bumps on her shoulder.

"As soon as everyone can get here."

"Whatever you want, my queen." She smiles when I say those words, and we make quick work of washing up, eager to get to bed.

She reaches it before I do and drops, scooting back to the headboard, her eyes never leaving mine.

"I can't wait," she whispers, motioning for me to come closer.

Heaven and earth collide when we christen my bed. As far as I'm concerned, I don't need a wedding to know she's already my bride. From now and throughout eternity.

Our family stands on the highest peak in Farrow, overlooking the glassy water. Light flurries swirl around us, and it feels like we're all tucked in the middle of a snow globe. Nearby heaters help soften the chill. Ava and Gentry stand next to me, with Star panting by my feet, and Luka and Eden where Delilah will stand, along with Kathryn. Our extended family is here too—Elias and Mara, Alex, Brienne, Chelsea, and of course, the guards who have fought by our side...one big, happy kingdom. Quincie got his license just so he could marry us. When I asked him to officiate, he cried and then pretended to have something stuck in his eye.

A cello begins to play and I look back to see Basile standing next to Delilah. He says something to her and she laughs, her head falling back and the blond sending streaks of light across the mountain. God, I love her. She is in my every heartbeat.

As she walks toward me and Basile hands her to me, his hands clasping both of ours before letting go, I thank every hard, every good, every painful moment...because they all culminated in this one perfect moment of her saying yes to me again.

Her eyes light up when she takes my hand and I feel the compression of a thousand butterflies lifting off of my chest when I feel her skin against mine.

"Are you ready to be mine forever?" I ask.

"I already am. For this forever and as many forevers as we are allowed."

I kiss her then, unable to wait to feel her lips—we are the ones making our own rules—why not kiss at the beginning of a wedding? I kiss her until her body grows limp and weightless, and the feeling is powerful. I am drunk on her.

"I am yours and you are mine," we begin to quote the long passage of vows that we wrote together.

Where you begin, I will expand, and where I end, you will begin anew.

Our fire will never extinguish, a flame that once caught, only snags onto another more brilliant flame, setting new life to all the beginnings we will become together.

One king and one queen, our kingdoms will forge together, starting a new kingdom of peace and hope for our children and our children's children. Forever bound in love and trust.

Let it be so, today and always.

Amen."

Our vows are cemented with a kiss.

And then we dance the night away, both with our family and then later, alone, in our bed.

It's the most magical night of all...and only the beginning.

EPILOGUE 1

Delilah

Five years later

We travel to Niaps for the wedding. There was great indecision about where the location would be since Basile has been a fixture in all the kingdoms. Ultimately, the choice was left to Chelsea and she's chosen to be married in Niaps since that's where they first fell in love.

Luka, Eden, and Kathryn greet us at the door, little Selene running and leaping into Jadon's arms when she sees him.

"Uncle Jadon!" she yells.

He twirls her around and she laughs until she gets the hiccups. She runs to me for hugs next and I am basking in her kisses when she demands to know where Elijah is. I press my lips together, holding in my laugh.

"I wonder if he decided to stay home," I tell her, pulling a sad face.

"No," she gasps.

"I think you should look outside, he might've gotten carried away hiding..." Jadon tells her.

She claps her hands together and runs outside. We all laugh when we hear him jump out and startle her and then they both dissolve into a fit of giggles. There's nothing like the glee of cousins getting together when they're crazy about each other. Selene is nine months younger than our son, Elijah, but she thinks she's the oldest and the boss. He lets her think it most of the time.

I hug Kathryn hard. She's been a changed woman since she was released. She's kind to Jadon and dotes on all the grandkids, never has a negative word to say. Next, I hug Brienne—it's been the longest since I've seen her since she's usually watching over things in Niaps when Luka and Eden visit.

"You get more beautiful every time I see you," I say, holding her hands out and giving her another hug.

Next, I pat Eden's huge belly—she's due any day, another reason the wedding is here—and hug her while still keeping an ear on our kids just outside the door.

"Where's the clan?" I hear Elijah asking Selene.

"My mom says they're on the way and that we should get some of the danger out of our system before they get here so we don't lead them astray. Do you know what *astray* is?"

"It's that cat we found out by the water that time. 'Member when you were at my house last? Got to keep him and named him Socks," Elijah says proudly.

We all smooth out our faces by the time they reach the

door because they only like to be laughed at when it's intentional.

The "clan" pulls up later and I see them before I see their parents. Elias and Mara were the last couple we expected to have all the kids, but they're the best parents I know. They have a set of twins that are almost four, boys, and a set of twins that are two, girls. I'd lose my mind, but Mara has settled into motherhood like a boss. She is my idol, her endless patience with her kids never fails to amaze me, and doing it all while still making the executive decisions on her fashion line from home. We've become good friends over the years through Luka and Eden, and whenever I start to think about having another baby, I decide we're due a visit to Niaps. I get my fill of children when I visit.

The house gets louder as it fills up, and Basile and Chelsea arrive a little later, beaming at all of us.

"All under one roof...I couldn't be happier," he says. He waves a bottle of wine. "I've made a special blend for the occasion. Can't wait for you to try it." He wrinkles his nose. "Ava and Gentry haven't made it yet?"

"I thought they'd beat us here," Jadon says. "They spent a few days in Yuman, but I thought they left today before we did."

Gentry and Ava have been living in Farrow for the past year, finally settling down and helping us run both Farrow and Alidonia. It's taken all of us to get Alidonia in good shape again, all of the kingdoms uniting and working together. I'm proud of what our kingdom is now, proud of my home. But Farrow will always have a special place in my heart. I actually miss it when I'm not there.

Just then, the door bursts open and Ava and Gentry walk in. The kids all go nuts and swarm around them like little pesky puppies, tumbling over themselves. They are definitely the favorite aunt and uncle in the family. Mara's girls start climbing up Gentry's legs and he holds their arms as they do flip after flip. Selene jumps up and down, "My turn, my turn!"

Elijah and Mara's boys run to Ava and ask her if she brought her favorite sword this time. She laughs, shaking her head, but then pulls a coin out from behind their ears so the sword is quickly forgotten.

Jadon's eyes meet mine and he presses a kiss to my forehead. "Never a dull moment, is there?"

"I wouldn't trade it for anything," I whisper.

He pulls me closer to him, wrapping his arms around my waist. "Yeah? Think we need to add to the brood any time soon?"

I shrug and wink, leaning into his ear. "Too late," I whisper. "There's already one in the oven."

I lean back and watch as the realization hits him and love the awe in his eyes when he looks at me in shock.

"I love you, my queen," he says.

"I love you back."

The wedding is festive from sundown to sun-up. The kids dance until they can't keep their eyes open and we set up makeshift beds for them while we stay up talking all night. Since the day I married Jadon, I've gained a family that has far surpassed anything I could've imagined. They had every reason to not let me in, the sins of my father could've been held against me forever, but as my husband says, *"We are not our parents. We can't let pride dictate who we are. We don't have to repeat history; we've been given a chance to forge a new path."*

And that's exactly what all of us have done.

We've embraced each other with arms wide open.

We've set aside our kingdoms' past mistakes, and we've created a future that's brighter every day.

A world that is beautiful for future generations...

EPILOGUE 2

Jadon

Seven months later

"Breathe, breathe!" Ava whispers.

I'm holding Delilah's hand—or actually she has a death grip on me—and my sisters and Kathryn are surrounding us, along with a midwife. Star is guarding the door, looking concerned by the sounds coming from her favorite woman human. Our son is in the other room with his uncles, and soon we will be welcoming our baby girl into the world.

Delilah moans and looks up at me, her violet eyes shooting daggers into me. "This is the last baby," she shouts. "A boy and a girl, I hope you're happy..." She pants quickly and her face turns bright red as she breathes through a hard contraction.

I don't dare remind her that she was the one who stopped birth control months before Basile's wedding unbeknownst to me. She said she wanted to surprise me because she knew how much I love being a father. And it's true, I was all too happy to have another baby, as many as she wanted. But it's always been about *her*.

"You make me happier than I've ever dreamed of being," I whisper, wiping her hair back from her face. "I love our life, our son, this baby that's coming...but it all started with you in the Cave of Stars. It's because of you that I smile. I love every facet of the woman you are. It'll end with me loving you too."

Her eyes soften and then she groans. "It's not fair how perfect you are," she whimpers. "At this rate, I'll never stop having your babies." She leans up and starts pushing, as Ava yells along with her. "If this one would give us a niece or nephew so we could stop popping them out ourselves," Delilah says to Ava as she lies back again, breathing hard.

Ava chuckles and gives Delilah ice chips to chew. When Ava lowers the glass, she pats her stomach and lifts one eyebrow. "Working on that..."

Kathryn and Eden gasp, along with Delilah and me.

"*What?*"

"*When?*"

The questions fly at once.

"Are you finally gonna marry your baby daddy?" I ask and Ava slugs me in the arm.

"Yes," Ava giggles, "I finally said yes to his hundredth proposal."

We all laugh, even Delilah through a contraction. I hug Ava with my free arm and then Delilah does a mighty claw of reckoning: she's as deadly as some of the fights I've been in with her grip. She groans and pushes with all her strength, and we hear a little blustery cry. The tears are flowing among all of us and I reach down and help our midwife wipe her off before I take her in my arms and put her on Delilah's chest.

"Astra Kathryn," Delilah whispers. "What a little beauty."

"Just like her mama." I lean my forehead on my wife's and feel my heart cinch tightly in my chest. The love I have for my family. "Mother, will you get Elijah?" I ask Kathryn.

Her mouth falls open, a tear dropping down her face. She reaches out and takes my hand. "You've never called me Mother before," she says, her lips trembling.

"I think it's time, don't you?" My heart pounds a little harder.

"Long past time." She smiles and pats my cheek then hurries out to get Elijah.

When he comes in, his face brightens when he sees his sister. "She's really mine?"

"She is. You'll have to be the best big brother ever...see how she's gripping your finger? She trusts you already." I look up at my sisters and grin at their teary faces.

Everyone I love is in this house and I couldn't be happier. I remember the days of thinking loneliness was all I'd ever know, but I couldn't have been more wrong. Each day is full of beauty, a revelation of how good life can be...of more love than I can contain.

"Jadon?" Delilah says. "You deserve all of the best things. I'll give you all the babies in the world if it means seeing this look on your face."

I kiss her, our tears and sweat mingling with the sweet scent that is *her*. "I have everything I want right here."

The End

NOTE TO THE READER

If you enjoy angsty love stories, give one of these a try:

True Love Story
Lilith

ACKNOWLEDGMENTS

Thank you to my husband and my kids, my family...I love you so much. You're the ones who truly keep me going. Thank you for loving me during every part of the process.

Thank you to Christine Estevez for being my cheerleader and support (and so much more) throughout the writing process and beyond. I'm so grateful for you and your friendship!

Thank you to the betas who worked hard on this book: Jennifer Mirabelli, Christine Estevez, Tosha Khoury, Laura Pavlov, Christine Bowden, Natalie Burtner, Vicki Cuic, and Kathleen Pathi. Your input has been so helpful and has made the process *way* more fun!

A huge thank you to Laura Pavlov for becoming my sprinting partner —your encouragement motivates me SO MUCH! And you're just so great and positive and wonderful.

Thank you to Hang Le for this amazing cover! I love working with you.

Thank you to Wander Aguiar for the beautiful photographs...thanks to Neil Ingham, for this one in particular.

Thank you to all the bloggers and readers out there who spread the word about the books and authors they love. Thank you to everyone who has given this series a chance! I love all of you who have tried it out with me.

Thank you to my Asters FB group!

Thank you to my dear friends who support and love me whether you read my books or not. Your love means the world to me.

XO,
Willow

ABOUT THE AUTHOR

Willow Aster is a USA Today Bestselling author and lover of anything book-related. She lives in St. Paul, MN with her husband, kids, rescue dog, and grandcat.

For ARCs, please join my master list: https://bit.ly/3CMKz5y

For behind-the-scenes of my books and freebies every month, sign up for my newsletter: http://www.willowaster.com/newsletter

www.willowaster.com

ALSO BY WILLOW ASTER

Standalones

True Love Story

Fade to Red

In the Fields

Maybe Maby (also available on all retailer sites)

Lilith (also available on all retailer sites)

Miles Apart (also available on all retailer sites)

Falling in Eden

Standalones with Interconnected Characters

Summertime

Autumn Nights

Landmark Mountain Series

Unforgettable

Someday

Irresistible

Falling

Stay

Kingdoms of Sin Series

Downfall

Exposed

Ruin

Pride

The End of Men Series with Tarryn Fisher

Folsom

Jackal

The G.D. Taylors Series with Laura Pavlov

Wanted Wed or Alive

The Bold and the Bullheaded

Another Motherfaker

Don't Cry Over Spilled MILF

Friends with Benefactors

FOLLOW ME

JOIN MY MASTER LIST...
https://bit.ly/3CMKz5y

Website willowaster.com
Newsletter willowaster.com
Facebook @willowasterauthor
Instagram @willowaster
Amazon @willowaster
Bookbub @willow-aster
TikTok @willowaster1
Goodreads @willow_aster
Asters group @Astersgroup
Pinterest@willowaster